THE DEVIL'S LANDSCAPE

KEN McCLURE is an award-winning medical scientist as well as a global selling author. He was born and brought up in Edinburgh, Scotland, where he studied medical sciences and cultivated a career that has seen him become a prize-winning researcher in his field. Using this strong background to base his thrillers in the world of science and medicine, he is currently the author of twenty-five novels and his work is available across the globe in over twenty languages. He has visited and stayed in many countries in the course of his research but now lives in the county of East Lothian, just outside Edinburgh.

Other Titles by Ken McClure

The Steven Dunbar Series

THE SECRET
LOST CAUSES
DUST TO DUST
WHITE DEATH
THE LAZARUS STRAIN
EYE OF THE RAVEN
THE GULF CONSPIRACY
WILDCARD
DECEPTION
DONOR

Other Novels

HYPOCRITES' ISLE
PAST LIVES
TANGLED WEB
RESURRECTION
PANDORA'S HELIX
TRAUMA
CHAMELEON
CRISIS
REQUIEM
PESTILENCE
FENTON'S WINTER
THE SCORPION'S ADVANCE
THE TROJAN BOY
THE ANVIL

THE DEVIL'S LANDSCAPE

KEN McCLURE

Saltoun

This edition published by Saltoun in October 2017

ISBN 9781973402701

Copyright © Ken McClure 2017

The right of Ken McClure to be identified as the author of this work has been asserted in accordance with sections 77 and 78 of the Copyright, Designs and Patent act, 1988

This book is a work of fiction. Names, characters, places and incidents are either the product of the author's imagination or used fictitiously. Any resemblance to actual people either living or dead, events or locales is entirely coincidental.

PROLOGUE

Dr Owen Barrowman thought that the long stretch of cracked and broken track was never going to end. It seemed an age since he'd left the main road, having almost missed the small, neglected turn-off sign for Moorlock Hall and was now surrounded on all sides by barren moorland. It had been raining heavily and there was no way of estimating the true depth of potholes filled with water until his wheels hit them. The rain had stopped but fog was drifting across the track, varying in density and prompting him to wonder why anyone would want to build a hospital in the middle of nowhere, but of course, he knew. It had been constructed when Queen Victoria was on the throne and Hansom cabs had plied their trade on cobbled, gas-lit streets, a time when polite society preferred not to acknowledge the existence of unpleasant things. Moorlock Hall had been built to house the criminally insane – out of sight, out of mind.

Society had changed, but Moorlock Hall hadn't. Fourteen men whose insanity had caused them to commit almost unimaginably heinous crimes were being held there and where they would remain until they died. They had been deemed beyond redemption, not only by a public outraged at their crimes, but also by the practitioners of psychiatric medicine who had done little more than assign vaguely descriptive labels to their conditions and nothing at all to cure them.

Barrowman, a post-doctoral research fellow at London's Capital University, was here to complete his study of psychopathic killers after getting special permission to approach the Moorlock Hall authorities with a request that their patients might assist his research. He already had samples from patients in Broadmoor, Rampton and Ashworth hospitals in England and from the State Mental Hospital at Carstairs in Scotland when he belatedly became aware of the existence of Moorlock Hall.

The research group Barrowman had joined after getting his PhD from Edinburgh was led by Professor Dorothy Lindstrom who had recently returned from Yale University in the USA. She and her new group were currently existing on limited start-up funding from a pharmaceutical company and what temporary accommodation the university had provided. Expansion in terms of staff and equipment would be dependent on attracting UK government support in the upcoming round of grant applications.

Barrowman had never heard of Moorlock Hall but a careless remark let slip by a government official at a scientific meeting had alerted his old supervisor in Edinburgh to its existence and he had passed on the information as being a possible source of more volunteers for his study. According to the official, Moorlock Hall was 'for the real baddies'.

Professor Lindstrom had not been too keen on him making the approach, sensing that there might be problems if no one was supposed to know about the place, but his assertion that the inmates of such a place were exactly what he was looking for and the fact that interviewing a few more study subjects and collecting samples from them wouldn't require much in the way of finance had gained her reluctant permission to go ahead. After initial interest from the inmates however, only one had agreed to co-operate. The others had backed out after learning that there would be no *quid pro quo*. No privileges would be on offer and any possibility of parole would definitely remain out of the question.

Barrowman crested a small rise and the building came into view. He expected it be of its time, but wasn't prepared for something that pushed the boundaries of 'forbidding' to the limit. Perhaps it was its sheer size that took him by surprise for it had obviously been built to house many more than it currently did with three stories and towers at both ends of its front elevation and its stone walls blackened by well over a hundred years exposure to wind and rain.

He stopped the car some way short of the building, feeling the need to prepare himself and gather his thoughts. The fact that there were no standard hospital signs displaying directions to clinics and departments, no ambulance bays and no busy car parks gave the impression that the building was deserted, but of course, it wasn't. In Barrowman's mind, the invisible residents had an undeniable presence.

There was a row of cottages to the left and at right angles to the main building, which Barrowman thought might be staff accommodation. One of them boasted a washing line, its clothes hanging limply in the still air but providing welcome assurance that there was some normality to be found here for there was precious little else to suggest that he wasn't on the set of some Gothic horror movie. There were only four vehicles parked outside the main building. He made it five.

Pushing the button by the door resulted in an electronic hiss as a grill on the wall sprang into life.

'Yes?'

'Dr Barrowman. Dr Groves is expecting me.'

Barrowman winced as a steel slat in the door slid back with a bang and a pair of eyes darted over him before the small door inset in the substantial main one was opened. He was admitted, but only as far as a gate house some two metres beyond where he waited until the main door was secured behind him.

'Sorry,' said a middle-aged man wearing green hospital scrubs, 'we have procedures.'

Barrowman put his briefcase down and stretched out his arms for a security pat-down.

'I'm afraid I'll have to ask you to open your case, sir.'

Barrowman felt embarrassed. His black leather case with the gold combination locks and his initials – a present from his wife Lucy at Christmas – contained nothing more than a copy of The Guardian and a plastic box containing the detritus of what had been his pack lunch – sauce-stained sandwich wrapping, an apple core and a crushed Coke can.

'Thankyou sir,' said the man without change of expression although Barrowman felt sure he'd be telling the tale over supper. 'Snazzy case, all leather and locks and do you know what he had in it? . . .'

'And now your fingerprints, sir . . .'

Barrowman complied without comment and was then submitted to an iris recognition procedure. He was finally led through another locked door, which gave access to the ground floor of the main building where he was escorted along a corridor, as far as a further door protected by a number code before stopping there and being shown into a room leading off to the right and marked, Medical Director. It was empty.

'Dr Groves apologises. He'll be with you shortly, sir. Please make yourself comfortable.'

Comfortable was the last thing Barrowman expected to feel. He was in an office with a desk, a computer, a swivel chair for the desk user and a static one for visitors, rows of medical journals along one wall, a painting of yachts under sail and a wildlife calendar on another. The thing that made it so oppressive apart from its sparseness and institute-green walls was the lack of a window. Above him, a high ceiling bedecked with cobwebs suggested that spiders were the only things to have made contact with it in a long time. There was also a marked absence of sound, no hum of machinery, no air conditioning or distant sounds of activity. There was silence until the door opened and Groves entered, uttering apologies for having been delayed.

Barrowman rose and shook hands with a gaunt man of around six feet tall with a sallow, lined complexion and a comb-over hair style. He wore a brown suit that had seen better days and a faded college tie that secured a shirt collar a bit too large for his wrinkled neck. Barrowman noted that Groves' mouth drooped on the left side and his left arm seemed limp. He guessed at a stroke in the not too distant past.

'Quite a red-letter day,' said Groves. 'We don't get many visitors,' he added with an attempt at a smile. 'Sometimes I think we're the place that time forgot.'

Barrowman felt slightly uncomfortable. He thought he'd detected an undertone of bitterness in the comment. 'You're certainly off the beaten track.'

Groves managed a lop-sided smile and moved on. 'I take it you know that only one of our patients agreed to your request?'

'I had heard.'

'The others didn't feel inclined to assist medical research after learning there was nothing in it for them I'm afraid.'

'And the one who did?'

'Malcolm Lawler, curious I should think.'

Barrowman nodded.

'I understand this is a preliminary visit so you can tell Lawler about the project and what you need from him?'

'Yes,' agreed Barrowman. 'Actually, I was rather hoping you might be able to give me a heads-up on him.'

'A heads-up?' repeated Groves and Barrowman noticed his change of tone to vague distaste. 'Don't you know what he did?'

'Well, I've read the trial transcript of course and the newspaper reports of the time. I suppose I was hoping for a more personal slant. You must know him better than anyone.'

Groves stared at Barrowman for a long moment, the droop in his mouth exaggerating a look of annoyance. 'The trial record will have told you that expert opinion at the time decided that Lawler was a paranoid schizophrenic who was incapable of feeling guilt or remorse. He tortured, raped and murdered five people and would do the same again if released. I don't think I have anything to add to that.'

'Well, I suppose I should be grateful they didn't just call it a personality disorder,' said Barrowman.

There was an awkward moment when Barrowman thought he might have gone too far and Groves was about to take offence, but it passed and to his surprise the man appeared to relax.

'I take it that you, like me, do not hold the practitioners of psychiatry in high regard?'

This time Barrowman could not keep the surprise from his face. The 'like me' was a bit of a show-stopper.

Groves noticed. 'Yes, I'm a psychiatrist, but I understand and even sympathise with what many people feel about our specialty,' he said. 'In many ways, it's at the stage medicine was a hundred years ago. My own mistake was in voicing this opinion to my colleagues – in particular to those blessed with more self-confidence than common sense.'

Groves took an exaggerated look around his surroundings. 'And you can see where it got me.'

'I'm sorry,' said Barrowman, but it seemed painfully inadequate. 'I suppose I'm just finding it hard to believe I'm hearing this from a psychiatrist.'

Groves nodded but didn't comment.

'The people you have here . . .' began Barrowman.

'Have had the key thrown away.'

'That bad?'

Groves nodded. 'I'm sure human rights lawyers, given the chance, would milk the cash-cow but that isn't going to happen. These people are going nowhere.'

'Lawler?'

'Worst of the lot.'

Barrowman swallowed and Groves noticed. He said, 'I thought you'd be pleased. Isn't he exactly what you're looking for?'

Barrowman smiled weakly and said, 'Well, of course . . . in an academic sense, but . . .'

'Real life is different?'

'I suppose,' Barrowman conceded. 'I take it Lawler didn't managed to convince the colleagues you spoke of that he should be freed?'

'I'm sure he would have if circumstances had been different,' said Groves with a pained look that suggested old wounds had been re-opened. 'But he didn't get that chance, thank God. A fellow Broadmoor prisoner at the time, Clifford Sutton – a name you may remember – beat him to it. He was returned to society a changed and contrite man according to my erstwhile colleagues . . . only to resume his career of rape and murder. Ironically his last victim was one of the panel who had freed him. When asked why, he replied, "She voted against".'

Barrowman grimaced. 'And that's where Moorlock Hall comes into the picture?'

'Yes, it was that case which made me speak out. The Daily Mail whipped up public fury after I suggested to my colleagues it could happen again if people like Sutton and Lawler and a number of others who were capable of manipulating the system were subject to regular review by people who weren't as clever as those they were reviewing. It didn't go down too well and I hope you appreciate the irony now that Lawler and I are locked up together.'

'I'm sorry.'

'How did you find out about Moorlock Hall? It's supposed to be a secret.'

'Someone enjoying the hospitality of a drug company at a scientific meeting let the name slip and my old supervisor made a note of it. He thought you might be an interesting final source of volunteers for my project. I jumped at the chance.'

'Tell me about your project,' said Groves.

'Progress in genetics has uncovered several genes which appear to be linked to extreme psychiatric conditions. I'm a biochemist. I'm working in a group who hope to find out more about what these genes do and how they're controlled by looking at DNA sequences and spotting enzyme differences in the blood of very different types of people.'

'Lawler is certainly different.'

Barrowman nodded and said, 'Because the work is at a very early stage we're obliged to look at extremes of human behaviour, comparing people who seem absurdly happy and optimistic with others who only see the dark side of life. We've got people looking at those who devote their lives to religion – praying for the salvation of others – and, of course, my interest in people who apparently kill without compunction.'

'As you seek to *populate* the epigenetic landscape?' said Groves thoughtfully.

Barrowman smiled. 'I see you're familiar with the jargon. You obviously read the journals.'

'I have time.'

Barrowman nodded.

Groves said, 'I remember reading that less than twenty percent of our DNA comprises actual genes. What does the rest do?'

'For years it's been called junk DNA,' said Barrowman, 'simply because no function could be assigned to it, but recently, biochemical activity has been credited to at least some of it. There is wide disagreement about how much, so I think the answer to your question at the moment is . . . we don't know.'

'Not something one hears too often from academics,' said Groves. He glanced at his watch. 'Perhaps it's time for you to meet Mr Lawler?'

The smile disappeared from Barrowman's face and he gave a less than enthusiastic nod.

'We're all on the ground floor here,' said Groves as they left the office. 'A modern prison unit inside a Victorian shell. The rest of the building is sealed off and uninhabited apart from the rats and the rolling tumbleweed of times past.'

Groves stabbed numbers into a key pad on the wall and the steel door opened to reveal a brightly lit corridor.

'I've asked that Lawler be put in the interview suite. He tends to have the television on all the time in his own accommodation and there would be extraneous noise from those adjoining. You won't be disturbed in there. It's private. You can speak on a one to one basis.'

Barrowman felt a hollow appear in his stomach. Being left alone with a serial killer was not exactly top of his wish list.

Groves read his mind. 'The room will be under camera surveillance. Lawler will be under restraint.

Barrowman pretended he'd never imagined anything else.

They stopped and Groves spoke into a grill on the wall. 'Groves with Dr Barrowman.'

'Password three please.'

'Pine tree.'

The door opened and a tall, thickset man wearing the uniform scrubs of a male nurse but displaying the physique of a nightclub bouncer ushered them inside.

'This,' said Groves walking over to where a man in his fifties sat in a chair, 'is Malcolm Lawler.' Barrowman immediately took in that the chair was bolted to the floor and its occupant had his wrists and ankles restrained by straps securing them to the frame.

Had he met him under different circumstances Barrowman thought he might have taken Lawler to be a professional man. He seemed to exude an air of quiet self-confidence, the sort that UK public schools worked so hard to instil in their pupils, understated but definitely there – the kind of assurance that got you the job when exam results might have dictated otherwise.

The hollow in Barrowman's stomach grew more insistent as he recognised that he was about to come face to face with a monster. The moment their eyes met would be significant. He wasn't quite sure why, but it had something to do with the relinquishing of anonymity. He would no longer be a face in the crowd. Lawler would know him. He would register as someone known inside a killer's head.

He looked at the hands resting limply over the ends of the chair arms. These hands had carried out acts that had made him gag in horror when he'd read about them in the trial reports, but when he looked up, the face gave no clue.

'Thank you for agreeing to see me, Mr Lawler.'

Lawler's eyes moved over Barrowman appraisingly. Eventually he said in a well-modulated voice, 'You'll have to excuse me if I don't get up.'

Barrowman smiled weakly at the joke. 'I understand I may be interrupting your television viewing?'

Lawler's lip curled. 'I don't watch television; I have it on. The game-show idiots, the clothes-horse presenters, the endless bickering in soaps . . . they all serve to remind me what I miss so much about society . . .'

'I see,' said Barrowman, chilled by the humourless smirk that appeared on Lawler's face.

'Do you?' Do you really?'

'I suppose not,' admitted Barrowman, deciding to face the challenge head on. 'There's really no way I could.'

Lawler gave a slight nod acknowledging both agreement and approval.

'I'll think I'll leave you now,' said Groves turning towards the door. He and the nurse left the room.

Barrowman was hyper-aware of the sound of the door closing behind them.

'I understand you're a scientist,' said Lawler. 'What kind? Groves didn't think to say.'

'PhD in biochemistry.'

'Ah, a PhD,' purred Lawler, 'a specialist. You learn more and more about less and less until finally you know absolutely everything about fuck all.'

'That's one way of looking at it I suppose,' said Barrowman, beginning to feel as if he were sitting some sort of test with Lawler as examiner.'

'And what exactly does a biochemist want from me?'

'I'd like to take a few samples, nothing too invasive – a few millilitres of blood from time to time and some scrapings from the inside of your mouth.'

'With a view to?'

'Analysing them.'

'Who'd have thought?'

Barrowman bit his tongue and paused before responding. 'Medical science is coming ever closer to understanding what makes us all tick as individuals, Mr Lawler, identifying which genes are responsible for which traits and how they are controlled and regulated.'

Lawler snorted dismissively. 'It's one thing knowing which gene causes which condition, quite another being able to do anything about it.' said Lawler. 'You can't change an individual's DNA.'

'True,' said Barrowman feeling slightly uncomfortable at Lawler apparently knowing about the drawbacks inherent in gene therapy. 'But people are working on that.'

'So, you think you will discover why I am . . . what shall we say? alternatively blessed to the good folks on the Jeremy Kyle show?'

Barrowman had been making a point of looking Lawler in the eye when replying, but had found nothing there to support the possibility of establishing any sort of rapport with the man. He was looking into stagnant pools. 'Yes, that sort of thing,' he said.

'Sounds fun.'

Barrowman shuddered inwardly at the thought of what 'fun' might mean to a man like Lawler, but also realised why he was continuing to feel so uncomfortable. It wasn't the fact that he was alone with a rapist and a murderer, it was that Lawler was intent on establishing himself as his intellectual superior.

'Blood and scrapings, is that all you want from me?'

Barrowman hesitated before risking, 'It would be useful if you might consider conversation from time to time, talking to me, telling me about yourself . . . about anything really . . . just what you feel about things in general . . .'

'My hopes, my dreams, my ambitions . . .' said Lawler, making a point of looking up at the walls and then at the bindings securing his arms before assuming his superior grin. 'What exactly do you want to hear from me? What exactly are you hoping for? What do you need for your results? Just tell me and I'll play along . . . Psychopath? Schizophrenic? Paranoid schizo? I can do them all. Remorseful? Contrite? Born-again Christian? – that's my favourite. Just say.'

'I'm not interested in pinning labels on anyone,' said Barrowman. It's data I'm after.'

'Of course,' conceded Lawler. 'I forgot. You're not a psychiatrist, you're a scientist, cold, unemotional, observant, but ultimately seeking a scientific truth you can never understand.'

Barrowman looked at him quizzically.

'The big question, Doctor. What's it all about?'

Lawler used his eyes to create an arc above his head. 'It's the one question waiting at the end of the line for all you scientists, the one you can never answer because it's beyond comprehension. Everything is derived from something else. The law of conservation of matter. Matter cannot be created or destroyed. Correct? And yet, science proceeds like a hamster on a wheel, carefully examining the running surface in minute detail as it continues on its way to the end of a journey that isn't coming. How could the first molecule arise if there was nothing there to begin with? The big bang? What exploded if there was nothing there to explode? Maybe that wasn't the beginning of our universe, Doctor. 'Maybe it was the end of another . . . and where did that come from? Same problem.'

Lawler seemed pleased to have Barrowman's rapt attention. 'Or maybe it's all down to a man in the sky with a long white beard. Yes, that's it. That's what the chaps in frilly dresses and pointy hats would have us believe so why not? There we are. Sorted. Anything else we should talk about?'

'I'm sure there's lots,' said Barrowman, uncertain if that were true, but feeling slightly mesmerised.

'Maybe next time,' said Lawler. 'Deal or no Deal will be on shortly; I'd hate to miss that.'

ONE

London 2014

Dr Steven Dunbar arrived at the Home Office and climbed the stairs to the small suite of offices allocated to the Sci-Med Inspectorate. He was greeted by Jean Roberts, secretary to the unit and PA to his boss, Sir John Macmillan. She smiled as he entered then frowned and looked him up and down before saying, 'You look like a TV reporter.'

Steven grinned, understanding the allusion to the Berghaus jacket he was wearing. 'You're right. I should be standing outside 10 Downing Street telling people that nothing had happened in the six hours I'd been waiting there.'

'Or wading through knee-deep floods in the west country to show us dumb folks what water looks like,' added Jean.

'It was just so cold this morning,' said Steven, removing the Berghaus and shrugging his shoulders into his suit jacket. 'This winter seems to be going on for ever. Is John in yet?'

Jean shook her head. 'Time enough. The meeting's not till eleven.'

She referred to the Whitehall committee meeting that Macmillan and Steven were due to attend to hear decisions about government research funding for the coming year. Sci-Med had been for some time concerned about the possible use of biological weapons against the UK and had been urging government action to step up vaccine production to protect the public. This particular elephant had been in the room for a very long time but there was still a reluctance to acknowledge it.

This was not due to any underestimate of the damage that such weapons could do – quite the contrary, the nightmare possibilities were endless – but more down to a general embarrassment over not knowing what to do about an event which couldn't be defined in advance. You knew where you were with explosions – even nuclear ones – you could coordinate the actions of the emergency services, practice the drills, refine the responses ahead of the incident, but to come under attack without warning from an invisible enemy – a bacterium or virus – would be very different. It would create a scenario where the emergency services would be severely limited in what they could do in any practical sense. People running around in biohazard suits spraying disinfectant everywhere would be little more than a public relations exercise. They wouldn't know what they were looking for or where it was coming from. This would spread panic in a population who didn't have the benefit of protective suiting. Them and us. Always bad.

No meaningful response could be mounted until the identity and characteristics of the infecting agent had been established and chances were by then it would be too late. The wait for analysis would put the authorities on the back foot and they'd probably never catch up. It was conceivable that citizens living in towns and cities in the twenty-first century would have no more recourse to help and protection than people living in these same towns back in the fourteenth century when Black Death came to call.

John Macmillan arrived as Steven was pouring coffee from the machine. He said, 'Me too please.' and rubbed his hands vigorously before scanning through his appointments for the day in Jean's desk diary which she turned and pushed in his direction.

The Sci-Med Inspectorate was Sir John Macmillan's brainchild, a small group of scientific and medical investigators which he'd managed to convince government there was a need for some years before when it was his belief that science and medicine were progressing at such a rate that the police lacked expertise to investigate successfully in these areas.

Despite eventual cross-party agreement for the concept, the unit had suffered a difficult birth due to Macmillan's prescient insistence that it must be allowed to operate independently and with guaranteed freedom from government-of-the-day interference. He had foreseen that high level wrong-doing might well involve people in high places, people in authority and with perhaps intimidating amounts of power and so it had proved. The unit's success in occasionally exposing the *errors of judgement* of the rich and powerful had not won it a great deal of popularity in the corridors of power, but had earned it respect and continued autonomy. Macmillan had wryly pointed out on more than one occasion that Sci-Med's greatest ally was Her Majesty's Opposition – whoever they might be. Those in power knew that any attempt to muzzle Sci-Med would inevitably result in howls of synthetic fury from the opposition followed by the need for a humiliating climb-down.

Steven, a qualified doctor who had rebelled against a conventional medical career path and joined the army after admitting to himself that he had studied medicine for all the wrong reasons – parents and teachers had thought it a good idea. *Our son the doctor. A credit to the school*

As an athletic type with a love of the outdoors and a thirst for adventure. he had found himself well suited to army life although his new employers had not completely overlooked his medical background. A compromise had resulted in his becoming an expert in field medicine – the medicine of the battlefield – as well as acquiring the skills and attributes of a Special Forces soldier. He had served with distinction in areas ranging from the deserts of the Middle East to the jungles of South America.

When the time had come for him to leave the army in his midthirties – Special Forces operations were a young man's game and his body had started pointing this out – he'd found himself facing a depressingly small number of unattractive career options open to a man who could perform surgery under fire in the desert or jungle and who boasted an impressive range of combat skills . . . drug company rep, cruise-ship doctor, in-house medic for big business. His spirits had been at a low ebb when John Macmillan had come along at the right moment to ensure that the round peg that was Steven Dunbar ended up in the round hole that was Sci-Med investigator.

Steven had built up a record of success in his new role and had become Sci-Med's principal investigator. His personal life however, had not run as smoothly. His wife, Lisa, a nurse whom he'd met in the course of an early investigation in a Glasgow hospital, had died of a brain tumour when their daughter Jenny was only two years old, leaving him without hope or purpose until time had worked its healing magic and allowed him to climb out of the abyss to face the world again. Jenny had gone to live with Lisa's sister, Sue, her husband Richard and their two children in Glenvane, a small village in Dumfriesshire in Scotland where she was currently being brought up as one of their own.

Although female company had come and gone in the following years, finding a lasting relationship had eluded Steven until Dr Natalie Simmons had come along. Tally had been working in paediatric medicine at a Leicester children's hospital when she and Steven had met during the course of one of his investigations. Respect and an immediate liking for each other had evolved quickly – as these things tended to do when fear and uncertainty were present to act as a catalyst – and it didn't take Steven long to realise that Tally was special. For her part, Tally had been reluctant to embark on a relationship with someone who lived and worked in a different part of the country – perhaps seeing the difficulties more clearly than Steven who had so quickly lost his heart to her – but his persistence and the undeniable strength of her own feelings had made it inevitable that they would give it a go.

The relationship had had its ups and downs with Tally never feeling at ease with the dangers present in Steven's job – something she had witnessed for herself after their initial meeting – and the distance that existed between them for most of the week, but after a change in circumstances which had seen Tally apply for and get a position at Great Ormond Street Hospital for Children in London. Tally had sold her flat in Leicester and they had set up home together in Steven's flat in Marlborough Court in London.

'How is Dr Simmons these days?' asked Macmillan as he settled into his chair.

Steven smiled inwardly at Macmillan's insistence on formality when referring to Tally. He supposed it was an age thing. 'I think she's still finding it a bit strange.'

'How so?'

'She's been so used to having to fight for everything on a daily basis that coming to Great Ormond Street has been a bit of an eye opener.'

Macmillan smiled. 'Makes all the difference working in an establishment with a world-wide reputation.'

'I think it's money that makes the difference.'

'One begets the other,' said Macmillan. 'Wealthy people like to be associated with heart-warming good causes. Show business people fall over each other to front-up sick children's charities – there's nothing quite like being filmed handing out presents in a children's ward when it comes to furthering your career.'

'And I thought I was the cynic in this outfit.'

'You are, but I'm becoming increasingly-aware of the role of imagery in medical care in our country. We're all being manipulated and I don't like it. '

Steven nodded and said, 'If you're going to develop a condition, make sure it's a fashionable one or you could be in trouble. No one gives three pounds a month to fight arthritis or deafness.'

'Quite.'

'What's the plan for the meeting today?'

'Rumour has it our suggestion will be turned down again.'

'Surprise, surprise,' said Steven. 'But then politicians always tend to see bio-defence as a poisoned chalice.'

'Vaccination isn't sexy and won't get you votes.' They'll pay lip service to the need for it, but when push comes to shove, other interests will come first. I understand we'll be in competition with cancer research, genetic engineering, stem cell development and some new kid on the block, epigenetics I think it's called. I'm told it's the coming thing?'

'There's been a lot about it in the scientific journals,' replied Steven. 'It's going to explain why we are all individuals and just what makes us different from each other.'

Macmillan's expression suggested that he was less than impressed but he didn't say so, obliging Steven to continue, 'Some of the concepts are difficult to get across,' he conceded. 'But if you stick with it you just might get a sense of how big it's going to be.'

'I'll await my epiphany.'

Steven was reluctant to let it go at that. 'Look at it this way. Think of our DNA as our hardware – we can't change it: we've got four trillion cells inside us and nearly all of them carry an exact copy of our genome. We can't hope to replace a faulty gene in each and every one. But the good news is that we also have what those in the know are calling the epigenome. This can be regarded as our software – the tools we need to switch genes on and off. If we can get control of that, we could start telling our hardware what to do or what to stop doing.'

'And how do we go about doing that?'

'That's the million-dollar question.'

'That new?'

Steven nodded. 'They've recently demonstrated strong epigenetic involvement in brain function, particularly during the change from childhood into adulthood. Some genes are switched on and others switched off and hey presto the ugly duckling with an attitude problem becomes a rational swan leaving for university to study history of art.'

'Actually,' said Macmillan thoughtfully and making a steeple with his fingers, 'I do seem to remember reading something recently about identifying brain differences between optimists and pessimists.'

'That's all part of it,' agreed Steven.

'Be that as it may, I can't see epithingy standing much of a chance in the competition for funds against the big boys unless they've got some kind of scientific superstar making the pitch.'

'I think they just might,' said Steven.

Macmillan opened his eyes wide. 'Please God, not another telegenic pretty-boy.'

Steven shook his head. 'I don't think Professor Dorothy Lindstrom falls into that category.'

'A woman . . . name seems familiar.'

'She hit the headlines a few years ago, never off the telly, regarded as brilliant and not afraid to speak her mind but ruffled a few feathers in her time. There were a few sighs of relief when she went off to Yale.'

'Of course,' exclaimed Macmillan, relaxing back into his chair, 'Now I remember. She was a bit unusual, wasn't she, a big player in science who didn't worship at the feet of Charles Darwin.'

'That's her,' Steven agreed. 'She's a committed Christian, a Roman Catholic who thought there were just too many convenient evolutionary accidents required by Darwinists and wasn't afraid to say so.'

'So, what made Professor Lindstrom return to these shores?'

'Tragedy.'

Macmillan looked over his glasses. 'What happened?'

'Just over a year ago there was a fire in her lab. It happened at night but two of her young post-doctoral workers were working there at the time and perished in the flames. The lab was completely destroyed.'

Macmillan made a face.

'Dorothy took it very badly.'

'Understandable.'

'Yale were very supportive, told her to take as long as she needed to recover and assured her that her lab would be rebuilt as quickly as possible, but that didn't happen. Dorothy told Yale she wouldn't be needing a new lab, she was resigning. She did her best to have her people re-assigned to other research groups and took the decision to return to the UK.'

'That really is taking it badly,' said Macmillan.

'She also decided to change her field from neuroscience to epigenetics.'

'No small step.'

'It certainly wasn't. Most people at the top of their game are happy to drift along, dotting 'i's and crossing 't's on their previous success.'

'But not Professor Lindstrom.'

'No, she moved back across the Atlantic after persuading a drug company to give her a year of start-up funding and Capital University here in London to give her lab space. One of her younger post-docs elected to come with her and she recruited new staff here. Things have been going well and she's had a couple of papers published recently in good journals.'

'What's in it for Capital?'

'Publicity. Dorothy is high profile. Every time she publishes a paper the press turns up to interview her. She's good at . . . maximising the potential of her discoveries.'

'They all are these days,' said Macmillan.

'Publicity means grants.'

'You'd have thought the press would have wised up to their weekly *breakthroughs* by now,' said Macmillan.

'Symbiosis,' said Steven. 'The scientist gets a grant; the press gets a story.'

'Well, I guess we'll see how successful she's been in attracting funding from the wise old owls of a government grants committee.'

TWO

Sir Robert Dalrymple, secretary to the government's bio-research grants committee, got to his feet and looked around the table, checking that all expected were present before calling the meeting to order.

'Ladies and Gentlemen, thank you all for coming although I have to say that I am the bearer of not very encouraging news. I'm afraid the treasury has been even less generous than we anticipated this year.'

There were groans and looks of exasperation were exchanged, but Steven and Macmillan remained impassive: they had expected little else.

'The chancellor has resolved to keep a tight rein on spending and research funding is to be no exception. You will be aware that major annual research council funding has already been frozen at its current level and we thought that supplementary funds might suffer a similar fate. Unfortunately, we have been cut by a further ten percent.'

'But there'll still be enough cash for Trident submarines and Middle Eastern wars,' said Sir Nigel Carter, a distinguished-looking, white-haired man representing the interests of cancer research.

Dalrymple did not respond.

'All that public posturing about how important health care is and in reality, our hands are being tied behind our backs,' said the scientist representing genetic engineering interests, Sir Keith Walman.

Once again Dalrymple took it on the chin and said nothing, choosing neither to argue nor agree – a Whitehall speciality.

'What will this mean in practice?' asked Professor Simon Laing from the UK Stem Cell Research Monitor.

Dalrymple took a deep breath and made a weak joke about not shooting the messenger then paused as if about to announce the winner of an Oscar.

'The committee has decided that Sci-Med's request that the government actively engage with drug companies to introduce a vaccination programme for the general public to provide protection against agents likely to be used in biological attack . . . be declined.'

Macmillan nodded and exchanged a look with Steven who risked a small smile.

'The application from Professor Dorothy Lindstrom for funding to continue and expand her work on epigenetic control mechanisms . . . has also been declined.'

'Totally?' exclaimed Lindstrom clearly taken aback.

'I'm afraid so.'

'What short-sighted stupidity. Unbelievable.'

Dalrymple seemed momentarily startled but decided to ignore Lindstrom's outburst and continued. 'The supplementary grant to cancer research will remain at its current level.'

Sir Nigel Carter nodded and accepted the decision without comment but Dorothy Lindstrom was reluctant to retire from the fray. 'Why?' she demanded.

Dalrymple recovered quickly from his obvious surprise. 'I'm sure I need hardly remind you that cancer is a major killer in our country, Professor.'

'It's a major killer in every country,' said Lindstrom. It has been for a *very long time.*'

'Your point, Professor?'

'Isn't it about time they cured it rather than gobble up money *sine diem*?'

'Oh, come on, Dorothy, you know it's not that simple,' protested Carter. 'We have been making real progress.'

'No, you haven't' retorted Lindstrom, something that brought gasps from round the table.

Carter was becoming agitated. 'The cancer figures are plain to see. People are living longer and longer. No one disputes that.'

'People are living longer and longer *with* cancer,' said Lindstrom. 'You're keeping people alive for longer and longer *with* cancer. Their quality of life can be poor to bloody awful but that doesn't appear in your figures, does it? Quality of life never does. The bulk of your research is concerned with diagnosing the disease, telling us what causes it, screening for it, everything but curing it! You've got money streaming in from slick advertising which costs a bundle and makes people feel guilty if they don't start shelling out on a monthly basis or running a marathon backwards dressed as a blooming kangaroo and you still want more!'

'Professor Lindstrom, I know you are disappointed but I really must ask you to desist,' Dalrymple intervened.

'I'm not disappointed; I'm furious and I hoped I might be allowed to put my point of view,' said Lindstrom.

'You've certainly done that, Professor. We must move on.'

Dalrymple shuffled papers in front of him unnecessarily, still reeling from what had happened. 'The committee has decided that funding for therapeutic genetic engineering be held at its current level.'

'Why?' interjected Lindstrom.

'Really, Professor. This is completely unprecedented. The committee is under no obligation to explain its decisions to anyone . . . but I will tell you that it felt that the putative treatment of disease by genetic engineering techniques continue to be given a priority rating.'

'A priority rating,' repeated Lindstrom quietly. She took a moment before saying in deliberately controlled fashion. 'Science discovered the gene for cystic fibrosis in 1979. Money poured in to fund a genetically engineered cure and here we are in 2014 no further forward apart from having a regiment of scientists on the CF payroll.'

'That is monstrously unfair,' said Walman. 'The problems involved in inserting a replacement gene are enormous.'

'That's an excuse for failure not a claim for success,' retorted Lindstrom. 'You may never come up with a suitable vector.'

'That's not a reason for stopping trying,' said Walman, clearly rattled.

'No, it isn't,' agreed Lindstrom. 'But it is a reason for reconsidering priorities before they become traditions,' she added with a glance towards Carter.

'If I may be allowed to continue . . .' said a clearly stressed Dalrymple, raising his voice to overcome the hubbub. 'The committee has granted a ten percent increase to the stem cell research budget.'

'Quite right too,' said Lindstrom to Dalrymple's obvious relief. 'It's our brightest hope.'

'I'm glad you concur, Professor,' said Dalrymple.

Simon Laing nodded his satisfaction. 'Not as much as we'd hoped for, but in the circumstances, very welcome.'

Carter, still smarting from Lindstrom's attack, said, 'Perhaps Professor Lindstrom would be good enough to tell us why she considers her work more important than research into cancer and genetic engineering?'

Walman nodded his approval of the question.

'Because it's new and I know where I'm going with my research. Your people are going up side streets, around in circles, doing the same things over and over again because of a lack of vision. It's fresh ideas you need not more cash.'

'Whereas,' said Walman angrily, 'piddling around with what makes us happy, and what makes us sad is really important?'

'It's a start,' said Lindstrom evenly, 'but my research group have come a bit further than that. We accept we can't make changes to the human genome when there are copies of it in nearly every cell in the body but it's becoming clear that we can exercise control over it and we're coming ever closer to learning how to turn genes on and off. We're pretty sure we know why placebos work. It's not magic; it's the epigenome in action, the switchgear working. When one patient is given a drug and another a sugar pill and both get better it's the *belief* that he had been given an appropriate drug that triggers the response in the placebo patient. It's not a positive attitude in itself that helps patients deal with illness and overcome it, it's the genetic switches that are thrown when a patient develops one. There's a genetic reason why certain people have photographic memories and others not. There's a genetic reason why some autistic savants can perform the most amazing calculations and others sit down and play a Beethoven sonata on the piano after hearing it for the first time. It's all down to the switches and we are homing in on them. We may all have these abilities within us; it could just be a matter of learning how to throw the switches and in the right order.'

'Or not,' said Carter sourly.

'Mind over matter,' said Walman with a shrug of disbelief.

'You're right; it is mind over matter,' said Lindstrom. 'But what we have to do is translate the vagaries of mind into actual chemical reactions, identify them and simulate them.'

'That does indeed sound an exciting prospect, Professor,' said Dalrymple, attempting to mend fences. 'I'm truly sorry that the committee could not see their way to offer support at this stage.'

'No matter,' said Lindstrom, getting up to leave, 'I'm sure not all grant-funding bodies will be so short-sighted.'

'Ouch,' whispered Steven as this was taken to signal an end to the meeting.

'Well, what do you think?' asked Steven as he and Macmillan walked through to where coffee was being served.

'She's a formidable woman . . . but not exactly a sad loss to the Diplomatic Corps.'

'Do you think she'll find alternative funding?'

'I suspect you'd have to be closer to finding these chemical switches before the pharma companies come on board, but it would be pretty wonderful if they could do it,' said Macmillan. 'Imagine being able to cure debilitating conditions through triggering a switch.'

'I'm beginning to feel gutted she didn't get support,' said Steven.

'Didn't you say she had some?'

'The drug company which paid for her relocation from the states gave her start-up money for the first year, but they would be counting on government cash appearing. I can't see them picking up the tab much longer unless Lindstrom's people were suddenly to hit the jackpot.'

'How about the university helping out?'

'No chance. Universities are like sponges. They would have been expecting grant money too so they could mop up a large chunk of it for providing accommodation and basic services. Now that there isn't to be any . . . well, who knows?'

'Life's rich tapestry,' sighed Macmillan. 'Why don't you see what the feeling is in the Lindstrom group? I noticed Dorothy wasn't alone this morning.'

'Good idea,' said Steven, looking across the room to where Dorothy was making sure no one was left uncertain of her point of view. He saw the young man who had been sitting beside her earlier detach himself and head for the sandwich table. He walked over to create a chance meeting.'

'Steven Dunbar,' he said with a smile.

'Owen Barrowman.'

The pair shook hands.

'Bad luck this morning,' said Steven.

'You too,' replied Owen Barrowman, picking and choosing to fill his plate 'I noticed you came up empty handed too.'

'We're used to it,' replied Steven. 'One day soon I might just buy a lance and start looking for windmills.'

'Barrowman grinned and Steven added, 'Happily, we weren't looking for grant funding to continue our existence. We were trying to get the government to take public vaccination seriously. Your situation seems more precarious.'

'You're right,' agreed Barrowman. 'We were all hoping for government money. Everything depended on it. Jobs, careers, degrees, mortgage payments, you name it.'

'For what it's worth, I'm truly sorry you drew a blank. It sounds like a really exciting field to be in right now.'

'If only the suits could see that too. I don't think anyone saw a complete turn-down coming, least of all, Dorothy. I thought someone with her credentials was a cert for funding.'

'Have you been with her long?'

'I joined her group when she returned to the UK from the states. I did my PhD on epigenetics at Edinburgh and was looking around for a post-doc position, which would allow me to continue my own research interest but without much success when I read that Dorothy had moved into the field and was looking for people to join her. It sounded just right for me.'

'For her too I should think,' said Steven. 'PhDs in epigenetics can't be too thick on the ground.'

Barrowman grinned. 'Yeah, well I guess it looked like working both ways. I thought I'd landed on my feet: now I find it was my backside.'

'You said, continue your research?'

'Most advertised post-doc positions are to work on specific projects, which is fair enough, but I was hoping for one that would allow me to continue what I'd started during the last year of my

PhD project. My old PhD supervisor got me a small grant for six months to tide me over until Dorothy arrived from the states.'

'So, what are you studying?'

'Genetic and biochemical patterns in psychopathic killers.'

'Are you serious?'

'Absolutely.

Steven was taken aback. 'How on earth do you do that?'

'I got the university to approach high security prisons and prison hospitals across the country with a view to me interviewing selected prisoners – those convicted of murder while classed as criminally insane – hoping to recruit them as volunteers in my project. They would have to provide lab samples for analysis.'

'And they agreed?'

Barrowman smiled. 'It took a while to get through all the red tape but, in the end, all the prisons agreed although not all prisoners did, but I've managed to get a reasonable number to provide blood, buccal swabs etc.'

'I take it Professor Lindstrom was happy for you to continue this line of research?'

'I wouldn't say she was over the moon but she wanted someone to bring her new people up to speed in the latest epigenetic techniques. It's worked out well.'

'Dorothy's goal is to understand everything connected with human behaviour.''

'Is that your goal too?'

'I'm more specific,' said Barrowman. 'I'd like to find a cure for psychotic behaviour.'

'That's a pretty high bar too,' Steven pointed out. 'I'm impressed. Seriously, this field is just too important to be ignored. It can only be a matter of time before support appears.'

'I hope you're right, but I'm beginning to suspect that the people Dorothy upset in the past might be thinking it's payback time. She's not the easiest person to get along with.'

'We should keep in touch, maybe have a beer some time,' said Steven. 'I'd like to know more about your work.'

The two men exchanged contact details.

Steven and Macmillan walked back across Green Park.

'You two seemed to get on,' said Macmillan.

'He's gutted that the group didn't get funding when he'd gambled that they would. He's at that time in his career when he needs to get a few good publications out there to establish himself as a researcher and start thinking about a lectureship somewhere. I think he's worried that there might be some kind of vendetta against Dorothy.'

'Mm,' said Macmillan non-committally. 'I'm having lunch with a couple of ministers tomorrow. I'll see what I can find out.'

'Good, we agreed to keep in touch.'

It was just after six in the evening when Steven got back to Marlborough Court to find that Tally hadn't yet arrived home. He made himself coffee and stood at the window, catching glimpses of the Thames river traffic through the gap in the buildings across the street while he considered the events of the day. He was feeling numb and wondering why this should be when the sound of Tally coming in broke his train of thought.

'Well, how did it go?' she asked, dumping her bag on a chair and shrugging off her coat. 'Is HMG going to take up the challenge and offer the public protection at last?'

Steven shook his head. 'They turned us down.'

'I'm sorry,' said Tally coming over to wrap her arms round him. How do you feel about that?'

'It's what we expected.'

'That's not what I asked.'

'No,' agreed Steven, 'Defence against biological attack should be a priority and here I am neither pissed off nor angry that the government is still sitting on its hands over it. Why's that?'

Tally looked up at him, mildly amused. 'Because . . .you don't know what to do about it any more than they do. If you did you'd be absolutely furious. Instead you probably just feel numb.'

Steven smiled, appreciating the fact that Tally had hit the nail on the head. He squeezed the hand resting on his shoulder. 'I think I'm more concerned about someone else being turned down for funding.'

'Really? Who?'

Steven told her about the Lindstrom group and their failure to attract government support.

'Well, I suppose there's only a limited amount of money to go around.'

'Mm,' said Steven thoughtfully. 'Trouble is I'm not entirely convinced that was the reason.' He told Tally about his conversation with Barrowman.

'I suppose you take on the establishment at your peril,' said Tally, 'but didn't you say Dorothy Lindstrom had been a darling of the media?'

'There's a world of difference between that and being embraced by academe, said Steven. 'Anyone who crosses their invisible line and strays into what might be considered show-business can be in for a very hard time indeed.'

'Something you don't realise until the knife goes into your back,' smiled Tally.

Steven told her about the opinions Dorothy had expressed at the meeting about the direction of current research funding.

'Wow.'

'Wow indeed, but not entirely without foundation,' said Steven quietly.

'Maybe . . . but I mean . . .'

'Not the wisest thing to come out with?'

'Quite, I mean you've got to play the game, haven't you?'

'Maybe it should depend on how clean the game is,' said Steven.

'You don't think it is?'

'People are people. Human nature rules at whatever level of society you're in.'

'Not a happy thought if you really believe that the research grants system is corrupt. Do you?'

Steven shook his head. 'No,' he conceded. 'Well, not at the level of cash exchanging hands in brown paper bags, but it's not above having an old boys' network who scratch each other's backs. As to whether it extends to standing in the way of first rate research in order to settle old scores . . . who knows? John is going to try and find out at one of his lunches.'

Tally smiled. 'Where the real truth leaks out.'

Steven nodded and asked, 'How was your day?'

'Life is good,' replied Tally. 'I am practicing medicine instead of spending my time arguing about targets and filling in forms.'

'Being a consultant suits you.'

'Nothing to do with that,' said Tally. 'We're well funded and well managed. I now work in a proper hospital instead of being treated as a form-filling, box-ticking piece in a board game for third rate politicians and mediocre managers. *It's all about choice for patients,* my backside. It's all about money. Period.'

Steven smiled. He was used to hearing Tally sound off about the shortcomings of the National Health Service He was even pleased that her promotion and move had apparently done little to blunt her views, but felt obliged to point out what John Macmillan had said about special funding for Great Ormond Street.

'I suppose,' Tally conceded. 'Maybe I should keep my mouth shut, smile sweetly and be terribly sympathetic to medics less fortunate than myself.

'Well, I was wondering how long it would be before the establishment gets to you and bends you to its will. You'll be co-opted on to one committee after another until you can't say a word without offending someone you shouldn't.'

'Aint gonna happen.'

'Mm, maybe we should go out to eat before you start wearing a bow tie and playing golf.' said Steven.

'Maybe we should go out to eat before I pour the contents of this kettle over your head?'

The food at the Jade Garden Chinese restaurant was as good as it always was. Steven had been a regular there since joining Sci Med; Tally had only been there twice before – with Steven when she'd come to visit – but it was now a favourite haunt for them both.

'Will John continue to lobby on mass vaccination?' asked Tally after they'd placed their order.

'I'm sure he will,' said Steven, 'but I think we're both resigned to failure until . . .'

'Until what?'

'Until something actually happens . . . either by deliberate attack or through some awful epidemic arriving on our shores through chance or circumstance.'

Tally ended the ensuing pause. 'Would you like to hear a happy story?' she asked.

'You bet. Have you got one?'

'One of my patients, a little blind girl; is going to get her sight back.'

'Surgery?'

Tally shook her head. 'Stem cells. Isn't that just brilliant?'

'Now that is a happy story.'

'Stem cell technology is just so exciting. It's going to bring about such a revolution in medicine.'

'Even if it's a bit of embarrassment to science,' said Steven.

Tally raised an eye.

'Science doesn't really understand how stem cells do what they do.'

'As a clinician, I must say I don't really care. It's then end result I'm interested in. What's their problem anyway?'

'Differentiation,' said Steven, 'the holy grail of biology. How do absolutely identical cells in terms of their DNA diverge to become limbs and organs which are totally different from each other? Science doesn't know but stem cells do. If we put them in the right place they'll do the job for us.'

'And that's all I care about,' said Tally. 'If stem cells can make my patient see again, they can keep their secret.'

Steven nodded. 'Actually,' he said thoughtfully, 'they may not be keeping their secret that much longer.' He told Tally about Dorothy Lindstrom's claims for epigenetics. 'It makes so much sense,' he added. 'The DNA can't change so it must be the switchgear that does the trick.'

Tally made thoughtful imaginary circles on her napkin with her forefinger. Eventually she looked up and said, 'You know, there are times when I think we know so much and then, quite suddenly, I feel like we know nothing at all.'

'Join the club.'

THREE

A month passed before John Macmillan decided that his unofficial enquiries as to why the Lindstrom group had been turned down for funding were not going to bear fruit and he said as much to Steven.

'It's very strange,' he said. 'I don't usually have trouble finding out what I want to know from Whitehall people, but everyone I spoke to below the Home Secretary herself genuinely didn't seem to know. I'll keep trying of course, but I'll have to think of a different approach.'

'Ask the Home Secretary?'

'Maybe not. A bit difficult if personal vendettas are involved.'

Steven thanked him for trying and said he planned to set up a meeting soon with Owen Barrowman to find out how things were going. He'd pass on the bad news.

* * * *

Owen Barrowman entered, The Moorings, the riverside pub where he had agreed to meet Steven at eight. It was a quarter past. He spotted Steven sitting in a corner, reading a newspaper and nursing a half empty glass.

'Sorry I'm late, good to see you again,' said Barrowman shrugging off his jacket and asking if Steven was ready for another. Steven said not and waited while his companion got himself a beer from the bar.

'My sincere apologies, I hate being late but I forgot I had a meeting with my volunteer at Moorlock Hall today and it took longer than I'd anticipated.

'Moorlock Hall?'

Barrowman tapped his fingertips lightly off his forehead before saying, 'Sorry, I'm not thinking straight, there's no reason why you should know about it. I hadn't heard of it myself until a few months ago. It's all very hush hush.' Barrowman leaned across the table to explain in muted tones just who were being held in Moorlock Hall.

Steven let out his breath in a low whistle. 'I can see why they might want to keep that quiet,' he murmured. 'It probably contravenes every human rights regulation in the book. Do you know who sanctioned the place?'

'I didn't ask. To be honest, I don't care. I just saw it as an opportunity to get data from some of the worst criminal psychopaths on the planet.'

Steven smiled at the single mindedness of the career scientist. 'And has it turned out that way?'

Barrowman paused before saying, 'Only one of the inmates agreed to take part in the study, a bit of a disappointment, but there's something scarily special about this guy – one of the worst according to the medical superintendent and he's certainly the most intriguing subject I've come across. Maybe you've heard of him, Malcolm Lawler?'

'God, yes,' Steven replied. 'It was a long time ago, but I remember him, an absolute monster. He was all over the papers for weeks. Why did someone like him agree?'

'The director thinks he was curious.'

'I can't say I envy you your choice of project,' said Steven with a shake of the head. 'You must have to read up on what these people have done before you meet them, go all through the details?'

'That's part of it, yes. I need to know everything in order to link up possible traits with genetic or biochemical factors.'

'Doesn't it get to you?'

'I have the occasional wobble.'

Steven raised his eyes at the word 'wobble'.

'Bad dreams, the occasional sleepless night, a certain loss of belief in human nature, shall we say.'

Steven nodded. 'I can empathise with that.'

It was Barrowman's turn to raise his eyes.

'Army,' said Steven. 'I saw a bit of human nature in my time. It was quite an eye-opener to see what human beings will do to each other when they think they have some sort of official approval.'

'There's a difference between what you witnessed and the horrors my lot got up to,' said Barrowman. 'Mine needed no approval from anyone.'

'A different level of evil,' said Steven. 'You should be careful.'

Barrowman's eyes asked the question.

'Continued exposure to evil can be . . . problematic. People have been known to change after such exposure.'

'Cold war brainwashing?'

'Actually, I was thinking more about the studies done in Nazi Germany before the second world war. Ordinary decent people who felt outraged by what was happening to their country went along to Nazi party rallies to protest and came away as committed Nazis. Their anger and outrage had left them vulnerable to the power of suggestion. The filth flooded in and changed them forever.'

Barrowman nodded. 'It works both ways,' he said. 'Many people went along to the Billy Graham rallies in the nineteen fifties, curious to see what was going on and came away as committed Christians. They got swept up in the fervour they experienced in the huge venues that were used.'

Steven smiled and said, 'Somehow I suspect you are about to suggest it was all down to epigenetics.'

'Absolutely, throwing the right switches . . . and the wrong ones.'

'Scary, but you and the group are going to be able to explain it soon?'

'Frankly I'm not sure how much longer the group is going to last,' said Barrowman. 'We're running out of money.'

'Still no sign of funding?'

'Afraid not.'

'It's bizarre,' said Steven. 'I take it Dorothy kept trying for funding after the government turned her down?'

Barrowman nodded. 'She drew a blank everywhere. I keep thinking it doesn't make any sense. She has a worldwide scientific reputation and epigenetics has to be the coming thing in research. Maybe the public don't know too much about it, but everyone in science is saying so.'

Steven nodded. 'My boss is still trying to find out why government support didn't materialise, but he's hit a brick wall.'

'Thank him for trying.'

'Correct me if I'm wrong, but I got the impression you're in a slightly better position than the other members of the group in that you had accumulated quite a lot of data before you joined Dorothy?'

'I was able to collect quite a lot of samples from prisoners in high security places and I've done some preliminary analysis, but we have to depend a lot on favours from other labs when it comes to use of equipment for screening and sequencing.'

'Any interesting results?'

Steven noticed a slight reluctance to answer the question. He smiled and said, 'No details, just a general enquiry.'

'I've seen some marked differences in the data but not enough to be absolutely sure. It's so frustrating. I just wish I had discovered Malcolm Lawler earlier. I'm convinced he's going to be something really special.'

'But you'd have enough to publish if the worst came to the worst and the group collapsed?' Steven probed.

'I'll be able to get a couple of decent papers out of what I have, but that's not what I really want.'

'Of course not,' said Steven. 'It's *Nature* or nothing.' He couldn't help but think that naked ambition was sometimes very unattractive. 'How about the rest of the group?'

'Again, a few promising lines, but we're all in the same boat really; we need more time and more data.'

'And that requires money,' said Steven before finishing his drink. 'Another one?'

'I don't think so,' said Barrowman. 'It's been a long day.'

Steven smiled. 'Sounds like it. Well, I look forward to hearing how you get on, especially with your *real baddie*.'

'I'll keep you in the loop,' said Barrowman. 'I'm going to make as many visits to Moorlock Hall as I can in the next few weeks just in case the university pulls the plug. At least, if I have the samples, they can sit in the fridge until happier times. Maybe you'll let me know if Sir John finds out anything?

'Of course.'

'How did your meeting go?' Tally asked when Steven got home.

'Things are getting pretty desperate for the Lindstrom group. They can't go on for much longer without new funding and people are starting to look through the jobs pages of *New Scientist*.'

'Does that include your man, Barrowman?'

Steven explained why Barrowman was in a better position than most. 'He managed to collect quite a lot of samples for his study before Dorothy relocated, but he thinks he might be on to something special with a prisoner being held in a secret place . . . but that's another story.'

'I've got time if you have, said Tally.

Steven told her about Moorlock Hall and watched her mouth fall open.

'That sounds like a real fun place to work. Is that legal? I mean keeping it a secret?'

'Probably not,' said Steven with a shrug. 'But it sounds like a damned good idea to me. They've let out too many monsters to walk the streets and commit mayhem all over again.'

'Surely, you're not questioning the competence of our psychiatric colleagues?' asked Tally, tongue in cheek.

'No, no,' replied Steven. 'I think the emperor's new clothes are absolutely lovely.'

Tally fell silent and Steven sensed that she was thinking about something else he'd said earlier – he knew that look.

'Did anyone come from the US with Dorothy?'

'Just one I think, a young post-doc, Jane Lincoln.'

'I suppose I was wondering why anyone would do that. I mean, Dorothy decides to change her field, gives up a position at Yale – one of the finest universities in the USA – crosses the Atlantic without any guarantees for the future and one of her post-docs says, count me in. Does that sound right to you?'

'Now you come to mention it . . . I suppose it does sound like a bit of a leap in the dark. Mind you, she might have been keen to stay with a big name.

'Suppose you're right,' Tally agreed, 'but travelling three thousand miles to end up working in an English university few people have ever heard of for only a few months before being told you're out of a job doesn't sound like a brilliant career move to me.'

'Ah, the insight of hindsight,' said Steven. 'Dorothy's a very persuasive woman and I don't think she imagined for a moment she'd be turned down for funding.'

The Home Office

'I have a question for you,' said Steven to his boss. 'What do you know about Moorlock Hall?'

John Macmillan shook his head slowly before admitting, 'Never heard of it. Should I?'

Steven filled him in on the details as given to him by Barrowman.'

Macmillan frowned. 'Good God, where is this place?'

'Middle of nowhere according to Barrowman. It's an old Victorian asylum which now plays host to fourteen people who would have been executed in times past.'

'So why are they keeping them there instead of somewhere like Broadmoor?'

'A decision was made that they would be taken out of the system, never be subject to review and therefore never be released.'

'By whom?'

'That's not clear, but it seems it was taken after a killer named Clifford Sutton was released from Broadmoor, having been "cured" and went on to rape and kill again. The press and the public were furious and a plan was hatched to make sure nothing like it could happen again. Prisoners – or patients depending on your point of view – from across the UK who were judged beyond redemption were quietly transferred to Moorlock Hall, never to be released or even considered for release. Officially it doesn't exist.'

'So how the hell did Barrowman find out about it?'

Steven told him.

'The old story, two can keep a secret if one of them is dead.'

'Should we be interested?'

Macmillan made a face and leaned back in his chair. 'I don't think it's a matter for Sci-Med, do you?'

'Personally, I think it a pity that the cat ever got out the bag.

'I'm inclined to agree: it wouldn't worry me greatly if they transported these people to the planet Zog, but my concern is that Sci-Med might be thought negligent if we knew about this situation and neither said nor did anything. What do you think?''

Steven considered for a few moments before saying, 'I've forgotten what we were talking about . . .'

Macmillan smiled. 'So be it, but chances are it's not going to stay a secret for much longer. Once this gets around Whitehall there are those who will be bound to see a way of using it for their own ends.'

FOUR

'Well, here we are again,' said Malcolm Lawler as Owen Barrowman was shown into the interview room at Moorlock Hall where Lawler had been strapped to his chair in preparation.

Barrowman felt his teeth go on edge, reading more into what on the surface was a polite greeting. What was it? Mockery? Derision? A patronising acknowledgement that someone mildly amusing had arrived?

'Afternoon, Mr Lawler.'

Although this was their eighth meeting, Barrowman stuck doggedly to formality, something Lawler had made easy for him with his smug air of superiority. Barrowman loathed the man but also found him spell-bindingly interesting. It was like speaking to a creature from another planet. There was much to learn.

'So, what has science learned from my blood, doctor? Is a ground-breaking paper about to rock the British Medical Journal?'

'Too soon for that, Mr Lawler, but there are certain enzyme levels that look interesting. They just need more investigation.'

'Ah, that's always the way with science,' mused Lawler. 'More research needs to be done . . . progress always lies round the next corner.'

Barrowman smiled. Lawler's preliminary blood results from samples taken on the last three visits had revealed more than he cared to talk about, least of all to Lawler, but it needed checking – thorough checking. Publishing conclusions which later proved to be wrong could end up in scientific crucifixion. Scientists liked seeing what they expected to see: they liked hearing what they expected to hear. Beware. Check, check and check again.

As a researcher, Barrowman knew the importance of being observant – perhaps that above all else. In the early stages of an investigation there was no way of knowing what was important and what was not. The smallest detail could be the key to a much bigger truth. When they'd first met, Groves, the medical superintendent at Moorlock Hall, had complained bitterly that Lawler could fool psychiatric assessors by telling them exactly what they wanted to hear and making sure they saw exactly what they were looking for. When later, Lawler had bragged to him personally that he could assume the persona of whatever psychiatric label he cared to assign to him, Barrowman had put him to the test. He had manoeuvred the conversation around to the difficulties inherent in psychiatric diagnosis and Lawler had taken up the challenge to demonstrate his skills in faking mental conditions.

Barrowman had not only made a point of flattering Lawler over his ability, he had collected lab samples immediately afterwards. His plan had been to compare the biochemical profiles of someone pretending to suffer from a recognised psychiatric condition with those he'd already obtained from officially diagnosed cases in other institutions. He hoped that, as a side interest, he might be able to establish a blood test to expose the fakers – those who sought to use mental illness as a way of escaping the full weight of the law when it came to punishment.

Barrowman had spent the previous evening examining Lawler's biochemical results – which had just come back from the lab – with those he had on file from patients in Broadmoor and Rampton. What he saw had excited him and then caused him to stop and wonder. The most likely explanation for what he was seeing was that there had been some kind of mix-up in the specimens he had given to the lab – embarrassing as he'd been solely responsible for this, but it had to be checked. Earlier this morning he had taken up what was left in the fridge of Lawler's blood sample from the date and time in question and asked if the lab might hurry through repeat tests as a favour. Barrowman could be very charming when it suited him, the results would be ready when he got back.

'So, what is it today?' asked Lawler. 'How are we going to progress the great discovery? More blood?'

'Of course,' Barrowman replied a little hesitantly, 'but to reach any firm conclusions I'd like to understand more about you. I need to differentiate between nature and nurture. I don't want to waste time looking for a genetic reason for behaviour that is really down to an experience you had in childhood, if you know what I mean?'

Lawler gave Barrowman a withering look. 'I'm perfectly familiar with the concepts of nature and nurture, thank you.'

'I'm sorry, I didn't mean to be patronising. It's just that I know so little about what makes you tick. I know why you're here of course and I've heard your views on mental illness and the people who treat it, but I need to understand . . . more about what goes on in your head as a person . . . what you think about when you're alone . . . when you're not performing for your own amusement . . .'

Owen saw the expression on Lawler's face darken and sensed that he'd got it all wrong.'

Lawler saw his unease and paused to revel in it. He leaned forward in his chair, the restraints on his arms forcing him into the body shape of a cat about to spring. 'What you really want to know is why I did it,' he snapped. 'Just like all the rest. How could anyone bring themselves to do the things I've done? How could anyone in their right mind – woops, but I'm not, am I? – even conceive of some of the things I've done? *My god, Marjorie* – Lawler affected a posh matronly voice – '*it makes me quite ill to think about it.*'

Barrowman felt the hairs on the back of his neck rise and a feeling of trepidation engulf him as Lawler's unblinking stare transfixed him. He made a weak attempt at arguing that this wasn't the case but Lawler ignored him. 'What goes on in my head, Doctor? What goes on in my head? . . . all right.'

Barrowman heard the last two words as his ticket to a place he really didn't want to go to.

Lawler, still straining forward, said quietly, 'I think about fear, doctor. Fear is the key to my world. Sweat glistening on skin, gasps for breath – music to my ears. My god, let me tell you, doctor, the smell of fear is quite intoxicating, but it's only an aperitif, a joyous hint of what's to come as you strip away every veneer, every vestige of dignity, every scrap of belief and hope from . . . your subject.'

'I don't want to hear this, Lawler. Stop there!'

'But you must, doctor,' hissed Lawler. 'You're a cold, dispassionate scientist, remember? You have to hear it or you're no longer a genuine investigator. You'll be a fraud. You'll be leaving out the bits that YOU have decided should not be recorded. You'll be left with flawed data, doctor. FLAWED DATA, the enemy of science.'

Lawler took Barrowman's nervous swallow as acquiescence and continued as if he'd only been momentarily distracted. 'Where was I? Ah, yes, pain, I was coming to pain. Drugs are fine but they are as nothing compared to the high you can reach in the presence of someone in complete and absolute agony . . . Mona Styles for instance.'

Barrowman knew that Mona Styles had been one of Lawler's victims and had read with horror what had been done to her. He had no wish to hear the perpetrator go through it in detail, but Lawler had engineered the situation perfectly. He couldn't get up and leave without losing credibility. *FLAWED DATA,* the enemy of science.

Barrowman fought the urge to vomit as Lawler guided him through a tale that touched the outer limits of depravity.

It was obvious to him that Lawler was feeding off his disgust, stage-managing his revelations with the deliberate introduction of pauses which forced Barrowman to fill in the blanks for himself before trumping him with yet more horrendous details.

'The moment when she realised there was yet more to come, doctor, . . . yet another level . . . of exquisite agony to encounter . . . Let me tell you, I touched the stars . . .'

Lawler relaxed his grip on the chair arms and closed his eyes, leaning back to relive the moment as if caught up in some hellish rapture.

Barrowman sat, immobile and wide-eyed like a waxwork, waiting for Lawler to return to the present before steeling himself to say in as controlled a fashion as he could, 'I'll take your blood sample now, Mr Lawler.' He managed it without a quaver in his voice, a triumph of self-control over utter revulsion.

The merest suggestion of doubt appeared in Lawler's eyes. He had been expecting a different response, some overt sign of disgust, at best a complete collapse of professional demeanour, perhaps even a descent into abusive rant, but it didn't happen.

Two nurse/attendants came into the room, opened the mesh barrier and stood by while Barrowman took a blood sample from Lawler's arm before thanking him as matter-of-factly as he could. He left the room and paused while the door was closed behind him before half running, half stumbling along the corridor to the staff toilet where he threw up helplessly into a wash basin. Every thought of what he'd heard resulted in yet another retch until the pain from his stomach muscles made him wince. He was still holding the plastic blood sample tube in one hand as he struggled to turn on the taps with the other to wash away the mess and the smell . . . *the smell of fear, Doctor, an aperitif.*

The sound of Groves' voice behind him startled him. He hadn't heard him come in.

'I understand our Mr Lawler has been entertaining you with his trips down memory lane, doctor . . .'

Barrowman shook his head, risking taking it out of range of the basin to stand up and turn around. 'I'm sorry, that was . . . unprofessional.'

A slight smile appeared on Groves' lips. He said, 'The day when feeling like a decent human being is less important than being professional will be a very sad one indeed. I keep a decent malt in my desk drawer for when things just become . . . too much. Join me?'

Back in his office, Groves handed Barrowman whisky in a glass tumbler with a chip out of the rim. 'Do you really think this is going to be a worthwhile exercise?' he asked.

Barrowman examined his glass in silence. It seemed to match his surroundings perfectly, he thought, noting that the rim on Groves' glass had more than one chip out of it. There was an awkward moment when he raised the glass to his lips and the strong aroma of the whisky threatened to provoke another protest from his fragile stomach, but the moment passed and the fire in his throat from his first sip seemed to signal an end to the nightmare. 'God, that's good,' he exclaimed.

'Ardbeg,' said Groves. 'A reason to live.'

'In answer to your question, I wasn't counting on what happened today. That was something else. but I've been getting some interesting data from Lawler's blood results. I have to stick with it.'

'You don't think you just might end up with a new label for someone like Lawler?'

'That would be the very worst thing that could happen. Labels are pointless in my book: They don't change anything. Learning that the man who's just murdered your daughter suffers from a condition involving twenty-three syllables and a silent "p" doesn't change a thing. She's still dead and that bastard killed her.'

Groves tipped his glass slightly in agreement. 'There are those in my profession for whom labels are an end in themselves and then of course, there is the legal profession.'

Barrowman smiled. 'Who will extend proceedings as long as possible to accommodate long-winded and often contradictory expert opinions.' He declined the offer of the whisky bottle and shook his head. 'I have to drive.'

'There does seem to be a reluctance among both professions to acknowledge even the possibility of the existence of evil,' said Groves.

'But you do?'

'I'm surrounded by it. Evil has a presence, doctor . . . a very real presence.'

The look in Groves' eyes asked a question which Barrowman answered with a slight nod. He knew exactly what Groves meant. He'd started to feel it too. His mind had filled with disgust, terror, but with a degree of alertness he'd never experienced before.

The drive back to London left him feeling all over the place. He had completely failed to compartmentalise Lawler – something he'd always managed with the other killers he'd dealt with. There seemed to be nothing he could do to escape from what he'd heard from Lawler and it left him feeling exposed and damaged in terms of self-confidence. Despite that, he could appreciate the irony in Lawler having been the one who'd reminded him of the cold, dispassionate nature of science when, here he was, floating like a cork in a maelstrom of mixed emotions. He detested Lawler yet was still transfixed by him. He felt sorry for Groves and understood his decline into self-defensive cynicism, joking about he and Lawler being locked up together. But it was no joke. It was so evidently true and, what was worse, Lawler had got the better of the deal.

It had gone five when Barrowman drew into the university car park and people were leaving. He planned to do exactly the same after putting away Lawler's blood sample in the lab fridge, but he met one of the junior technicians, Molly Bearsden, on the stairs.

'Hi Owen, Dorothy was looking for you earlier. I think she's still in her room.'

The prospect of a debriefing session with Dorothy Lindstrom when he desperately just wanted to go home did little to fill him with joy. He even considered slipping away after he'd stored the blood, but then thought better of it, He went along the corridor and knocked on Dorothy's door.

'Come on in, Owen. Sit down. How was your day?'

Barrowman struggled for words. His reluctance to relive the interview with Lawler was overriding everything else. He shook his head and gestured with his hands to suggest he didn't know where to start.

'No matter,' said Dorothy, 'You've obviously had a long day. We can talk about it tomorrow. What I did want to tell you is that I had some rather wonderful news today.'

'Really?'

'I've got funding.'

'You're kidding. Wow, that's great news. How much are we talking about?'

'A lot,' said Dorothy, putting her elbows on the desk and leaning forward conspiratorially. 'Enough to keep the university happy for the foreseeable future, enough to make everyone in the group secure and enough to expand the lab to at least twice our size. We can even have our own biochemistry section, working exclusively for us instead of having to wait our turn to have things put through the analysers.'

'So, who's come up with that sort of cash? Did the drug company have second thoughts?'

Dorothy seemed to hesitate for a moment before saying, 'No, it's all a bit mysterious, but the funding organisation wishes to remain anonymous for the time being.'

Barrowman was dumbstruck for a few moments. 'I don't understand. Why on earth would they want to do that?'

'I don't know, but you know what they say about looking a gift horse in the mouth.'

'How long is the agreement for?'

'They've agreed to support an expanded group and equip it for three years.

'That's what you asked the government for. This is wonderful, but what do these people hope to get out of their investment?'

Dorothy made a vague gesture with her hands.

Barrowman was clearly bemused. 'I'm sorry . . . I feel as if I'm being asked to believe in Santa Claus. There must be strings attached, conditions?

Dorothy approached her answer as if walking on broken glass. 'They insist on seeing our results before they're submitted for publication.'

'And?'

Dorothy broke off eye contact and looked down at the table. 'They would have the final say over what gets made public and what doesn't.'

'What?' Barrowman exclaimed, prompting Dorothy to raise her hands in a mock defensive gesture.

'Calm down, think about it. It's not going to be a problem. Why would they want to hush up important findings if they were actually funding the project?''

Barrowman fell silent for a few moments, feeling that this was all a bit much to take in after the day he'd had. Eventually he confessed, 'This is giving me such a bad feeling.'

'Frankly, I'd happily take money from a baby's piggy bank right now,' said Dorothy. 'Look, if our research went well, these people would probably just want to make sure their contribution was fully recognised in the papers we publish.'

Barrowman shook his head. 'I hate the idea of other people – anonymous people – people we don't know anything about – having control. It could be a money laundering scheme.'

Dorothy looked extremely doubtful about that suggestion.

'All right, I don't know what a money laundering scheme is, but we could work for years on something and if they didn't want our findings made public that would be an end to it – and probably the careers of all those of us involved.'

'Oh, come on, Owen.'

'So what aspect of our research attracted them?'

'Yours.'

Barrowman's mouth fell open. It had been a pretty awful day, but unbelievably it was getting worse. 'How could they possibly know what I've been doing?'

'I told them.'

'You told them?' Barrowman exclaimed.

'Look, the university requested that I meet with some people who might possibly be interested in funding cutting edge research to use their term. These people weren't introduced to me by name or organisation so it was obvious they had little to do with the usual funding bodies. That suggests that they would be more interested in investment rather than scientific progress – venture capitalists if you like. I gave a talk about the work going on in my research group – I felt I had nothing to lose. I've just about run out of grant money and the technicians are already applying for other jobs. Why would I refuse?'

Barrowman ignored the question. 'How much did you tell them about what I'm doing?'

'I told them about your PhD work and said that I thought you might be on the trail of some interesting connections between genes associated with certain psychotic disorders and, if all went well, how they might be controlled.'

'I see.'

Dorothy picked up on the annoyance in Barrowman's voice. 'Owen, you've had a hard day: you're not in a position to think clearly. Why don't we stop here and get a good night's sleep, we'll have a full group meeting tomorrow and talk things through rationally.'

Barrowman gave a reluctant nod before getting up and leaving without further comment.

Lucy Barrowman looked on in bemusement as her husband headed straight for the whisky bottle – a half full bottle of Bell's which had lain largely untouched since New Year time – and poured himself a large measure before swilling it down.

'Well, hello to you too,' she said accusingly. 'I take it we've not had the best of days?'

'Sorry,' grunted Barrowman, fighting the fire in his throat. 'Shit awful. I think I'm going to be looking for a job.'

'Well?' Lucy prompted as the silence continued. 'Are you going to tell me why?'

Barrowman told her.

'Does it really matter where the money comes from?'

'Of course, it matters. These anonymous donors could screw up my whole career.'

'Does that matter more than being out of a job?'

'I expected more support from my wife.'

'The baby and I will be expecting some support too.'

'What bab . . .Oh Christ, I forgot, you were seeing the doctor today. You're pregnant. Oh God . . . that's . . . wonderful.'

'Yeah,' said Lucy, getting to her feet and leaving the room.

'Oh, come on Lucy,' Barrowman called out. 'C'mon, you know I'm delighted . . . It's just been such an awful day and not just because of the funding thing . . . this guy at Moorlock Hall . . . he's really getting to me.

The bedroom door slammed.

FIVE

'You look thoughtful,' said John Macmillan.

'Sorry,' smiled Steven, 'a lot on my mind. Owen Barrowman phoned me late last night. An anonymous outfit has come up with funding for the Lindstrom group.'

'Well, well,' said Macmillan. 'I heard a rumour to that effect at dinner last night. Apparently, the fact that her group is looking for genetic links to extreme criminal behaviour attracted someone's attention, someone to whom money is no object.'

'Barrowman's work,' said Steven. He's been collecting data from psychopaths in high security units all over the UK. He's looking for genetic and biochemical differences that might point the way to possible treatments.''

'A cure for psychopaths?' exclaimed Macmillan.

'The Lindstrom group are looking at a wide range of extreme human behaviour. It's the old story, if you understand how something works you're coming close to controlling it.'

Macmillan looked as if his mind had strayed off somewhere else. 'You know, this is all getting quite . . . bizarre. I had a note delivered to me just before you arrived. It was unsigned.'

'Was it the kind you have to swallow after you've read it?' asked Steven with a grin, which attracted a withering look from Macmillan.

Thinking that Macmillan had been told the identity of the anonymous Lindstrom benefactors, he said, 'I take it your *billet-doux* has given you the name of the funders?'

'Nothing to do with that,' said Macmillan. 'My anonymous informant was telling me why government-sponsored funding had been turned down for Professor Lindstrom's group.'

'Payback time for standing on too many toes in the past?'

'Nothing so banal,' said Macmillan, looking Steven straight in the eye. 'Our intelligence services warned them off.'

Steven let out a low whistle followed by a quiet, 'Oh dear.'

'And for the life of me I can't work out why,' Macmillan continued. 'You'd think any research into the working of the human mind and how to control it would be right up their street'

'Shades of, *The Manchurian Candidate*,' smiled Steven.

'I was thinking more of *The Quiller Memorandum*,' said Macmillan. 'Better music.'

'Maybe it's just a case of mental illness always being the poor relation when it comes to handing out cash,' said Steven.

'That wouldn't explain MI5's involvement,' said Macmillan.

'True.'

'Anyway, your friend Barrowman must be very relieved that money has come in from somewhere.'

'Actually, he's not,' said Steven. 'He'd obviously been drinking when he called last night, but he was angry; he'd much rather the money had come from one of the more usual sources. He's been told the holders of the purse strings will have the final say about what gets made public and what doesn't and he doesn't like the sound of that, thinks it could screw up his career.'

'Some people are never happy,' said Macmillan with a world-weary shrug and a wave of his hand.'

'He has a point,' said Steven. 'Young scientists have to get their work published to get a foot on the career ladder. To work hard, make a breakthrough and then be told to keep quiet about it could lead to being seriously pissed off.'

'Nothing's ever straightforward these days.'

Steven gave a wry smile. He said, 'You know, I came in this morning to suggest we keep an eye on the situation and then you drop the bombshell about Five's involvement. That sort of changes everything.'

'What was your concern before that?'

'Supposing . . . just supposing Owen Barrowman *did* come up with a way of treating psychoses and the funding body wanted to hush it up . . . for whatever reason.'

'How could they stop publication?'

'You can bet your house that top lawyers will have been involved in drawing up the conditions attached to the grant.'

'See what you mean,' Macmillan conceded with a sigh. 'So, what does your friend do about that?'

'Barrowman's a bright guy. He'll have seen that scenario on the horizon.'

'Ah,' said Macmillan appreciating what Steven was getting at. 'And be tempted to be economical with reports of his success?'

'Exactly. I gather he works alone so he's in a position to decide who gets told about his results . . . and who doesn't . . . '

''You're right,' agreed Macmillan. 'So, he hides what he finds out under the bed. What does he do next?'

Steven thought for a moment before saying, 'He has a first-class degree and a PhD, but he's probably never been involved in doing anything devious in his life. He'll be out of his league.'

'Unlike you,' said Macmillan.

'Not sure that was a compliment.'

'Just a fact.'

'He'll come up with what he thinks is a cunning plan. He'll resign and take his findings with him. He'll apply for a new job somewhere else, pretend to begin his research all over again. After a while he'll announce his discovery, accept the congratulations of his colleagues and submit his paper to *Nature*.'

'Something tells me that isn't going to work,' said Macmillan.

'We don't know who the funding body is, but, for the moment, let's call them the opposition.'

Macmillan nodded.

'The one thing we can safely assume is that they'll be pretty bright too.'

'And maybe even streetwise and devious,' added Macmillan with a smile.

'That we don't know, but even if they are perfectly respectable and completely above board, they'll figure out what Barrowman's up to and go after him with charges of theft of intellectual property. They'll inform the scientific journals of pending proceedings and they'll immediately put a hold on publication.'

'You said theft?'

'It won't be hard to prove that the data really came from Barrowman's work while he was in the Lindstrom group at Capital and, as such, it'll belong to the funding body not the scientist under the terms of their agreement. Under these circumstances no one would dare publish it. The opposition might even suggest he made the whole lot up if they were so inclined. One way or another Barrowman's career would be over.'

'Maybe someone . . . a friend should warn him if he's considering going down that route?'

The look on Macmillan's face suggested that someone should be Steven. 'He trusts you.'

'Not sure if a late-night phone call under the influence amounts to that, but I could give it a try . . . if only because there's another possible scenario.'

'Go on.'

What I outlined is what might happen if the funding body is a respectable outfit with entirely innocent reasons for maintaining anonymity.'

'Anonymous philanthropy? Not that common.'

'So, let us consider they might not be all that innocent, said Steven. 'We simply don't know. But again, for the sake of argument, let's suppose they are a ruthless bunch of venture capitalists backing the research for some reason we haven't worked out. Young Barrowman might find himself being persuaded to hand over his data by virtue of having his kneecaps removed.'

Macmillan recoiled at the thought. He got up and walked over to the cupboard where he kept his much-loved Amontillado sherry. He poured two glasses and, in accepting one, Steven recognised this as the ritual, performed by Macmillan when he was about to commit Sci-Med formally to an investigation.

Macmillan took a sip and relaxed back into his chair. He took a moment to get his thoughts in order before looking up at the ceiling and saying, 'We have a backer for medical research who doesn't want to be identified, a scientist who might not want to share his results with anyone and an intelligence community who doesn't want the research to be carried out in the first place.'

'About sums it up

'What the hell's going on?'

'I don't know, but I take it you think this is a problem for Sci-Med?'

'We can't ignore it,' said Macmillan. 'Apart from anything else we can't sit back and let MI5 interfere with legitimate medical research.'

Steven murmured his agreement.

'And we can't stand by idly while a young scientist possibly conceals knowledge which could have huge benefits for mankind.'

'More difficult,' said Steven. 'We don't know what Dorothy Lindstrom has signed up to and what the nature of the funding body is.'

'You mean *they* might want to keep it under wraps?' asked Macmillan, sounding surprised. 'But why would they fund it if they wanted to bury the results?'

'Maybe they'd just want exclusive use of them,' Steven suggested. 'And, as you have pointed out on more than one occasion, John, discoveries that can be used for good . . .'

'Can also be used for evil,' Macmillan intoned with a weary sigh.

Macmillan's phone rang and Steven made to leave but Macmillan signalled him back as he reached the door.

'Well, well,' said Macmillan replacing the phone. 'That didn't take long. After what you told me about Moorlock Hall I asked my sources to keep me informed if any mention of it should crop up in the corridors of Whitehall. There's to be an inspection of the place by an *ad hoc* parliamentary committee.'

Steven shook his head and said, 'They couldn't leave well alone.'

'It never rains . . .'

'Do you know when?'

Macmillan shook his head.

'I think I'll contact Barrowman and arrange a meeting, ostensibly to tell him what's about to happen,' said Steven, 'but it'll give me a chance to assess how he's feeling about things.'

'Like I said . . . devious . . . street wise.'

* * * *

Dorothy Lindstrom entered the seminar room just after two o'clock to find her research group waiting expectantly for her. She plumped her heavy shopping bag on to the speaker's desk and withdrew three bottles of sparkling Italian wine to a murmur of approval.

'Do you think you could get us some beakers, Molly?' she asked Molly Bearsden who was sitting at the end of the row nearest the door as chatter broke out all round. 'We're going to have a little celebration.'

The girl returned from the sterile glassware unit with a wire basket containing a jumble of glass beakers. She helped Dorothy strip the metal foil covers from the rim of each before whispering, 'I don't think Mrs Cotter was too pleased.' Vera Cotter was in charge of the washing and sterilising of laboratory glassware and not a woman to be trifled with.

'Ask her to join us,' said Dorothy, popping the first cork and starting to pour. 'Help yourselves everyone. We've had some good news.'

An orderly line, alive with chatter, formed in front of the desk.'

Owen Barrowman was the last to accept a beaker, insisting that Vera and Molly precede him. He and Dorothy exchanged glances. 'All right, Owen?'

'I'm fine.'

'Any happier?'

'Lucy's pregnant.'

'That's wonderful news. Congratulations. We can have a double celebration.'

Dorothy looked for signs of agreement but found only a slight nod. She waited until he'd sat down with the others before announcing that funding had been secured. She basked for a few moments in the smiles and expressions of relief that filled the room before continuing, 'I hope those of you who were considering applying for other jobs might reconsider so that we can continue together to enjoy the exciting times and discoveries that lie ahead.

The murmurs were positive.

'There is something however, that has been brought to my attention and I feel I should mention it at the outset. The money has certain strings attached to it. We will not have the usual academic freedom to submit our findings to the journals of our choice or indeed speak about our work at scientific meetings. This doesn't mean we won't be allowed to do that, it just means we'll have to run it past our fund providers beforehand for approval. This won't affect many of us but it might be something that will concern a few.

' Dorothy looked directly at Barrowman who looked down at the floor.

'Personally, I can't see this becoming a major issue. I'm sure it'll just be a case of rubber stamping.'

Someone asked where the funding was coming from.

Dorothy looked slightly embarrassed but made light of it. 'I don't know,' she said. 'The donor prefers to remain anonymous, Owen thinks it's the Mafia.'

Owen continued to look at the floor but did his best to adopt a slight grin.

When the laughter subsided Dorothy continued, 'The donors have instructed a legal firm to act on their behalf and act as intermediaries, which I think suits us very well. I can't see lawyers wanting to poke around the labs all the time.'

'Maybe they'll just ask for written reports . . . all the time,' said Owen.

'That's a possibility,' Dorothy conceded, 'but if they do we can complain and point out they're interfering with research. It's in the donors' interests to keep us happy, don't you think?'

Owen conceded with a nod but added, 'The real problems will arise when we want to publish our findings and the donors say no.'

'But, why would they?' Dorothy argued. 'It's not as if we're working on anything secret. We're not designing chemical weapons or nuclear missiles. We're simply trying to work out why people are the way they are . . .'

'Supposing there *was* a disagreement, what's to stop us publishing anyway?' asked one of the technicians

'Lawyers,' said Dorothy in a way that suggested what she thought of the profession. The laughter suggested she wasn't alone. 'The university lawyers tell me the contract has been drawn up by people who knew what they were doing.'

'Some of us will be obliged to sign binding secrecy agreements which would make us personally liable – in a legal sense – should we breach them.'

Jane Lincoln, the American post doc who had worked with Dorothy at Yale and who had moved with her to the UK, broke into laughter.

'Something amusing you, Jane?'

'Sorry, I was just thinking I've been working with a group of schoolgirls at a boarding school in Wales who more or less simultaneously developed a rash on their bottoms. I suppose it's the idea of a rash on the bum being some kind of official secret . . . For your eyes only, Mr Bond.'

Everyone joined in the laughter including Dorothy. Even Barrowman managed a smile.

'Well, there you go. I'm sure our funding body would see the funny side too,' said Dorothy. 'I honestly don't think we have anything to worry about.'

This view satisfied the room.

'Okay people, perhaps we can now talk about science and you can tell me what you've all been up to since our last get together. As you've already whetted our appetite, perhaps you'd like to start, Jane? You've got us all intrigued?'

Jane adopted a dramatic pose and announced, 'This is the tale of the giant spider of Felinbach, a fearsome beast that stalks the corridors of the Aberconwy School for Girls in North Wales.'

Several people went, 'Wooo,' to add atmosphere.

'Just over a month ago a young girl reported to matron that she had a rash on her bottom. When asked if she had any idea what might have caused it she claimed that she had been bitten by a large spider in the toilets but had been too afraid to tell anyone. She had been "in a state of shock" to use her words.

Word got around the school about a giant spider lying in wait for the unwary in the john and, in all, twenty-three girls developed a rash on the buttocks, reporting that they had been bitten too.'

'Did you get blood samples?' Dorothy asked.

'I didn't get there in time for the early ones but I did manage to get bloods and buccal smears from the final three to report the appearance of a rash.'

'Well done. What are the medics saying?'

'No sign of bite marks on anyone.'

'Ah,' said Dorothy.

'Ah indeed,' Jane agreed. 'It turns out the original girl made up the story about the spider. She used stinging nettles to give herself a rash to get out of games which she hates.'

'Her and me both,' said Dorothy. 'But presumably not all the others were similarly averse?'

'No, but they all developed rashes.'

'Nettle rashes?'

'No.' Jane paused for effect. 'They had rashes consistent with insect bites.'

Jane achieved the desired effect. Eyes opened wide and mouths fell open.

'Isn't the mind just wonderful?' said Dorothy to break the hush that had fallen over the room. 'These girls believed they had been bitten and their brains managed to convince their bodies to respond appropriately.'

'Frightening,' said someone.

'Intriguing,' said another.

'Both,' said someone else.

The meeting continued with a report from a graduate student, John Spiegelman, who was monitoring volunteers recruited to the study by virtue of either being unusually happy, content and optimistic or continually low in spirits and pessimistic although not regarded as clinically depressed.

'I've added details of another ten of each type and their DNA is being sequenced as we speak,' said Spiegelman. 'That'll bring the total for the study so far to thirty of each and we have blood samples awaiting analysis should the computers come up with something interesting,' he added.

'Good. Dare I ask how things are going with our suicidal subjects?'

Dorothy had turned to a red-haired girl who had been tasked with investigating more extreme subjects – those receiving treatment for clinical depression.

'I'm working on my tenth patient,' replied Linda McLeod, Dorothy's youngest researcher, a girl who had recently gained her PhD from Newcastle University. 'Mary Lennox has tried three times to take her own life without being able to tell anyone why. She's proving quite harrowing to be with.'

'Understandable,' said Dorothy.

'I'm finding it hard to think of her objectively as a subject in a scientific study. I mean she's first and foremost a person, a human being, and my instinct is to want to help her, but I can't because I don't know how. She always seems to be beyond my reach as if there's some kind of invisible barrier between us and she's . . . floating away.'

'Nothing to be ashamed of,' said Dorothy abruptly, 'but ultimately the best way to help Mary and people like her is going to be through the successful application of science. We're not social workers. Others can provide shoulders to cry on and the short-term fixes of pills and potions, but at the end of the day and sooner or later, we're the ones who are going to come up with long term solutions. Understanding the scientific basis for anything is the key to controlling it. We should all remember that.'

'Yes, Dorothy,' said a rather sheepish Linda.

'Tell me if it gets too much for you.'

Dorothy turned to the others and said, 'We must all keep our focus.' She paused until she got the nods she was looking for. 'I've been discussing our new financial situation with the university and our DNA sequencing requirements are to be given top priority in a soon-to-be-expanded facility. We will also be re-equipping with the latest biochemical analysis equipment and advertising for new technical staff will begin next week. We should be in a position to start generating serious amounts of data within a month.

'Thinking ahead, I'd also like our studies to expand to include people who have apparently experienced miracle cures. You know the sort of thing; they've been suffering from cancer and their tumour miraculously disappears. Good for selling newspapers, but maybe, just maybe – and for whatever reason – the right switches were thrown at the right time.'

Dorothy held up a couple of empty wine bottles to lament the fact that they were empty. 'Maybe we should get started,' she said with a smile. 'I'd like the post docs and post-grads to stay behind.'

The technicians, lab assistants and undergrads left the room wearing smiles and chattering about a future that looked much more positive.

SIX

The door closed, leaving Dorothy alone with her senior staff. 'Well, she said, 'what do we really think about the schoolgirls' rashes?'

'On the surface, a classic example of mass hysteria,' said Jane Lincoln. 'The literature is full of such reports.'

'What about below the surface?'

'We seem to have quite a bit of information this time,' said John Spiegelman. 'The fact that the girl who was lying displayed a nettle rash while the others – our mass hysteria girls – the interesting ones – had the real deal, an insect bite rash. That is pretty cool.'

'No spider, but clear evidence of its bite on all these girls. Now that really is spooky,' said Linda McLeod.

'Cool and spooky are not quite what I'm looking for,' said Dorothy acidly. 'How do we explain it?'

'Something happened to make all these girls display evidence of an insect bite without them having been bitten.'

'Is stating the obvious,' said Dorothy. 'What happened?'

'I'd guess at a switch being thrown,' said Linda.

Dorothy rubbed her forehead lightly. 'Well, yes. I think that's why we're all here,' she said, betraying a hint of irritation that just stopped short of open sarcasm. 'But why? What made it happen? What happened to throw the switch?'

'Fear,' said Owen Barrowman.

'Go on,' said Dorothy quietly as all eyes turned towards Owen.

'They were young girls, frightened of spiders, terrified in fact, so much so that the report of a giant one in their presence and evidence of what it had done to one of their friends triggered off a response in their own bodies to something that actually hadn't happened.'

'Wow,' said Spiegelman. 'You're suggesting that if you manage to convince someone that something bad has happened to them, their body will respond as if it really had?'

There was a short silence before doubt surfaced and Jane Lincoln said, 'No, there's something missing. There has to be, otherwise . . .'

'You're right,' acknowledged Spiegelman. 'Otherwise this sort of thing would happen all the time and it doesn't. . . but state of mind must play a part.'

'Agreed,' said Dorothy. 'And in this case, I think Owen was right. The strong emotional factor was fear. Fear was the key.'

Dorothy looked to Owen who had paled visibly. 'Are you feeling all right?'

Barrowman appeared not to have heard, causing the others to become concerned. Jane Lincoln touched his arm and his gaze returned from the middle distance.

'Sorry, yes,' he stammered. 'I'm fine.'

Dorothy looked doubtful but let it go at that. 'Well, I think we've all been given food for thought. The girls' anxious state allowed some factor to take control of their bodies and make them react in the way . . . it thought appropriate.'

All traces of humour surrounding mass hysteria disappeared in an instant as people found themselves focussing on the word 'it'.

'Well,' said Dorothy resting both elbows on the table, 'Let's all have a think and meet again, say on Friday? In the meantime, Owen, could you stay behind?'

Dorothy waited until the door had closed after the departing post docs before saying, 'I didn't ask you to report on your work because Mr Anthony Medici from Scarman, Medici and Weiss, the lawyers acting for our benefactors is going to be joining us. I'd like you to brief us privately.'

'He's the go-between?'

'Yes, and before you ask what you say to a lawyer, he'll be bringing a scientific adviser with him.'

Owen nodded but said nothing. Dorothy knew that anger still simmered inside him, a source of some irritation to her. 'It's always a good idea not to bite the hand that feeds you,' she said.

'Fine, let me know when I'm to perform,' said Barrowman getting up.

'You've changed, Owen, and it's not just the funding business. I don't know what the problem is, but sort it out.'

Barrowman returned to his lab, swore out loud and slapped his notebook down on his desk. He was sick to the back teeth of people questioning his mood or telling him he'd changed. If it wasn't Lucy it was Dorothy. Most of all he was sick of constant distractions. He was on the verge of an important discovery and he needed peace and quiet and time to think. He hadn't had time to go through the biochemical results he'd asked the lab to repeat so he'd have to do that at home tonight, but that meant more moaning from Lucy.

The phone rang and he snatched it from its cradle, growling, 'Barrowman.'

'Owen? It's Steven Dunbar. Bad time?'

''Oh, Steven, sorry about that . . . having a bit of a bad day. Look, I'm sorry about bending your ear last night . . . I guess I went on a bit.'

'Not at all. Actually, I'm ringing to suggest we might meet up and have a proper conversation and I've got a bit of news for you . . . about Moorlock Hall.'

'Really? I'm all ears.'

'Maybe not over the phone. How about this evening? Same place as last time? Any time suits me.'

'Yeah . . . God, there aren't enough hours in the day at the moment. Let me see, I've got a meeting with the money people or rather their representatives this afternoon and I promised Lucy I'd try to make it home for dinner this evening . . .'

He was still dithering when he heard Dorothy's voice outside and that of a stranger. The man who paid the piper was about to call the tune.

'Oh shit . . . got to go . . . okay, this evening, eight o'clock . . .the Moorings.'

Steven looked at his phone as it went dead. 'A man on the edge,' he murmured.

Steven noticed that Barrowman's hands were shaking slightly as he poured his beer from bottle into glass. 'Are you sure you should be here?' he asked.

'Yeah, I'm fine. You said you had some news about Moorlock Hall?'

'It's no longer a secret,' said Steven. 'A parliamentary committee is being set up to investigate what's been going on. You seemed excited about the progress you were making there and I wasn't sure how this might affect your research so I thought I'd let you know.'

'Shit, that's all I need, a bunch of interfering busybodies sticking their noses in.'

'You said you just had the one patient there, Malcolm Lawler. Do you still have a lot of work to do with him, or are you close to having all you need?'

'Why do you want to know?'

The question startled Steven. 'I don't really,' he replied. 'I just thought I might ask John to see if he could delay things for a bit if you needed more time.'

The fact that Steven had maintained unwavering eye contact with him while giving his answer made Barrowman realise that his snapped question and what lay behind it might have been out of order. 'I'm sorry,' he said, 'I'm under pressure from all sides at the moment to explain myself and what I'm doing. That was very decent of you, I'm grateful.'

'So, do I ask him?'

'Yes, thanks, I do have quite a lot of samples but I need Lawler to talk to me some more. He holds the key to something I'd really like to understand and there's no way of knowing how a distraction might affect that.'

'You say you're under pressure. I don't understand. Why's that?''

'There's a chance I'm on to something big,' Barrowman confided, 'something really big.'

'Surely that's something you should be pleased about, not a source of anguish?'

'You don't understand the research community,' said Barrowman.

'Tell me.'

Barrowman took a swig of his beer and sighed. 'People imagine researchers all work for the common good, they share ideas and results and encourage and help each other in any way they can in the fight to cure disease and understand what makes us the way we are.'

'I guess.'

'Wrong. It's one big competition. You don't help the opposition, you beat them any way you can. You don't get a Nobel prize for being second to discover something. Pharmaceutical companies aren't interested in curing disease – that doesn't make money –

they make money from *treating* it. Designing products to treat chronic conditions is the real name of the game. Why produce vaccines to prevent disease when you can produce pills that people will need and perhaps will take for the rest of their lives. Vaccines wipe out potential customers.'

Steven remembered Sci-Med's latest turndown, but said, 'Surely there must be some good guys out there?'

Barrowman pursed his lips but didn't say more.

'Another beer?'

Barrowman nodded.

Steven went up to the bar and used the wait to figure out where he went from here. Barrowman sounded completely paranoid, but he suspected there was more to it? Paranoid was an adjective applied freely to everyone who felt put-upon and for whatever reason. Barrowman was a researcher at the top of his game who believed he was on the verge of discovering something important, but he seemed convinced that he was surrounded by people who wanted to steal the glory from him. To compound the situation, he had been keeping company with psychotic criminals to such an extent that he might even be seeing life through their eyes. What a mess.

Steven paid for the beers and brought them to the table, still undecided as to whether he should proceed with more questions or call it a night. Barrowman looked up and smiled self-consciously. 'Sorry about that. I think I needed to let off steam.'

The fact that Barrowman had calmed down helped Steven make his decision. 'So where do you fit into this fun-filled picture of science?' he asked. 'You're a researcher on to something you think might be big and you'd like recognition if it works out. Who do you see standing in your way? Professor Lindstrom?'

'The head of the group always takes credit for whatever comes up in the lab. Her name will be on the paper, which she will probably insist on writing, and there will be an asterisk next her name making herself corresponding author.'

Steven gave him a questioning look.

'People will write to her with comments and questions.'

'Does that make you feel bitter?'

'That's just the way it is, but . . .'

'But what?'

'She used my work to get funds for her whole group without any reference to me. That still pisses me off, particularly as it turns out we don't know where the money's coming from or why they're giving it.'

'Ah,' said Steven, 'I can understand you feeling upset about that.'

Barrowman seemed pleased to hear what he took as support.

'You said you were having a meeting with your benefactors this afternoon,' said Steven. 'How did that go?'

'It was a bit bizarre really. They sent along a lawyer and some scientific advisor guy. Dorothy asked me to give them a run down on what I'd been up to and then take questions from their advisor.'

'Sensible questions?'

Barrowman thought for a moment before saying, 'Yes, he seemed to know what he was talking about . . . maybe a bit too informed if you ask me.'

Steven adopted a puzzled look.

'I didn't mention Moorlock Hall in my talk because I didn't want to say anything about Lawler. I wanted to keep that to myself for the time being so I confined my report to my work with the prisoners I'd seen in other establishments and stressed it was too soon to come to any conclusions about anything as we haven't had the facilities for sample analysis.'

Sounds like you really didn't want to tell them anything at all,' said Steven.

Barrowman shrugged.

'Not something you can keep up for too long.'

'I suppose not,' Barrowman conceded.

'What did you mean when you said you thought the advisor might be too well informed – did he have a name by the way?' Steven's inquiry was a long way from being 'by the way'.

'He was introduced as Dr Neil Tyler, Scottish by the sound of him, a forensic psychologist. He asked about the number of samples I'd collected, whether I had enough and was finished doing that or whether there were still more to come . . . and where from. I suspected he knew about Moorlock Hall and was trying to wheedle information out of me.'

'Was he successful?'

'I felt I had to tell him I was still working with a patient.'

'At Moorlock Hall?'

'I thought I'd better say that in case Dorothy had already told him.'

'Had she?'

'She said not when I asked her afterwards.'

'Did Tyler know about Moorlock Hall?'

'He said he'd never heard of it. It could have been an act of course.'

Or it could be paranoia on your part, Steven thought. 'Did the lawyer have much to say?'

'Very little, struck me as a cold fish. Dorothy introduced him as Mr. Medici from a law firm with three names. His was one, I can't remember the other two.'

'I can see why the Medici name stuck,' said Steven with a smile. 'Any jokes made about Venice?'

'I don't think Mr. Medici would recognise a joke if it kicked him up the arse.'

'So, no clues dropped about who the funders are?

'None at all.'

Steven took a deep breath. 'You know, I think it would be in both our interests to find out who they are

'What's your interest?'

Steven ignored the defensive edge in the question and said, 'Sci-Med likes to know what's going on in science and medicine; it's our job and we're talking about a big investment here. I think we'd both feel better if we knew everything was above board, don't you?''

Barrowman nodded although Steven noted signs on his face that said real paranoia was still in the mix.

SEVEN

If there was anything that could make Moorlock Hall look even worse than it usually did, it was rain. This was Owen Barrowman's conclusion as once more he crested the hill under leaden skies and saw the building come into view. He found himself wishing the wipers could sweep away the building and all thoughts of it so that he could wake up and find it had all been a bad dream, but it hadn't. He was living in the real world but his real world had changed out of all recognition over the past few months. It had turned against him; they had turned against him. Who? Everyone, his boss who blamed him for having changed when it was her who had changed with her desire to get money for what she was about to call *her* research, Jesus! The colleagues he'd thought of as friends who'd grown distant as they chose to side with whoever had the money and could offer them security.

Even his wife had turned on him with her constant questioning about what he was doing and whingeing about how long he spent working in the evenings. Christ, he was on the very edge of making a great discovery and she wanted to talk about a bloody baby they hadn't planned for and what bloody colour the nursery should be. Would it be easier if they knew the sex before the birth? He didn't give a damn about the nursery or the sex of the sprog for that matter. He had other things on his mind. Why couldn't they all offer him support instead of constant criticism? The answer if he could work it out would have to wait. It was time for another session with Malcolm Lawler

Barrowman kept small talk with Groves to a minimum although he did feel obliged to bring up the upcoming inspection that Steven Dunbar had told him about. 'I thought this place was supposed to be a secret.'

'So did we,' said Groves. 'We're not supposed to be subject to inspection or anything else for that matter. Officially we don't exist.'

'Let's hope it's just a formality.'

Groves smiled his lop-sided smile but didn't comment further.

Lawler watched as Barrowman sat down and took out a notebook from his briefcase. As he snapped it shut, Lawler asked, 'So, where is it?'

'Where's what?'

'The elixir you've been designing that's going to make me one of the chaps, a decent human being, a pillar of society, member of a golf club, chair of the round table and all-round good egg.'

'I'm afraid we've still got a bit to go,' said Barrowman through gritted teeth but affecting a small smile, 'but we're definitely getting there . . .'

'You disappoint me, doctor. Didn't you say last time you had identified certain interesting enzyme differences?'

'Yes, but these things take time, everything needs to be checked and verified.'

'Ah, I see. You've made one of these discoveries where you folks say, *hopefully within five to ten years this will lead to blah blah blah . . . a cure for cancer . . . all our power from nuclear fusion . . . transmutation of lead into gold.*'

'I'm doing my best.'

'And what does your best require of me today?'

'I'd like you to sell yourself to me.'

'What are you talking about?'

'Imagine you're being interviewed for a very senior post in an international company. I'd like you to tell me all about you, presenting yourself in the best possible light, emphasising your good points, highlighting your skills and abilities. Would you do that?

'No.'

Barrowman was disappointed. He felt sure Lawler would have been keen to seize the chance to show off. 'Why not?'

'The last time we spoke I told you all about me and what went on in my head . . . as you put it.'

Barrowman swallowed involuntarily as the awful memories surfaced inside him. 'I remember.'

'Well, I want to know what's going on in yours. It's only fair . . .'

'What exactly do you want to know?'

'You're married.' Lawler stared pointedly at the wedding ring on Barrowman's finger. 'Who is she? Tell me . . . all . . . about her.'

Barrowman felt instantly uneasy. Apprehension filled him as it so often did in his times with Lawler. Lawler's eyes remained fixed on him.

'This won't help the research at all,' Barrowman tried. 'You're just delaying your golf club membership.'

The joke fell flat.

'What's her name?' demanded Lawler. He drove the words home like rivets.

'Lucy, her name is Lucy.

'Lucy,' repeated Lawler. 'There, that wasn't so bad, was it?'

Oh yes it was, Barrowman thought. Hearing Lawler utter his wife's name was not a good feeling.

'So, tell me about Lucy . . . is she good looking? Nice body? Of course, she has . . . Tell me . . . what sort of things does she like to wear?

The thought of Lawler getting off on what Lucy wore made Barrowman shudder inside. He was being asked to pimp his wife's image. 'Clothes,' he snapped.

Lawler smiled as he read Barrowman's mind. 'Children? Do you have children?'

A shake of the head.

'Plans?'

'One on the way.' *Jesus, why did I say that?*

'A baby? Aw . . .' crooned Lawler adopting a sing song voice. 'Owen and Loocee and baby makes three . . .I bet you have a house with a garden?' he asked with feigned enthusiasm.'

'A flat.'

'Pity, still . . . there's plenty of time.'

It suddenly occurred to Barrowman through the anger simmering inside him that Lawler wasn't just playing a part. He had adopted the personality and mannerisms of someone he had seen on TV, a popular, daytime TV presenter. He was doing it so well that it triggered an idea. He had taken samples from Lawler when he had been simulating a number of psychotic conditions; this would be his chance to get specimens when he was simulating someone who would be regarded by society as normal. His gut feeling sensed that this could be a huge bonus, but his gut feeling was also insisting that his association with Lawler was making him ill.

He had known this for some weeks but couldn't bring himself to walk away because Lawler was the source of the data he needed to make a major breakthrough. The man was a genetic Rosetta stone and he wanted to be the one to unravel the secrets of the code. At least . . . he thought this was the reason, but there were times when he felt some other force was playing on him and he couldn't quite focus on it. Lack of sleep, the drive of burning ambition, growing resentment of others and the constant need for deceit were all playing their part in sponsoring short temper, impatience and evasiveness in him, but that didn't matter, it would be worth it in the end he kept telling himself.

In the lab, previous uncertainty about the future, lack of funding and the constant need for charitable help from other groups had been a useful smokescreen to explain away his apparent slowness in declaring results. It had been accepted as it had for the others in the group because it was to be expected in their impoverished circumstances. In his case, the truth was different. He had been very successful in getting help from other labs because of his previous popularity and he had been secretly taking data home to analyse, something that kept him working into the small hours nearly every night. Lucy had accepted his explanation at first – that he had to keep ahead of others in the field; there were no prizes for second place – but even she had begun to have her doubts about what he was really up to.

Barrowman had spent the previous late night session going through the results of the repeated tests on Lawler's samples yet again. Having established there had been no mix-up it now seemed clear after repeated checking that Lawler really could change his biochemical signature to emulate those recorded in a whole range of mental conditions. If the sample he'd just taken showed that he could also display the make-up of a normal person . . . this really would be something special . . .

Barrowman's excitement was short lived and suddenly eclipsed by a flood of uncertainty. If Lawler really could adopt the genetic state of a normal person, why hadn't he done just that? Why had he become what he had? Why the hell didn't he just go through life as a decent human being, making friends, falling in love, laughing, crying? Why would anyone *choose* to throw switches that made them a monster completely devoid of compassion, taking orgasmic pleasure in the fear he could induce in others, revelling in their agony?

Barrowman forced himself back into the present. 'Well, Mr Lawler,' he said, 'You know about me; I know about you. I think I'd like to take a blood sample now and call it a day.'

'But we've only just begun!' Lawler protested. 'I want to hear more about Lucy. What does she do? Is she a scientist too? Maybe you spend your evenings unravelling the secrets of the genetic code? Four little letters . . . ATCG, the basis of all living things. Amazing really, the rest of us can't even make a proper word out of them!' Lawler laughed like the TV presenter buttering up his scientific guest.

Lawler's knowledge of the chemical bases which comprise the spine of DNA registered with Barrowman even as he chose to put an end to any more conversation and call in the attendant so he could take a blood sample. 'Sorry,' he said to Lawler. 'There's a seminar at the university tonight I want to go to. It's being given by an old friend of mine from Edinburgh University.'

'Old pals from uni, eh? . . . nice.'

'I haven't seen him for ages. It'll be good to catch up,' said Barrowman, keen to keep the small talk going. He was anxious there should be no delay in taking the blood sample. He needed it to reflect Lawler's nice guy state of mind, not the angry individual he sensed he might become.

When the attendant came in Barrowman was surprised to see that it wasn't the one on duty when he arrived. 'Where's staff nurse Donovan?' he asked.

'He didn't think you'd be finished for a while yet,' the man replied. 'He nipped up to the kitchen for a coffee. I'm Staff Clements . . . Alan.'

'I need to take a blood sample from Mr Lawler, Alan.'

'Okay dokay.'

Barrowman turned away to get what he needed from his briefcase, a sterile twenty ml syringe and appropriate needle, two sterile plastic containers for the blood – one containing an anticoagulant, another without so that the blood would separate into serum and a clot – and an alcohol impregnated swab to sterilise the site on

Lawler's arm. If required he'd use one of the leather securing straps on the chair as a temporary tourniquet.

Lawler's lower right arm had been released from its binding and his sleeve rolled up to expose the inner aspect of his elbow. Clements was holding his arm steady on the chair arm. Owen cleaned the area where he could see a suitable prominent vein and murmured, 'Don't think we need a tourniquet, this looks fine.' He slipped the needle into the vein and slowly withdrew fifteen millilitres. 'Excellent,' he said. 'Thank you, Mr Lawler.'

Barrowman turned away and ejected the blood, half each into the two containers. When he turned around he was instantly aware of Lawler giving him the *stare*. It was something that reminded him of a raptor surveying what it held in its talons – seeing everything but feeling nothing. It was something he did when he was upset or felt he hadn't been accorded the respect he thought he deserved. It wasn't hard to work out that he obviously felt *he was the one to decide when an interview was over.*

Barrowman was just about to say something conciliatory when Lawler swung his arm round hard into Clements' face as he moved in to restore his binding. The blow knocked the nurse off balance and sent him sliding across the floor holding his jaw. Barrowman made the mistake of looking to Clements rather than Lawler and paid the price. Lawler's free right hand shot out and his fingers fastened on either side of his windpipe. He felt himself being pulled down towards Lawler's face while Clements struggled ineffectually to get up.

'Fear . . . I can smell it off you, doctor,' Lawler whispered. 'The smell of fear . . . soon to be absolute . . . bloody . . . terror . . . His fingers tightened on Barrowman's neck. 'Let me tell you, doctor, you're a loser . . . you just don't see the big picture . . . You play by their rules . . . the ones designed by the few to keep the rest in order . . . when it could all be so different . . . You've saddled yourself with Loocee . . . you've got a squalling brat on the way . . . that is the fucking highway to nowhere. You've been playing the game wrong, doctor . . . Don't you understand? Take what you want from life; don't bargain with it. Destroy anything and everything that gets in your way . . . set out to win . . . don't set out to . . . comply.'

Barrowman was seeing stars. He had almost used up all his strength in an attempt to prise Lawler's fingers apart but they were locked in a grip that was stifling his ability to breathe. His brain was telling him he must let go: he should go for Lawler's eyes with his thumbs. But his overwhelming fear that the instant he let go of Lawler's hands, his windpipe would be ripped out was proving stronger. He was losing consciousness. He barely heard the 'What the fuck!' exclamation coming from Nathan Donovan returning from his coffee break.

EIGHT

'Clements! You useless son of a . . . What d'you think you're doing?' Donovan slammed his fist against the alarm button on the wall, filling the air with deafening whoops and rushed over to help Barrowman. He freed him from Lawler's grip using sheer brute strength before slamming Lawler's arm back down on the chair arm and securing him tightly. 'Are you all right?' he asked Barrowman, getting a weak nod in reply before turning on Clements to continue his tirade.

'Sorry Nate, I thought these two got on,' mumbled Clements, still sitting on the floor nursing his jaw. 'I wasn't expecting it. Bastard took me by surprise, took a swing at me and grabbed the doc by the throat.'

Donovan raised his voice to be heard above the whoop of the siren and sound of running feet. 'Nothing ever takes you by surprise in this place, Clements Have you got that? You expect anything and everything at all times.'

Clements nodded.

'Get out of my sight. This isn't over.'

Barrowman sat massaging his throat and feeling disorientated.

'Are you sure you're okay?' Donovan asked, putting a hand on his shoulder and trying to look into his eyes.

'Yeah . . . fine.' Barrowman looked past him at the help arriving and then at Lawler who seemed to be looking at everything as if he were a disinterested party, an onlooker instead of a participant. There was no sign of the murderous violence he had displayed only a few moments before. Lawler saw him turn to look directly at him but the *stare* had gone. In fact, his expression was quite different, not one Barrowman recognised immediately although there was something vaguely and unsettlingly familiar about it. It was . . . as if . . . as if . . . He couldn't quite put his finger on it, but then it came to him. It was the look that passed between people who shared a secret, the fleeting glance that passed between two office colleagues who were having an affair. He found this bizarre in the extreme, not just unsettling, but scary.

The three attendants who had arrived, two with shields and batons, one wielding a Taser stun-gun, were stood down as Groves followed them into the room. He was full of apologies.

'My God, I'm so sorry,' he exclaimed. 'This should never have happened. I've called an ambulance. We'll get you off to hospital as quickly as possible.' He ushered Barrowman out of the room with his good arm resting lightly on the small of his back.

Without understanding why, Barrowman felt the urge to decline. 'No need,' he said, 'no real damage done. Let's go easy on the drama for all our sakes.'

Groves looked at him as if he couldn't quite believe his ears . . . or his luck. 'Well, if you're absolutely sure . . .'

'I am. Mind you, a drop of that malt of yours wouldn't go amiss right now?'

'Absolutely.'

Groves visibly relaxed and Barrowman knew that the man must have been looking ahead in trepidation to what the inspection team might make of what had happened just before their arrival.

A knock came to the door and Nathan Donovan came in. He placed the blood samples on the desk in front of Barrowman. 'Thought you might need these.'

'Thanks,' said Barrowman, adding sincerity to the word with a look and smile.

'No problem.'

Groves said, 'Nathan, we're having a debriefing session, perhaps you should join us. He turned to Barrowman, 'What exactly happened?'

'I'd just taken a blood sample from Lawler and Clements moved in to secure his free arm. Lawler suddenly caught Clements with a swing of his forearm. I saw it happen. The blow was enough to knock him off balance and he landed on the floor. Clements didn't get up. I was looking at him to see if he was alright when Lawler caught me by the throat.'

'Clements didn't get up?'

'He was still on the floor when I arrived,' said Donovan.

'As opposed to helping Dr Barrowman?'

'He was sitting there rubbing his jaw.'

'How hard did Lawler hid Clements?'

'Hard enough to knock him off balance,' said Barrowman.

'But not enough to knock him out?'

'I don't think so.'

'I don't think so either,' said Donovan. 'He was just sat there watching events when I arrived. There's hardly a mark on him.

'You probably know him better than I do. Do you think he froze?' asked Groves.

Donovan looked doubtful. 'No . . . I don't,' he said with plain meaning. 'Clements isn't the biggest guy on earth, but Lawler was still secured to the chair – he only had one arm free. If Clements had got off his backside and waded in, I'm sure he and Dr Barrowman could have put an end to Lawler's nonsense before he tried to rip out anyone's throat.'

'Oh dear,' said Groves. 'Not exactly what I wanted to hear.' He paused for a full five seconds before saying to Barrowman, 'Clements is a fairly new member of staff; he's a bit different; he was seconded to us after our existence became no longer a secret.'

Barrowman could see an attempt to improve things before the investigation but didn't say so.

'Different?' he asked.

'Our people here have to be screened thoroughly for suitability before being appointed.'

'And you don't think he was?'

'Oh no, nothing like that,' said Groves. 'He was subject to the same scrutiny as all the others and had signed the Official Secrets act. By different I simply meant that he has a qualification in art therapy,' said Groves, clearly making an effort to keep judgement out of his voice.

'He's been giving lessons to Lawler,' said Donovan.

'Ah,' said Barrowman.

'And instead of Clements influencing Lawler . . . '

'Clements will be cleaning Lawler's shoes by the end of the month,' said Groves. 'A weak personality in thrall to a strong one. I haven't seen this involve a member of staff before – it's usually been something between prisoners as was the case when Sutton and Lawler ruled the roost at Broadmoor. I was there at the time – the axis of evil as some of the staff called it. Their word was law. A whole wing danced to their tune'

'How many prisons was Barrowman in before he ended up here?'

'Just Broadmoor.'

Barrowman asked why Sutton hadn't been transferred to Moorlock.

'He died in Broadmoor. Cerebral haemorrhage.

Barrowman raised an eyebrow.

'No suspicious circumstances,' said Groves. He noticed that Barrowman kept feeling his throat. 'Are you sure you don't want to have a hospital check-up?'

'I'm fine.'

'Good,' said Groves cautiously tip-toeing up to a new question. 'Dare I ask where this leaves your research?'

Barrowman looked at the samples he'd taken from Lawler. 'I may have all I need here. If not . . . I'll be back. Lawler is something else, science should know about him.'

Groves applauded his dedication.

'Just don't have Clements riding shotgun on me.'

'Absolutely not, although he'll be difficult to get rid of without concrete evidence. The best I can do is probably keep him and Lawler apart. After all, the other inmates should be given the chance to benefit from his artistic skills.'

Barrowman sat in his car for a few minutes, his fingers alternately squeezing and releasing the steering wheel as he struggled with being an emotional mess. The adrenalin rush from the Lawler incident had dissipated, leaving him feeling confused, exhausted and depressed, but also strangely angry with himself. He didn't seem to be in control of anything. He should have gone to hospital but he hadn't. Instead, he had sought to cover the incident up, dismissing it as a minor blip in proceedings when it had been anything but. He could have died. Why? he wondered, why had he done that? Why had he stopped official procedure taking its course? Was his research really so important that nothing should be allowed to interfere with it? Were the secrets that Lawler held really worth risking absolutely everything for? The answers, when they came, brought with them a feeling of calm that settled over him like the morphine-induced relief given to those in severe pain. They were yes and yes again. Nothing must stand between him and Lawler.

Barrowman was ten minutes into the drive home when he managed to turn his thoughts to the evening seminar. He hadn't been lying when he'd given this as the reason for cutting short his time with Lawler, although he hadn't reckoned on it triggering the nightmare it had. His friend from his time in Scotland, Dan Glass, really was speaking tonight about his research on epigenetic changes and hormone levels in teenagers and Barrowman had volunteered to be the member of staff to take the guest speaker out for supper afterwards. He had been looking forward to catching up on news of contemporaries and talking about the old days over a few beers but now . . . He couldn't pull out now, he decided. If he did, it would demand explanations he didn't want to give.

He did his best to put all other thoughts out of his mind and concentrate on the evening ahead. He even managed a smile as he recalled animated discussions over pints of Belhaven Best beer in Bannermans bar in the heart of Edinburgh's old town. Pubs had been important in student days. Looking back now as he approached his thirties he suspected that many ideas in young minds might well have stayed there if expression had been confined to formal seminars and scientific meetings where established scientists ruled the roost, speaking long and loud of the road well-travelled and perhaps discouraging thoughts of any venture into uncharted side roads.

The smile faded as reality insisted that times had changed. Things would not be the same this evening. They couldn't be. He and Dan had been students in these far-off days, free to speak about the first thing that came into their heads and argue without restraint, but circumstances were different now. He wouldn't tell Dan anything about what he was working on. He couldn't. He couldn't risk telling anyone anything about it. He had too much to lose. The history of science was littered with the wrong people getting the credit for the ideas and discoveries of others.

He would say nothing until his work was safely in print, then he would speak of little else as the invitations rolled in. With one single publication in *Nature* he would secure his future in academe and more importantly a place in medical history as the man who explained the basis for psychopathic personality and how the condition might be reversed. No one was going to take that away from him. No one.

Thinking about Dan and the old days however, had given Barrowman an idea. Dan was still a pal and he might be useful. He had a favour to ask.

NINE

FOUR WEEKS LATER

'Ye gods,' John Macmillan exclaimed as he opened a Home Office confidential note that Jean Roberts had brought in. She exchanged a knowing look with Steven, suggesting that something unpleasant might be about to unfold.

'There's been a leak from the committee who inspected Moorlock Hall. The report was supposed to be kept confidential but the Press are on to it and have been phoning to check their facts. The existence of Moorlock Hall will be all over the papers in a couple of days unless the government can come up with a reason for a D notice.'

Steven cursed. 'I take it it was a damning report.'

'Yes,' Macmillan confirmed. 'It appears Mrs Lillian Leadbetter, chair of the committee was not at all pleased.'

'I wonder if the woman has given a moment's thought to the victims of these monsters and their families What's her angle anyway, do-gooder or self-interest?'

'I'd go for self-interest,' replied Macmillan. 'She's a Lib-Dem MP looking for a bit of a career hike now that her party has decided it's time to flex its muscles to show the voters they're not just Tory government gophers in the coalition.'

'And without a moment's thought to the consequences,' said Steven. 'What does she want for psychopathic killers? Five hundred lines? *I must not rape and murder.*

Macmillan smiled ruefully and said, 'There's a chance she's just having her moment in the sun. Maybe she'll move on and look for a new handhold on the greasy pole of political success.'

'It might not be that straightforward,' said Steven. 'If it suits their purpose, Labour will bring up the subject in a few weeks' time and point out that the Lib-Dem's complaint has been completely ignored by their Tory masters and that Labour's the only party who really cares about mental health issues. This in turn will force the lady to pretend that she's still deeply concerned and we'll have a very public competition to show who cares the most – the answer of course being none of them. The less they care the more they have to appear to care. It's one big game.'

Macmillan gave a resigned nod. 'I wish I could argue.'

'Well, I was about due to get in touch with Owen Barrowman anyway. I'll give him the news.

'How have your enquiries been going?'

'Thanks to some sterling work by Jean we now know something about the firm of lawyers fronting the anonymous backers, Messrs Scarman, Medici and Weiss. They are not a high-profile firm, but they did pop up in a case in the city a few years ago. They were representing the Catholic Church in some big claim against the church for compensation.'

'Abuse?'

Steven nodded.

'Were they successful?

'Let's say the claimants weren't happy with the outcome. Scarman and co. successfully argued that it was all a very long time ago, many of those being accused were now dead and distant memories from middle aged adults who were small children at the time could not be relied upon. In a damage limitation gambit, they did however, accept that there may have been shortcomings in behaviour of a few in positions of authority and offered apologies . . . along with small payments as a gesture of goodwill.'

'Bless 'em,' said Macmillan.

'As for Dr Tyler, he doesn't hold a post at any British university as far as we can see although Jean found it quite difficult to check.'

'Mm,' said Macmillan. 'Every pillar box seems to be a university these days. I'll get her to keep at it.'

When Steven got home he found Tally packing a bag.

'Was it something I said?'

Tally didn't laugh. 'It's Mum, she's had a fall. My sister, Laura, called: The home thinks she may have broken her femur.'

Steven screwed up his face. He knew as well as Tally that the breakage of a major bone in an old person was very serious, often leading to death through complications.

'I'm sorry.' He gave Tally a hug and asked if there was anything he could do. Tally said not. She would see her mother at the hospital up in Leicester and stay over with her sister.

Tally had always been close to her mother and had gone through a difficult time when it became clear that she would have to go into a home. It had been a guilt-ridden situation familiar to so many and she and her two sisters had gone to great efforts to find a home committed to top class care and comfort.

'And no bloody stupid names featuring havens of rest or bloody forest lawns,' her older sister Jackie had insisted. Jackie, who lived down in Dorset, had suggested at one point that her mother might like to live down by the sea near she and her husband, but, in the end, they had all agreed that home territory would be best. They had settled on the Granby Road Care Home in Leicester. It was near where Laura lived and in a part of the city their mother had known all her life.

'How was your day?' Tally asked.

'The newspapers are on to Moorlock Hall.'

'That doesn't sound good. Exposing this sort of secret will be right up their street. Heads must roll.'

Steven agreed but said, 'Let's not talk about it just now, you've got other things on your mind. Off you go. Love to your mum.'

'I'll call you.'

Tally left and Steven paused for a moment with his hand resting on the door, letting the silence engulf him. There was no escaping the feeling that one of life's milestones was looming.

Steven left it until seven thirty before calling Owen Barrowman. A young woman answered. 'I'm afraid he's not here at the moment. Can I give him a message?'

'You must be Lucy?'

'Who is this?'

'I'm sorry, we haven't met. My name's Steven Dunbar.'

Lucy Barrowman's voice relaxed slightly, but still gave Steven reason to think that all was not well. 'Oh yes, Owen mentioned you. You had a drink together a few weeks ago?'

'That's right, I learned something today that might interest him and was hoping we might meet up.'

'He's working in the lab, Steven. He said he wouldn't be home before midnight and then he'll probably be at his computer until all hours. Was it important?'

'Not really,' Steven replied. 'Owen's been keeping me in the picture about his research and I had a bit of relevant news for him if he hadn't already heard . . .'

'Does it concern Moorlock Hall?' Lucy interrupted.

'You know about Moorlock Hall?'

'I wish I didn't. I wish I'd never heard of it or that dreadful creature he goes to see there.'

Steven was surprised at the venom in her voice. 'I'm sorry. Has something happened? Is there anything I can do?'

'What's wrong with Owen, doctor? Do you know? He's changed. He's not right . . . He's just not Owen any more . . .'

The harshness in her voice had changed to anguish. Steven even heard the suggestion of a sob as she waited for an answer. 'Look, why don't I come over there? It'll be better than trying to speak over the phone.'

Anguish became embarrassment. 'I'm sorry, this is ridiculous. I'm so sorry. I'm pregnant; it must be my hormones.'

'Don't apologise, it's not ridiculous at all and I'd guess it has nothing to do with your hormones either,' said Steven gently. 'Your husband's been spending a lot of time with unsavoury people, convicted killers – psychopaths. That's not the sort of thing people can cope with without some price being paid. Owen and I have spoken about this. Look, give me your address and I'll come over. We'll talk things through. Maybe he needs help.'

Lucy gave Steven the address and he wrote it down. He decided to drive over, estimating a journey of around ten to twelve miles. He hadn't been out in his car for over a week and his Porsche Boxster didn't like being ignored. She needed regular driving or she might cough and splutter in slow-moving traffic to remind him that she didn't like being taken for granted. That's the way Steven saw it. Tally saw things differently. 'It's a bloody car, Steven.'

Steven took the lift down to the underground garage and grinned as the Porsche sprang into life. He blipped the throttle a couple of times before murmuring, 'Roll over Beethoven,' as he set off round the exit curve with a squeal of the tyres to join London's evening traffic.

The Barrowmans lived in a small block of flats in a pleasant avenue in north London It was flanked on both sides by mature English limes, which, judging by their height, had seen the comings and goings of many generations of residents. At nine in the evening the street lights struggled to penetrate their branches, but any loss of illumination was compensated for by an aura of calm respectability.

Steven ran his index finger down the list of those staying at number seven and pressed the appropriate button.

'Come on up.'

He was met on the second floor by Lucy Barrowman who immediately dispelled his telephone-inspired-notion that she would be small, dark and attractive. She was tall, fair and attractive. He had the impression that when she felt relaxed she would exude an air of quiet confidence, but, at the moment, her eyes showed nothing but anxiety. They shook hands.

'I'm Steven.'

'Lucy. I'm sorry, I feel so guilty for dragging you over here like this.'

'You didn't,' Steven assured her. 'I volunteered'.

'You said you had something to tell Owen about that awful place?' said Lucy as if she couldn't wait any longer to ask.

'Moorlock Hall is going to be all over the newspapers in the next few days and not in a good way. I think there's a very real chance it will have to be closed down when the dust settles.'

Lucy Barrowman's features seemed to freeze for a moment then she let out her breath in a long sigh as tension left her body and she exclaimed, 'Music to my ears. I can't tell you how happy that makes me feel.' She broke into a big smile before asking, 'Not that it matters . . . but why?'

'A House of Commons committee has carried out an impromptu inspection of the place and produced a damning report. The fact that the place has been kept a secret for so long will almost certainly ensure that it will turn into a political football'

It suddenly dawned on Lucy that she'd kept Steven standing just inside the front door. 'I'm so sorry,' she said, 'what am I thinking. Please come in, sit down. Can I get you something to drink?'

Steven declined reluctantly, 'A wine gum can get you three points on your license these days.'

Lucy smiled and offered alternatives. Steven jumped at the chance of espresso.

'So, you think that Owen has changed?'

Lucy shook her head as if struggling for words. 'Owen has always been ambitious, but that goes with being a researcher I suppose. There are no silver medals for researchers he kept reminding me, but, almost as soon as he started going to Moorlock Hall and spending time with that creature, Lawler, he started to change. He's become angry, secretive, suspicious of everyone and seems to imagine there's a conspiracy against him. He stays up all night, poring over reams of data, but never seems to take any of it with him to work. When I pointed this out he nearly snapped my head off, accused me of being "one of them" whatever that means. I'd never seen him so angry; his face was scarlet . . . spitting saliva . . . shaking. I thought he was going to hit me.'

Lucy paused and Steven could see she was finding it difficult to hold things together. 'I've become afraid of my own husband . . . I have to consider carefully before I open my mouth . . . I know I've led a sheltered life – even privileged – I'm a middle-class girl, the daughter of professionals who's never known anything but . . . niceness and decency, wanting for nothing. I never imagined for a moment I would end up talking to a stranger about being pregnant and in fear of attack by her husband.

'This sounds like a terrible situation.'

'I suppose you know that Lawler attacked him?' said Lucy.

'What?' Steven exclaimed, 'I had no idea.'

'He grabbed him by the throat while he was taking a blood sample. Another few moments and he would have died. He was saved by one of the attendants coming back from his break.

'You mean he was left alone with Lawler?' Steven sounded incredulous.

'I don't know the details,' said Lucy. 'He didn't want to talk about it and, despite what happened, he still wants to continue working with that animal.'

'I didn't know anything about this,' said Steven.

'Owen wanted it covered up and I suppose the people at Moorlock weren't that keen to have it made public. I think they all colluded.'

'Talk about tangled webs,' said Steven with a sigh.

'But, from what you say, his association with Lawler might well be over?' said Lucy, keen to have it confirmed and managing to regain control of her emotions.

'I'm pretty sure Moorlock Hall's days are almost certainly over. I can believe it was founded with the best of intentions, but it's a skeleton in the cupboard and the cupboard door has just been thrown open. Politicians are not the sort to look the other way when that happens. Someone will be sure to grasp the opportunity to storm the moral high ground and the blame game will begin in earnest.'

'You don't like politicians very much, do you?'

Steven gave a politician's answer. 'Well, it all depends on what you mean by "like". What I *am* saying – and I've made this perfectly clear in the past – the question of liking or not liking is subject to constant change and, as such . . .'

Lucy cottoned on to what Steven was doing and said, You're good at this. She became his interviewer, 'Answer the question!' she demanded. 'Yes or no?'

'Well, what I *am* saying – and you're absolutely right to ask the question – is Mary had a little lamb, its fleece was white as snow . . .'

'You're a natural,' conceded Lucy and they both laughed.

'Something tells me you're not a scientist?' said Steven.

'An English teacher,' said Lucy. 'Maybe it would have helped if I had been and understood more about what Owen was working on, but Bunsen burners and bad smells were never my scene.'

'I don't think it would have helped at all,' said Steven. 'Maybe a master's in psychology, but even then . . . Owen's been treading where angels fear to go.'

'I'm not with you.'

'Sorry, I'm struggling here myself,' Steven confessed. 'It's a bit like trying to define charisma. It's impossible, but we all recognise it when we come across it. Those who have it can often influence – even inspire the rest of us – and it's not unusual for some people to fall completely under their spell. In Owen's case he's come up against the evil equivalent of charisma. There are those who exude evil and malice to a spellbinding degree and unfortunately, these people exert influence too . . . sometimes with catastrophic consequences.'

'That sounds positively terrifying,' said Lucy. Her eyes widened and she seemed to take an age thinking about it before saying, 'Do you know what I think is the most alarming thing for me? . . . it's that Owen seemed to know that . . . He spoke about loathing Lawler but also being fascinated by him. He hated him for what he'd done, but the more he hated him the more interested he seemed to become in him. It sounded like an addiction being described by a scientist, but he was talking about himself.'

Steven nodded.

And now the big money question, what will happen if he can't see Lawler any more . . . will he come back to me? Will I get my husband back?'

'Let's hope so,' said Steven. 'Understanding what you're dealing with and what you're up against can be a big advantage in a situation like this. It helps you rationalise things and, from what you say, Owen knows what's been going on inside his head. He needed data for his study and he's been prepared to take the risk of associating with a number of absolute monsters for quite some time. 'He must have convinced himself he could handle it.'

'And then along came Lawler.'

'I remember when we spoke for the first time,' said Steven. 'He said there was something special about Lawler. He couldn't put his finger on it at the time but it seemed clear that Lawler was in some awful different league to the others in his study. It's no surprise to hear that Lawler has gotten to him, but he was obviously prepared to take the risk and maybe push his luck . . . too far.'

'I think that explains things perfectly,' said Lucy quietly.

Steven said, 'Many people who come into contact with the seamier side of life on a regular basis convince themselves that they can leave the job behind when they go home at the end of the day and then find they can't. They start seeking help from booze and pills and then resent anyone who notices they have a problem and tries to help – usually the ones who care the most. An unfortunate few discover just how few steps there are between having a secure family life and settling down for the night under a railway arch.

'Owen's started drinking.'

Steven saw the panic in Lucy's eyes and could see this wasn't the time to trot out glib assurances. He said, 'We should consider the positives.'

'Which are?'

'Lawler is the problem.'

'Agreed.'

Moorlock Hall is not going to exist for much longer. Its inmates will be transferred to other secure units. Owen will not be granted further access to Lawler.'

'How do you know?'

'I will see to it.'

'Can you do that?'

'Yes.'

'Owen told me you were a doctor,' said Lucy. 'but you're not a psychiatrist, are you?'

'So, what do I know . . .'

'I'm sorry, I didn't mean to imply . . .'

'I was an army medic,' said Steven. 'Let's just say I came across the evil dregs of humanity in my time and saw what they did. I learned from the experience.'

'I see, and now?'

'I'm chief investigator with Sci-Med.' Steven explained Sci-Med's function.

Lucy nodded. 'Okay, I believe you, no more meetings with Lawler. Happy days.'

'Owen probably has enough samples from Lawler to give him data for his research and, if not, he has material from prisoners in all the other secure units. There's no reason why he can't get on with analysing them and completing his project. Maybe once he gets back to working full time in the lab and stops spending so much time with deranged killers, he'll find his way back to normality.'

'I desperately want to believe you,' said Lucy with an attempt at a smile.

Steven got up to go and gave her his card. 'Call any time if you need me.'

'What should I do about warning Owen there's going to be stuff in the papers?' Lucy asked.

Steven could see the difficulty in the situation. Lucy wouldn't want to tell her husband she'd been seeking a shoulder to cry on. 'Don't,' he said. Have an early night. Go to bed. Leave a note for Owen telling him I phoned and that he should call me back when he got in. The time doesn't matter.'

TEN

Steven stood in the darkness of his empty flat for a few minutes looking out the window at the lights of the river traffic. It moved slowly and the lights were pretty. He felt uneasy and concerned about Lucy Barrowman. He had believed the situation to be manageable until she'd told him about the attack on her husband and the fact that, despite the experience, he still wanted to continue working with Lawler.

Although he hadn't said so to Lucy – because she needed reassurance not cause for further anxiety – that took things to a new level. This was not the normal behaviour of a person whose life had been in danger. Joe and Jill Public would have been more than happy to have the emergency services appear on the scene – the more the merrier – and to have had medical checks carried out and reassurance provided. There was a real risk that Barrowman had stopped rationalising his association with Lawler and had fallen completely under his spell. If that were so, Lucy could be in danger. One thing was for sure, if there was to be any chance of recovering the situation, Barrowman had to be stopped from seeing Lawler.

The phone rang and broke his train of thought. It was Tally.

'Where have you been?' I've called twice, the last time half an hour ago.

'I went to meet a young lady.'

'I should have known,' said Tally. 'Turn my back for ten minutes and you're out on the pull.'

'I can hear you sharpening your scalpel.'

'No, I'm going to use a blunt one.'

'I went to see Lucy Barrowman. She has fears for her husband.'

'With cause?' Tally asked.

'I think maybe.'

'Oh dear, so what's the plan?'

'He has to be kept away from Lawler. I'm going to speak to John in the morning and maybe I'll pay the director of Moorlock Hall a visit before the world and his wife turn up.'

'You don't think a D notice will be issued?'

'I can't see it,' said Steven. 'It's not a matter of national security and whoever set up Moorlock Hall in the first place was clearly in the wrong – legally, morally, politically. Common sense will be excluded from any argument to the contrary.'

'I suppose.'

'How's your mother?'

'She's stable and comfortable, but the next 48 hours will be crucial.'

'Of course. Did you ask to see the X-rays for yourself?'

'No,' growled Tally. 'I'm not the sort to mess with other people's egos and orthopaedic surgeons have big hammers and sharp saws.'

'Good thought.'

'Apart from that . . . a nurse told me it was a clean break.'

'Good,' said Steven with a smile.

'It's ages since we've been apart.'

'I know, I don't like it.'

'Me neither, talk to you tomorrow.'

Steven was conscious of the fact that Owen Barrowman had not phoned him and this was another source of worry. Maybe he hadn't seen the note . . . or maybe he hadn't come home and stayed in the lab working all night. He was about to try calling him when John Macmillan arrived and Steven told him all that had happened at Moorlock Hall. He unloaded all his fears about Barrowman's state of mind. 'We have to stop him having any further contact with Lawler.'

'No question,' agreed Macmillan.

'Did you tell the Home Secretary you were calling a code red on what was going on in Professor Lindstrom's lab and what was going on with the funding for her research?'

'I did, naming you as lead investigator.'

'Good. Any problems?'

'No,' mused Macmillan turning to gaze out of the window with an innocent expression. 'Mind you, I didn't mention we knew about MI5's involvement,' he murmured.

Steven smiled. 'An understandable oversight.'

'Well, she didn't mention it either.'

The signalling of a code red did not imply anything as dramatic as it sounded. It was simply a notification to all government bodies that Sci-Med was actively investigating something it deemed to be important. Any named investigator in the operation – in this case, Steven – was to be accorded every assistance from all public service bodies including the police in whichever area he was operating, should he request it. Cooperation was mandatory. He was also licensed to carry a firearm should he believe it necessary, although by choice he rarely did. There was also a dedicated phone line he could call at any hour of the day or night to seek expert technical information and advice.

Jean Roberts gave Steven her, 'here we go again' smile as he came out of Macmillan's office. 'How can I help?' she asked.

'I need to see Moorlock Hall for myself and talk to the medical director before any story breaks in the papers,' said Steven. 'I guess that means today.'

'Anything else?'

'I need to know where it is.'

Jean stifled a giggle. 'Give me thirty minutes to make some calls. Go have a coffee

Steven did as he was told and tried contacting Owen Barrowman, first at the lab where he was told he hadn't come in yet and then at home where there was no reply. He'd try later.

Steven explored a wide range of expletives as his Porsche struggled with the surface of the road leading up to Moorlock Hall. He even found himself apologising to it when he failed to avoid a particularly bad pothole. When he finally came to a halt in the small car park he sat for a couple minutes, just savouring the stillness broken only by metallic contraction sounds from the car.

Steven showed his Sci-Med ID and said that he was expected. The owner of the eyes behind the grill responded by admitting him and putting him through the standard security measures before taking him to see Groves who invited him to sit with a wave of his good hand.

'For a secret establishment, we seem to be doing quite a reasonable impression of a tourist attraction,' said Groves. 'What exactly is Sci-Med?'

Steven told him and got an approving nod. 'How can I help?'

'I believe Dr Owen Barrowman from Capital University has been coming here regularly as part of his research project into the genetic and biochemical make up of psychopathic killers.'

'He has, but only one of our inmates agreed to take part in his study.'

'Yes, Malcolm Lawler . . . who "took part" the other day by attempting to murder him.'

Groves froze for a moment. His eyes showed what Steven saw as a combination of disappointment and resignation. 'You know about that, do you,' he said quietly.

'His wife told me. I understand you all conspired to cover it up?'

'Owen said that he didn't want any fuss and I have to confess I didn't go to any great lengths to dissuade him. If I'm honest it was music to my ears. We had an inspection in the offing and an incident like that was the last thing we needed.'

Steven nodded, impressed by the man's honest appraisal of the situation. 'How did the inspection go?'

'They found failings,' replied Groves.

'Serious?'

'I'm to be retired.'

Steven was taken aback. He hadn't expected to hear anything like that. He'd been assuming that anything bad emerging from the inquiry would be concerned with the hiding of the existence of the place rather than any criticism of the way it was run. 'I don't understand. What sort of failings?'

'It would appear that certain elements of our coalition government are worried about the lack of spiritual and pastoral care being offered to our patients.'

'You can't be serious.'

Groves gave a little shake of the head as if he couldn't believe it himself. He sighed and said, 'There are those who would believe that no one is beyond redemption and that every effort should be made to achieve this. Our efforts in keeping the vilest creatures who ever walked the Earth away from society was not good enough for one such politician, Mrs Lillian Leadbetter. She and her band of all-party day-trippers wanted rehabilitation. She demanded that souls be saved and the hand of forgiveness extended. I, as the culprit who had made no effort to introduce remedial classes or even replace our last chaplain when he left over a year ago, was judged to be a major impediment to Mrs Leadbetter's reformist ambitions. As a consequence, I've been invited to consider my position.'

'Didn't she understand anything about what these people did?' Steven exclaimed.

'I think she put her hands over her ears and hummed la la la – metaphorically speaking. In her eyes, I was a dinosaur trying to excuse my insensitivity.'

'But didn't she understand anything about the reasons for setting up Moorlock Hall in the first place? Surely, she knew what happened when Clifford Sutton fooled all the experts and was returned to the community to rape and murder all over again? Wasn't that a wee clue for the honourable member?'

Groves made an attempt at a smile which only accentuated his lack of facial muscle control. 'The committee actually interviewed Lawler . . .'

'And?'

'He put on a performance that would have had him graduate *cum laudae* from RADA. I damned nearly applauded myself. He had them positively eating out of his hand. He was a poor misunderstood victim of an uncaring society that had never given him a chance. Yes, he had done wrong, terrible wrong, but he could see the error of his ways. He would give his very life if only he could turn the clock back and undo the harm he had done to all these "poor people" Well, I won't be here to see what the lying bastard gets out of it. Who said you couldn't fool all the people all of the time?'

'Surely there must be an appeal process you can go through?'

Groves shook his head. 'I don't have the stomach for a fight. My pension will see me to the end of the road with the occasional glass of malt. I'll settle for that.'

Steven nodded then asked as an afterthought, 'Why didn't you appoint a new chaplain?'

'Because I saw what they did to the last one.'

'Oh dear.'

'Father Patrick Burns was under no illusions when he came here. He knew – or at least thought he knew – what he was up against when he took on the task of persuading Lawler and the others that they should seek forgiveness from a higher power without reminding them too stridently or too often that they certainly weren't going to find it here on Earth. Despite having contact with them only twice a week, they utterly destroyed him. He lost his faith and was unable to continue as a parish priest after seeking solace at the bottom of too many glasses. The last I heard was that he was recovering in a seminary in France.'

'Good God.'

Groves raised his eyebrows at Steven's expression. 'I still remember what he said to me after seeing Lawler for the last time. He said, "It's not repentance Lawler needs . . . it's exorcism.'

Steven thought about this for a few moments before saying, 'I really came here today to talk about the growing influence that Lawler has been exerting over Owen Barrowman. I think the fact that he's a scientist and was aware of the dangers and could even talk about them tended to disguise the fact that he was succumbing to them.'

'I thought he was managing well,' said Groves. 'He's had a few bad experiences of course, when hearing what Lawler did first hand, but I thought he was on top of things. And then the attack happened . . . and I did wonder when he didn't want a fuss . . .'

'Why was he left alone with Lawler?'

'He wasn't,' replied Groves.

'I understood from his wife that he was alone when Lawler attacked him?'

'You've spoken to his wife recently?'

'Yes, his boss and his colleagues have all been noticing changes come over him since he started working with Lawler and, of course, his wife, Lucy, was subject to dealing with them more than anyone else. I saw her last night: she's a nervous wreck. She's afraid of him. His paranoia even includes her in some imagined conspiracy to steal his research. He mustn't be allowed anywhere near Lawler ever again.

'Good God, I knew there was a risk,' said Groves, 'but I really believed he could handle it . . . but maybe that's what I wanted to think.'

'In many ways he has himself to blame,' said Steven. 'He believes Lawler is the key to a big scientific discovery and he's the one who's going to make it, nobody else He needed Lawler for access to samples and data and hasn't been willing to let anything or anybody get in his way.'

'And now the tail is now wagging the dog,' said Groves.

'I think so,' said Steven.

Groves told Steven about Clements and his part in the attack on Barrowman. 'That's the way it seems to happen,' said Steven. 'One minute you're full of loathing for an individual, then quite suddenly it's replaced by unquestioning admiration and a willingness to lay down your life for them.'

'I should have cottoned on . . .' said Groves, hanging his head. 'It must have been the attack that opened up Owen's mind to suggestion from Lawler. His defences would have been minimal having been in fear of his life and it left him completely susceptible to what Lawler was filling his mind with . . . Lawler got to him. It was my fault.'

'I'm sure Barrowman's decision to have no action taken against Lawler would have sounded perfectly rational to you at the time,' said Steven. 'It may have been what you wanted to hear for other reasons, but you had no good cause to doubt him. It's hindsight that's illuminating the scene for both of us.'

'Thanks for that,' said Groves.

I take it you've been told the inspection report is going to make the papers if the government can't make a D notice stick?'

'I had heard. Someone from the Home Office rang me to apologise for the inspection – said it was all a mistake and should never have happened, but it was too late to do anything about it.'

'A nice touch,' said Steven sourly. 'It's amazing what damage a loose-tongued drunk at a party can end up doing.'

'Damn him to hell,' said Groves.

Steven asked a few questions about the organisation and running of Moorlock Hall, but this was more to justify his visit rather than be the basis of any kind of formal inquiry. Mrs Leadbetter's conclusions had changed all that. It was clear that there was no chance that the government was going to be able to hide her findings behind a D notice. He personally had decided that Groves was a perfectly decent man who was about to be pilloried in the press because some self-important politician had seen the chance to parade her precious liberal values on a stage provided for her by the press and all to catch the eye of the voters and advance her career.

'Did you particularly want to meet Lawler?' Groves asked.

'I don't think so.'

'I'll show you around anyway.'

Steven called Barrowman's lab number at Capital from the car, only to be told that he hadn't been in so he tried his home number again. A male voice answered but it wasn't Barrowman.

'Who is this?' Steven asked.

'Who's asking?'

'Dr Steven Dunbar. Who are you?'

'Detective Sergeant Riley. Can I ask your business please?'

'I'd like to speak to Owen Barrowman, what's going on?'

'I'm sorry, I can't tell you that.'

Steven said who he was, adding that he was on an active investigation and telling the policeman he could check his status with the Home Office. It was important he speak with Barrowman.

'Sorry sir, I can't see your ID over the phone.'

Steven ended the call and called John Macmillan.

'Steven, we've been trying to get in touch with you. Barrowman's wife is in hospital and he's disappeared.'

'Hospital?'

'She was badly beaten.'

Steven felt a crushing weight land on his shoulders. 'By Owen?' he asked in trepidation.

'They think so.'

'Oh my God, which hospital is she in?'

Macmillan told him.

'I'm going there.''

ELEVEN

'I'd much rather you left it until tomorrow?' the young doctor said when Steven asked to see Luc

'Steven put away his ID and went for a more personal approach. 'I understand you want what's best for your patient, doctor, and if you say no, I'll accept that without question, but I'm a doctor myself and I assure you I won't upset her in any way . . . if I could just have a few words?'

The doctor, who looked all of fourteen, took an age to weigh up imaginary pros and cons before stroking his chin and conceding. 'Five minutes, no longer.'

'Absolutely.'

Steven was accompanied by the doctor to Lucy's room where he had to show his ID again when asked by one of the two constables standing there. Steven wondered if the police really believed her life to be in danger.

'Five minutes,' he was reminded.

Steven had to swallow when he saw the state of Lucy's face. The bruising and swelling had made her practically unrecognisable. The only plus he could take from that was that the flesh around her eyes was so swollen that she probably couldn't see the look of shock on his face.

'Lucy,' he said gently. 'It's Steven Dunbar, they told me Owen did this to you. I'm so sorry, it must have had something to do with my visit last night?'

'Not your fault,' came the slurred reply through cut and swollen lips. 'You gave me your card . . . I left it lying around . . . Owen found it when he came home . . . didn't match with what I'd said in my note . . . had to tell him you'd been there . . . went crazy angry . . . lost it . . . clear you and I were part of the conspiracy . . . establishment had it in for him . . . going to steal his research . . . told him he needed help . . . made things worse . . . cue punch bag time.'

Steven winced at the thought. 'Do you know where he's gone Lucy?'

'He wasn't there when I came to.'

'The police were at your flat when I called.'

'Neighbour called them . . . my screams . . . couldn't help them much. They asked about motive . . . couldn't help . . . don't understand what's going on . . .'

'I don't think any of us do.'

'A politician's answer?'

'Sorry.

The young doctor appeared in the doorway and Steven nodded. He got up and said, softly, 'Get some sleep, I'll come back soon if that's all right?'

Lucy answered with a slight raise of her fingers.'

As they walked along the corridor, Steven asked the doctor if Lucy's parents had been informed.'

'She was adamant she didn't want that just yet.

Steven thought he understood. Lucy Barrowman was taking time to think things through herself before bringing mummy and daddy on to the scene. Respect.

'And now the big question, doctor, do you know about the baby yet?

'Don't know for sure. We didn't want to put her through any more trauma today. 'We'll do the tests tomorrow.'

Steven set out for the Home Office.

'What a day . . . what a bloody awful day,' Steven complained as he slumped down in a chair in the office.

Jean Roberts looked at him sympathetically. 'You couldn't have known something like that would happen,' she said softly.

Steven insisted. 'I could see the potential for danger.'

'Do you know what triggered it?'

Steven told her about giving his card to Lucy. 'In case she needed help!' he spluttered. 'Can you believe it?'

Jean looked puzzled and Steven explained. 'Lucy left it lying around and Barrowman found it when he came home late. The plan was not to tell him I'd been there in case he thought she was conspiring with people behind his back . . .It looks like that's exactly what he did think.'

'Don't blame yourself, Steven, it was her crazy husband who did this.'

'Jean's right,' said John Macmillan who had heard from next door and had now joined them. 'Life has a habit of doing this to people who don't deserve it. There was no way you could have foreseen such a violent outburst.'

Steven was unconvinced but let it go.

'How was your trip to Moorlock Hall?'

'Pretty awful. The medical director is about to be hung out to dry to divert attention away from politicians. A pity, he seems like a decent enough bloke. Mind you, I didn't get around to asking him how he'd ended up in a place like Moorlock.'

'The news at this end isn't any better,' said Macmillan. 'No chance of a D notice and I've just seen a transcript of the report that was leaked to the papers.'

Macmillan put on his glasses and read aloud from the A4 sheet he was holding. 'Questions have been asked by junior minister, Mrs Lillian Leadbetter regarding Moorlock Hall, an unlisted facility housing a number of convicted prisoners deemed criminally insane. She has accused HMG of covering up the existence of an establishment that would put a Stalinist gulag to shame. The patients, she claims, have been completely abandoned by society, locked away and left to rot without any attempt being made to rehabilitate them. Their only contact with the outside world is via television. They don't even have access to a chaplain to confide in.'

'They did have,' said Steven. He's hoping to recover his faith in a seminary in France.

'What a mess,' said Macmillan. 'Any idea where Barrowman might have gone?'

Steven said not. 'He'd disappeared by the time Lucy regained consciousness. The police were still in the flat when I phoned earlier; they're keeping a watch on the place.

'Do you think there's a chance he'll go back there?' asked Jean.

'There's no way of predicting what he'll do in his current state or what his options are, but we do know he is completely fixated on his research,' said Steven. 'Nothing else matters. He has just beaten the hell out of his wife because he imagined she was part of a plot to steal it from him. And now he's blown it, thrown it all away in one furious violent outburst. Talk about an unexploded bomb.'

'Do you think he's realised he's thrown it all away?' Jean asked.

'Or what he might do when he does,' added Macmillan.

'He'll destroy it,' said Steven. 'There's no way he's going to let others benefit from it.'

'Then we should do everything we can to stop him,' said Macmillan.

'Lucy told me he worked at home most evenings well into the night. I'll get over there and see what I can come up with. Let's hope he kept meticulous notes.'

'I'll call Professor Lindstrom, make her aware of the situation if she doesn't already know,' said Jean.

'Good,' said Macmillan. 'Ask her to gather all Barrowman's stuff together, disks, notebooks, everything and make it secure. Any computers used by him should be put in full shut-down with no access from outside sources especially wireless.'

Macmillan noticed that Steven had suddenly gone quiet. 'Something wrong?' he asked him.

'This is all a waste of time,' Steven replied . . . 'A complete waste of time. Barrowman's been showing signs of paranoia for some weeks. There's no way he would have left anything lying around on tablets or computers either at home or work. He would have stored all his work somewhere secure when he finished analysing the data he'd collected. We're not going to find anything.'

'So where would he keep it?'

'Pick a cloud,' said Steven.

'Damnation,' said Macmillan, but recognised that Steven had a point. 'Maybe we should still secure anything we can find. There might be a clue in it somewhere.'

Steven nodded but didn't feel confident.

'There's another thing,' Jean began. 'If Steven's right . . . it would mean that Barrowman could destroy his work any time he likes from anywhere he likes? All he has to do is access the distant server or cloud he's using and wipe everything out. He could do that from an internet café.'

'Or an i Pad or a smart phone,' added Steven. 'Jean's right. We'll just have to hope that he will be reluctant to do that until he's absolutely convinced all is lost.'

Macmillan looked at his watch and said, 'Not much more we can do tonight. 'I'll check that the police are aware of our interest and are keeping watch on Barrowman's home and lab. Anything else I should add?'

Steven said, 'If the police pick him up or he gives himself up – as he may well do after a night in the cold – he's not to be allowed to make a phone call and the police should oppose bail at our request if it reaches court.'

Jean brought up the statutory right to a phone call and Steven said, 'They can ask him who he'd like to call and what the number is. If it checks out someone can dial it for him. We don't want him punching in a code to a distant server and destroying something that could potentially benefit mankind.'

Steven picked up a kebab on his way home: he couldn't remember when he'd last eaten. It might not have passed as fine dining but by God it tasted good. He was munching on it when his phone rang and he had to take a few seconds to empty his mouth before he could speak.

'Are you all right?' asked Tally.

'Mm, fine.'

'Don't tell me you've got the dolly round at our place tonight. What's her name?'

'Donna,' Steven replied, pleased at his quick wit – so pleased that he couldn't quite stifle a splutter.

'Oh, very good, Dunbar. How come you're eating at this time?'

'First tell me about your mother. How is she?'

'She's okay, I think the nurse was right about it being a clean break. There's been no sign of bits coming off and threatening embolism problems.'

'Good.'

'Your turn, tell me about your long day.'

'Steven told her everything about a day he was mightily glad was coming to an end.

'And she's pregnant!' exclaimed Tally. 'How could he possibly do that to his wife and unborn baby over his obsession with some research project which will probably amount to nothing in the end as most of them do?'

'He's not in his right mind, Tally.'

'Damned right he's not. I hope they lock him up and melt the key.'

'No, Tally . . . you don't understand . . .'

'Don't understand? You can't possibly be making excuses for him.'

'I'm not making excuses for Barrowman,' said Steven. 'But he's no longer the Owen Barrowman everyone knew. His personality has changed dramatically, possibly through the company he's been keeping, in particular, his association with, Malcolm Lawler, the one he saw as being special. '

'Are you suggesting that Barrowman has become a psychopath himself?'

'Please God, no,' said Steven, 'but . . .'

'But what?'

'Maybe . . . We're in uncharted territory here. Everyone has heard about the power of suggestion but no one really knows what it means or what its limits are because no one understands how it works. Ironically, the person closest to being able to explain what happens in scientific terms is probably Barrowman himself. This is exactly what he's been working on.'

'Gene switching,' said Tally remembering an earlier conversation. 'but if this has happened to a clued-up researcher who presumably was well aware of the possible risks from the outset and on his guard, doesn't that suggest that psychopaths have a greater capacity to exercise the power of suggestion over the rest of us than other people . . . people who're not psychopaths?'

'Not a happy thought.'

'No, a frightening one.'

Steven related what Groves had told him about Lawler and Sutton taking control of a whole wing when they were held at Broadmoor.

'What a nightmare,' said Tally.

'What's really scary is that, in their case, we're not talking about the power of suggestion or the ability to influence others. With people like Lawler and Sutton, words don't come into it. Barrowman thinks that actual genetic switching is going on. These monsters have the ability to physically alter enzyme levels in others through inducing changes in their gene activity, which can lead to possible catastrophic personality change.'

'It's obvious Barrowman sees Lawler as the key to understanding how epigenetics work.'

'And he's been ignoring the dangers,' said Steven. 'When we first met, I warned him about the risks of spending too much time in the company of truly evil individuals, but I don't think he took it on board. He pointed out that it worked both ways.'

'How so?'

'I mentioned the instances of German citizens turning up at pre-Second World War rallies of the Nazi party to protest vigorously, but coming away as committed Nazis because their heightened emotional state had rendered them susceptible to the power of the rhetoric coming at them. He pointed out that much the same had gone on in the nineteen fifties when curious people had attended Pastor Billy Graham rallies only to emerge as committed evangelical Christians.'

Tally said, 'I think I'll take comfort from that. It's good to know it's not only the bad guys who have the power.'

'Steven gave a half laugh.

'What's funny?'

'Barrowman . . . the Lindstrom group . . . researchers working at the cutting edge of science . . . they're all caught up in a struggle that's been around since the beginning of time . . . Good versus evil.'

'And with that happy thought . . .'

'We'll say good night.'

'Love you.'

'Love you too.'

Thoughts of what had happened to Lucy Barrowman ensured that Steven couldn't find the sleep he needed and kept him awake into the wee small hours. Despite the assurances of the others he still felt guilty and could empathise with Lucy when she had once said that she wished she'd never heard of Moorlock Hall. That was exactly how he felt. The more he thought about it the more he understood the horror of having to work in a place like that – as its director, Groves had done for several years. People tended to fit into whatever sort of society they found themselves in. They adapted. They did as the Romans did as the old saying went, but when psychopathic killers comprised the overwhelming majority of the society you found yourself in . . . how did that work? How could you begin to establish any kind of working relationship with anyone?

Steven was still wondering about this when the phone rang.

'The police have Barrowman in custody,' said John Macmillan's voice.

'Thank God.'

'They found him wandering around in the rain and not making a great deal of sense when they approached him. The two officers didn't realise who he was at first. They'd been on the look-out for a dangerous, violent suspect and they had come across a confused character, soaked to the skin and talking nonsense.'

'Where are they holding him?'

'The police surgeon decided he needed proper assessment. He was organising a hospital transfer when I got the call.'

'Which hospital?'

'We'll find out in the morning.'

'Could be a day for hospital visits,' said Steven. 'I need to talk to Lucy again too.'

TWELVE

'She's had a good night,' said the nurse when Steven phoned, 'but the doctors want to run some more tests before any visitors are allowed.'

'When should I call back?'

'Give it a couple of hours.'

Steven went in to the Home Office and asked Jean if she'd heard anything about Barrowman's whereabouts.

'The police still haven't told us yet where he's being held.'

'What?'

'It does seem a bit odd.'

'Maybe we can get John to lean on someone when he comes in?'

'Of course. Anything else?'

'I need to talk to the Lindstrom group and interested parties to hear what happens now. Barrowman's work was the specific reason they were financed. Did you manage to contact Dorothy yesterday?'

Jean nodded. 'She was pretty shocked but agreed to secure Barrowman's stuff and keep it away from prying eyes. The police also confirmed last night that his home computer and any paperwork they came across has been removed from his flat for safe-keeping.'

'Good.'

'Won't the people who provided funding for the group consider Barrowman's results and data as their property?' asked Jean.

'Probably,' Steven replied, 'assuming there are any results and data to be found although I think Dorothy could counter-argue that she, as group leader and grant holder, should have the right to go through everything first and decide whether there's anything of importance there. She should also be the one to decide if Barrowman's research could be continued by other members of her group,'

'Why am I thinking of lawyers circling like sharks?' said Jean.

'Fear not,' said Steven. 'I have a cunning plan.'

'Do tell.'

'While they're all squabbling, I'm going to make sure that we get to take a good look at Barrowman's stuff.'

'Jean's eyes lit up. 'Lukas?' she said.

'Lukas.'

Sci-Med were too small an operation to have laboratories and employ their own technical experts so they had built up a number of agreements over the years with small, independent outfits who were among the best in their fields. Lukas Neubauer, biology section head at Lundborg Analytical in Crompton Lane, and an expert in all things biological was one of the consultants that Steven knew best and for whom he held high regard. Some people were bright and others knowledgeable: Neubauer, was both. A Czech expatriate and veritable polymath, he had come to the UK to do his PhD in the Medical Research Council labs in Cambridge and had never gone home. Meeting and subsequently marrying Janine, a Swiss mathematics student at the time, had eventually led to them establishing Lundborg Analytical.

'I'll call him sometime today and warn him we may be calling on his services,' said Steven.

'Whose services?' asked John Macmillan, arriving late and shaking rain from his white hair.

Steven told him of his plan.

'A good man,' said Macmillan, 'unlike the clown masquerading as a police inspector I've just wasted half an hour of my life speaking to. I thought I'd pop in on my way here to the station where Barrowman was taken to last night and find out where he'd been taken. I should have asked a traffic cone instead.'

Steven and Jean waited for more while Macmillan hung his overcoat on the stand by the door. 'He flatly refused to tell me where they took Barrowman last night.'

'In God's name, why not?' Steven exclaimed.

'Security,' the clown said . . . the standard reply of the clueless when they don't know what they're doing.'

Steven was astonished. 'Didn't you tell him who you were?'

'He had his orders and wasn't budging for anyone.

'More than his job's worth . . .' murmured Steven.

Macmillan let out his frustration in a long sigh before attempting a smile and saying, 'I'll ask the Home Secretary herself.'

'And I'll go see Lucy Barrowman,' said Steven.

Jean said, 'I'll see about setting up a meeting at Capital.'

Steven sensed that the atmosphere among those involved with Lucy Barrowman's care seemed much more relaxed than it had on the previous evening. The two policemen had disappeared from outside her door and the nurse who emerged as he reached it was smiling.

'Doctor Williams is still with her;' said the nurse. 'She'll be out in a few moments.'

Steven sat down and waited for what he thought must be good news.

'The baby's fine,' said the small woman wearing square frame glasses which seemed to magnify her eyes to an alarming degree and who introduced herself as Dr Williams, consultant obstetrician. 'Quite amazing really, considering the beating she took. Survival for baby must have been pre-ordained. The kicks missed vital areas.'

Details of the beating induced a surge of guilt in Steven.

'The doctor opened the door and inclined her head as a signal that Steven should enter. 'Not too long please.'

'Lucy, it's Steven.'

'Yes, I can just about see you,' said Lucy. 'They told me you were coming in this morning.'

'I hear you've had some good news.'

'Yes, baby's fine although he's had one hell of a change in circumstances before he's even been born.'

Steven saw her point but wasn't sure what to say. Anodyne rubbish about being sure everything would turn out fine was not for Lucy Barrowman, he wouldn't insult her with it. Likewise, never knowing what's around the corner or observations on life's rich pattern and the direction of curve balls would be non-starters.

'They told me yesterday that you didn't want your parents told?'

'Waves of parental anguish would have pushed me over the edge yesterday,' said Lucy.

Steven nodded. 'But maybe they should be told when you feel well enough . . .

'I just needed time to stand still for a bit, time to figure out what happens next. Does that make sense?'

'Perfect sense, but the medics say baby's fine and you're on the mend . . .'

'Your point?'

'Call your folks. Practical support is a good thing.'

Lucy nodded. 'Will do, the policemen on the door told me before they left that Owen had been taken into custody.'

'Late last night,' said Steven without adding details.

''Where are they holding him?

'I understand he was taken to hospital for assessment of his mental state. I'm not sure which one.'

'I see.'

'Lucy . . . pretty soon people are going to start asking you about Owen's research.'

'Me? Why ask me, why not him?' Lucy asked, becoming slightly agitated and aggravating the pain from her injuries because of it.

'They'll ask him of course, but chances are he won't tell them anything.'

'Ah, yes, his precious research,' said Lucy bitterly. 'Well, there's no point asking me about it. I've no idea what he was doing or what he came up with.'

Steven tiptoed onwards. 'It's not so much a question of knowing what he was doing, more a question of knowing what he's done with his data and results . . . You said he worked at home a lot . . .'

Lucy was quiet for some time before saying, 'Are you one of these people, Steven?'

'I am,' said Steven without any beating about the bush. 'It's Sci-Med's job to see to it that potentially beneficial information like Owen's work should not disappear or fall into the wrong hands. There's a chance he discovered something important about psychotic behaviour and how it might be . . . treated or manipulated.

'Manipulated? Lucy questioned. 'Treated, I understand, but manipulated?'

Steven gave an apologetic shrug. 'This is hypothetical of course, but if you understand the genetic details surrounding the condition, it's possible you might be able to alter, even cure it. Unfortunately, it's also theoretically possible you might also be able to induce it . . .'

'But who in their right mind . . .' Lucy stopped in mid-sentence.

Steven nodded and said, 'The people backing the research chose to remain anonymous – probably for innocent reasons, but. Sci-Med has to know for sure.'

'The changes that came over Owen . . .' Lucy began unsurely.

Steven watched Lucy's silent search for something that might excuse what her husband had done. It was understandable but something he was reluctant to encourage.

'You spoke of people falling under the influence of others . . . charisma and the like.'

'I did,' Steven agreed, 'and that is all tied up with this somewhere.'

'So, it's possible that Owen was under the influence of Lawler?'

'I don't think we can rule anything out,' said Steven, but his reluctance in saying so was obvious to Lucy.

'But?'

'It's just my opinion, but I don't think Owen was acting under anyone else's influence when he attacked you. I think he was the one making the decisions and for his own reasons.'

'Why do you think he did what he did to me? . . . The look in his eyes . . . it was like I was a complete stranger . . . not even a person.'

Steven listened with a sinking feeling in his stomach. Unspoken fears were being realised. 'You were the one who had crossed him; he acted as his new self . . . coldly, without empathy or sympathy.'

'So . . . you think he really has changed?'

'It's possible.'

'Could he have become a psychopath himself?'

Lucy took Steven's silence and a raise of his eyebrows as a yes. 'Ironic really,' she said, 'looking for a cure . . .'

'All the more important we find out what his research has uncovered about the condition and what might be done about it.'

'If you say so.'

'You said he worked a lot at home, do you share a computer?'

'He has a desktop, I use my laptop.'

'Did he ever mention data storage?'

'He used the university's servers.'

'He didn't worry about security?'

'Apart from thinking everyone on the planet was plotting to steal his work?'

'Sorry, stupid question, I was thinking more about the servers.'

'He was meticulous about secure passwords. He once gave me a lecture on how difficult it was to come up with random numbers and one of his favourite sayings was "don't put all your eggs in one basket."'

Any thoughts about other baskets?' Steven asked.

'He used cloud storage as well as servers. He said I should keep my photographs on one.'

''Which one?

'Microsoft Sky Drive . . . sorry, Steven . . . I'm feeling awfully tired . . .'

'God, I'm so thoughtless, forgive me.'

Lucy reassured him with a pat on his hand, but she was asleep by the time he reached the door.

Steven returned to the Home Office to find John Macmillan in a foul mood.

'No wonder they didn't want to tell me what hospital Barrowman was in,' he stormed. 'He isn't in one.'

'What?'

'The alarm was raised when the ambulance didn't arrive. It was found two hours later with Barrowman's police escort and the two ambulance attendants unconscious inside. None of them knows what happened.'

'They don't know?' exclaimed Steven.

'The driver remembers reporting he was being followed by what he thought was a private ambulance and shortly afterwards a police vehicle appeared – he thought in response. It flagged him down and he opened his window to talk. That's the last thing he remembers.'

'Sounds like gas was involved.'

'Someone wanted Dr Barrowman more than we did.'

'Someone with technical expertise when it comes to kidnapping, said Steven, 'not to mention inside information about his whereabouts which is even more worrying. Is this why they're keeping quiet?'

Macmillan nodded. 'No one can figure out what's going on and they certainly don't want anyone linking it with the Moorlock Hall story in the papers.'

'Why would they?' said Jean? 'I mean very few people know about Barrowman's connection with Moorlock.'

'I suspect Mrs Lillian Leadbetter does,' said Steven. 'Groves would have mentioned his involvement, I'm sure.'

'Oh dear.'

'I'm not sure there's anything in it for her,' said Macmillan, 'but it would be a godsend for the tabloids. *Scientist involved in experimentation on prisoners held in secret prison loses mind and tries to murder wife and unborn child before escaping police custody and going on run."*

'Not good.'

THIRTEEN

Steven walked by the embankment. He needed to clear his head; there were just too many variables floating around to prevent him seeing a clear course of action. He didn't think they'd find any useful information on Barrowman's computers and in his notes because of the man's paranoia. Lukas Neubauer and his colleagues at Lundborg might be able to crack passwords protecting data files if they found them but the odds must be against it. Lucy might remember something useful, some casual comment made in conversation before her husband became distant and hostile, but then again, she might not.

The only realistic source of information about Barrowman's discovery was Barrowman himself and unfortunately, someone else had concluded that too – and beaten them to it. There were two prime suspects for this, the intelligence services who had tried to prevent the research being done in the first place and secondly, those who had come up with the finance for Dorothy Lindstrom's research.

Steven decided that the first practical thing they all had to do, despite being pessimistic about the outcome, was to find out just how much information was on Barrowman's computers and in his notes. It was a fair bet that Dorothy Lindstrom was hard at work doing just that as he stood there, leaning on the wall, watching the rising tide. He had to concede that she had every right to do this as the future of her research group probably depended on coming up with some meaningful progress so that funding might be continued. She would probably be joined in her search by Tyler, the consultant retained by the funding body as soon as they heard what had happened, but Steven feared that this was something they might do even if they had had some involvement in the kidnapping and were currently interrogating Barrowman in some deep, dark cellar. That was the trouble with not knowing, Steven concluded, your imagination always made things worse.

Steven decided he would not request immediate access to the material found in Barrowman's lab. Dorothy and the money men's reps could do that while he did what they couldn't – get hold of what the police had taken from Barrowman's flat. He would ask Lukas Neubauer to go through it with a fine-tooth comb.

Steven was in the process of wondering whether he should give Lukas a call or go over to see him in person when Jean Roberts called.

'I've spoken to the principal at Capital. He and Professor Lindstrom have a meeting arranged for two thirty this afternoon to discuss the situation. You could join them if that's convenient?'

'Wonderful,' said Steven, who was well used to important people imagining their diaries were full until convinced otherwise.

'There's a bonus,' said Jean. 'The scientific consultant employed by the lawyers acting for the backers of the Lindstrom group will be attending too. Lots of birds with one stone?'

'What can I say?' Steven joked. 'A bottle of finest Prosecco will be yours.'

Capital was one of the new universities that had appeared in the UK in the past ten years having previously been a south London polytechnic. Attracting a high-profile scientist like Dorothy Lindstrom had been a major coup for them and her presence over the past year had put Capital on the academic map, ramping up its reputation in accordance with an unwritten rule that said that one outstanding scientist on the staff made you good, two made you a centre of excellence. The gamble of underwriting everything that Dorothy's start-up grant from the pharmaceutical company did not cover until government funding appeared had nearly misfired badly when her request had been turned down, but then the situation had been rescued by the anonymous injection of cash. Now it seemed that the roller coaster was about to plunge again following Barrowman's disappearance from the scene. So much was going to depend on being able to convince the anonymous backers that the research had not been entirely lost – or at the very least could be continued by the Lindstrom group.

Steven drove up to the collection of flat-roofed, white-painted buildings that comprised Capital University and found the image of a two-star hotel on the Spanish Costas coming to mind. The solar imagery made him think that if the worst came to the worst, their time in the sun was about to end as suddenly as it had begun. Attracting press attention would once more be dependent on handing out honorary degrees to pop stars and people who ran around in circles. '*Sic transit Gloria mundae*,' he murmured as he mounted the steps of the administration building, passing under another Latin inscription that he translated from vague schoolboy memory as having something to do with striving for the best.

'The principal is expecting you,' said the woman behind the desk when Steven presented his credentials. 'This way please.'

Steven was shown into a spacious room, requiring a long walk from the door across a deep pile carpet sporting the university's crest to where three people sat watching his progress – one behind a large antique desk whom he took to be the principal, Dorothy Lindstrom and another man on chairs in front. The man behind the desk rose and held out his hand. 'Charles Byford,' he said with a perfunctory smile and a look that suggested he had detected a vaguely unpleasant smell in the air. 'I'm principal here. I believe you've met Professor Lindstrom?'

'On the occasion when we were both declined government funding on the same day,' said Steven with a smile that was not returned.

'And this is Dr Neil Tyler, the scientific consultant who has been liaising with us and Professor Lindstrom's group on behalf of her financiers.'

Steven nodded to the second man who nodded back.

'Your Miss Roberts was kind enough to explain to me who and what Sci-Med did,' said Byford, 'but I'm afraid neither I nor Professor Lindstrom are clear what it is that you're investigating.'

It occurred to Steven that, if pomposity were an Olympic sport, Byford would be fed up hearing the national anthem. 'Let's see,' he said. 'One of Professor Lindstrom's post docs is carrying out research into criminal psychotic behaviour at a secret government establishment which no one is supposed to know about. His personality changes and he becomes secretive about what he's discovered to the point of paranoia. He descends into further psychosis and attacks his wife, coming close to murdering her and her unborn child. He is arrested by the police but is kidnapped by person or persons unknown when on the way to undergo psychiatric assessment. Call me picky, but I think there are quite a few things here needing investigation.'

Byford moved uncomfortably in his chair. 'I think Professor Lindstrom and I have been assuming that the police had everything in hand.'

'In matters scientific and medical where specific expertise is required the Sci-Med Inspectorate take precedent and will spearhead inquiries, to be assisted by the police where necessary.'

Byford acquiesced with a slight nod while Dorothy Lindstrom looked down at the floor.

Steven looked to Tyler and said, 'I'm afraid you have the better of me. We haven't met. You report to the people funding Dr Barrowman's research I understand?'

Dorothy Lindstrom interrupted angrily, saying, 'It's my research, Barrowman is one of my post-docs. The funding has been awarded to me.'

'Ah yes, sorry,' said Steven. 'Forgive me.' He smiled inwardly at being reminded how important it was that academic ego should be approached on tip-toe. He turned again to Tyler. 'Who are they?'

'Everyone seemed shocked.

Steven maintained eye contact with Tyler, hoping his directness was about to pay off, but Tyler didn't flinch. He gave the impression of searching through empty memory banks before saying, 'I really don't know.'

'You don't know,' Steven repeated.

'I've been retained by a firm of solicitors – Scarman, Medici and Weiss, if it helps. I report to them and they report to the donors who would prefer to remain anonymous.'

'I take it you have particular expertise in the area Owen Barrowman was working in?' Steven asked.

'I'm a forensic psychologist,' said Tyler.

'Ah,' said Byford, making a clumsy attempt to involve himself. 'Modern thumbscrews and the rack.'

Tyler acknowledged the comment with a slight smile and responded. 'I'm interested in the workings of the mind, Dr Byford, but I spend very little time torturing people. In fact, my particular interest lies in what makes people strap explosives to their bodies and blow themselves to kingdom come taking large numbers of our citizenry with them. I'm also interested in what makes young men leave the country of their birth to go to one completely foreign to them and of which they know nothing in order to be trained to slaughter the folks back home. I'd like to find a way of stopping them. From what I was told of Dr Barrowman's work when approached by Scarman et al, I didn't think our interests were a hundred miles apart. I'm sure we'd both like to put an end to psychotic behaviour, the difference being his subjects of study were securely locked up, mine aren't.'

Steven took a liking to Tyler and was willing to believe that he really didn't know who was behind Lindstrom's funding. He said, 'I think it's in all our interests to work together on what has happened. Police interest lies in finding Barrowman and his kidnappers so that they can be charged with criminal offences. Sci-Med's interest lies in finding out why it all happened. We'd like to know who's financing the research and why.'

Tyler nodded his understanding.

Steven continued. 'As I see it, Dr Tyler would like to be able to give his employers a detailed report on Barrowman's work so that they might make an informed decision about continued funding for the Lindstrom group. Professor Lindstrom and, of course, the university are hoping for a favourable decision and will be keen to find positives arising from Barrowman's work.' Steven turned to Dorothy. 'Perhaps you've already started examining Owen Barrowman's files, Professor?'

'I have.'

'I think we were all afraid that Owen in his paranoid state might have wiped the lot?

'That's not the case,' said Dorothy. 'There's actually a great deal of data on his computer and all of it is derived from his work in high security prisons up and down the country. We also found copious notes and some interesting conclusions.'

'That *is* good news,' said Tyler.

'Some of the DNA sequencing is incomplete as is some of the biochemical analysis, but it seems that Owen was well on the way to describing significant differences between criminal psychopaths and the rest of us and even some of the biochemical consequences of these differences.'

'Forgive my ignorance,' said Byford, 'I'm not a biologist, but that sounds as if he has discovered genes connected with the condition and what consequences they actually lead to?'

'Yes,' said Dorothy, letting the affirmative hang in the air. 'And if we know what a gene does in terms of what it produces . . . it's possible we can do something about it.'

'That sounds exciting.'

'At first glance, I don't think it's going to be too difficult to fill in the blanks in the data.'

'Wonderful,' said Byford. 'So, can I take it that, with a bit of work from your group, this will all be publishable?'

'I think you can,' said Dorothy with a glance towards Tyler.

'I look forward to seeing it,' he responded.

Steven was not so easily impressed and wondered if Dorothy was launching a PR offensive for Tyler's benefit, seeing what she'd found through rose-tinted spectacles when it was a view that might not be shared by a cold, dispassionate reviewer assessing a paper's suitability for inclusion in a good quality journal. Medical science had identified lots of genes connected with specific conditions but had been unable to do anything about it. Barrowman had really been looking for the switches that turned these genes on and off, not what they produced although, he conceded, identification was of primary importance.

'Did you find any data based on the Moorlock Hall prisoner?' he asked.

'Not specifically,' Dorothy replied, 'but it's early days. I've just been trying to get a broad overall picture.

'Of course,' replied Steven. *I'll take that as a no.* He felt depressed at what he thought he could see what was happening. Barrowman had left all the data surrounding his research on psychopathic prisoners on his work computer and probably the one he used at home too. This was exactly what you'd expect to find on the computer of a conscientious post-doctoral fellow who was hiding nothing from his boss or her colleagues. It sounded as if his findings were interesting and publishable so his group leader would and should be pleased – as would the university whose address would be on the published paper. Everything in the garden was lovely, wasn't it? What did it matter if studies on one prisoner were missing from the list. No one could be upset about that, could they? 'Oh yes, they could,' Steven murmured inside his head, 'Me.'

Despite Steven's suspicion that the one prisoner missing from the list, Malcolm Lawler, must be the sole source of Barrowman's exciting discovery and that they were not going to find anything about that in his notes or on his computers, he decided not to share his thoughts. He told the others that the Sci-Med labs would be examining the material taken from Barrowman's flat by the police and suggested they meet up again when everything had been scrutinised thoroughly.

Steven left with Neil Tyler who said, 'For what it's worth I understand why you want to know who's funding Barrowman's work, but I honestly don't know.'

'I believe you,' said Steven.

'Good. You people have probably been checking me out?'

'Probably,' agreed Steven with a smile.

'And getting nowhere?'

Steven gave a non-committal shrug but his smile was still there.

'In there, I told you what my interests were. What I didn't say was that my wife was a victim of terrorist bombing some five years ago.'

'My god, I'm sorry.'

'When I . . . got over it I gave up my academic position and became an independent investigator working to my own agenda. I tend to move around a lot and keep a low profile. I've managed to amass a great deal of data on the problem.'

Steven digested this and said, 'But someone knew how to find you and reckoned you were the right man to monitor what Barrowman was up to?'

'Yes.'

'Sounds like they made a good decision,' said Steven. 'Mind you, what interests me is how they knew all about you when my people came up with a blank.'

'I agree . . . that is interesting. By the way, the Moorlock Hall prisoner you asked about in there, was he Malcolm Lawler?'

'Yes.'

'Interesting, I read about the place in the papers this morning.'

The two men exchanged contact details, something that gave Steven a stab of conscience when he was reminded of the awful aftermath of giving someone his card. 'I'll call you if we find anything new in the stuff taken from Barrowman's flat.'

'Thanks,' said Tyler. 'Dorothy seems to have had very bad luck with her post-docs . . . Barrowman is the third who has come to a sticky end.'

They came to the parting of the ways but Steven felt he had been given food for thought. Had that been intentional?

FOURTEEN

Steven called Lukas Neubauer at the Lundborg labs and exchanged pleasantries before coming to the point. 'What are the chances of you dropping everything and going through the entire contents of a computer?'

'About the same as Arsenal winning the Premier League.'

'That good,' exclaimed Steven, knowing how big an Arsenal fan Lukas was.

'I wish. What are you looking for?'

Steven told him.

'So, let me see, you have DNA sequences from these people and you're looking for some clear differences from the norm that they all have in common?' asked Lukas.

'And anything else interesting you happen to notice along the way.'

'It might help if you tell me what's going on here.'

'How about I bring the computer round and then I'll take you for a pint and we can talk?'

'Do you think I'm that easy?''

'All right, two pints.'

It had been some time since the two men had last seen each other, but their history of having worked closely and successfully together and even faced danger in the past ensured that they quickly slipped into being comfortable in each other's company. Exchanges of family news – Lukas had twin boys – gave way to Steven giving Lukas a detailed rundown on what Owen Barrowman had been working on.

'Ah, epigenetics,' said Lukas without following up.

Steven gave him a full minute to stare at the surface of the table before asking, 'Is that a problem?'

Lukas came out of his trance and said, 'When Crick and Watson described the structure of DNA and how it replicated it was such a wonderful moment in science. The world smiled. Nothing but good could come from it.

'Absolutely,' said Steven.

'I have a very different feel about epigenetics,' said Lukas. 'I know it's early days but it holds so many secrets.'

'Is that bad?'

'There may be some we'll have difficulty coping with . . .'

Steven frowned and said, 'I never thought I'd hear that from a scientist.'

Lukas shrugged and said, When I was a young student in Prague one of my lecturers was very fond of quoting from an English poet. *He who pries into every cloud may be hit by a thunderbolt.*

'Hardly a comfort for researchers,' said Steven.

'I understand that protection can be achieved through the intake of Pilsner beer,' said Lukas eyeing his empty glass.'

'Coming up.'

Despite it being after seven Steven decided that he would go in to the Home Office to leave Jean Roberts a note. He was surprised to find her still there.

'No home to go to?'

'Choir practice night,' she replied. 'It's easier to go directly from here. I could ask the same of you.'

'I thought I'd come by and leave you a note. Tally's away at the moment.' Steven told Jean of her mother's accident.

'Nasty, I hope she pulls through. What can I do for you?''

Steven asked her if she could dig out information about the fire in Dorothy Lindstrom's lab at Yale University which had claimed the lives of two of her post docs.

'Will do.'

'I don't suppose John's still here?'

'You've just missed him. He's had a hugely frustrating day trying to get information out of the intelligence services about why they blocked funding for Professor Lindstrom.'

Steven nodded. It was no surprise. Sci-Med and MI5 had an uneasy relationship. Five thought Sci-Med lacked discipline, Sci-Med thought Five lacked imagination, but when push came to shove they tended to cover each other's backs.

'Any word from the police about Barrowman?'

'Not a peep.

'Really?' said Steven. 'That part of London must have more cameras than a Paparazzi party.'

'They picked up the private ambulance used in the kidnapping on CCTV, but it disappeared from view and was later found abandoned down a lane. They reckon a switch to another vehicle was made within a few minutes of the snatch and in a place where the kidnappers knew they'd be out of sight of cameras.'

'So, the bottom line is the police have no idea where he is?'

'Correct.'

Steven mulled over what he'd learned from the day as he walked home. Lukas had agreed to take a look at what was on Barrowman's computer, but the reservations he'd expressed about epigenetics had been a revelation. He'd asked him what he'd meant by there being too many secrets to cope with, but to no avail. Did he really think there were *some things better not to know*? Steven shook his head, subconsciously dismissing the notion. He'd always seen Lukas as the perfect model of a scientist, intelligent, endlessly curious and totally without bias. Facts were facts and were there to be discovered, but if someone like him thought that there might be a downside to discovery . . . maybe he should bear that in mind?

Steven turned his attention to John's problem with MI5. Five not answering questions was par for the course – secrets were their business and it was a way of life – but when the man asking the questions was Sir John Macmillan, a man with the highest security clearance and the ear of the Home Secretary, what did they think they were playing at? Surely, they must know that the next step would be John asking the Home Secretary personally. He felt sure that was exactly what would happen in the morning. In the meantime, he invoked the maxim about clouds having silver linings and decided that Five's continued awkwardness surrounding Dorothy Lindstrom's research made it easier for him to target them as prime suspect for having snatched Barrowman and not those who were funding the research. It would also explain the insider knowledge and expertise shown in the operation. All he had to do now was figure out what Five were up to.

Easy peasy, he thought as he remembered his daughter Jenny's favourite saying when she was younger; everything was easy peasy until proven otherwise. It had been a couple of months since he last made the trip up to Scotland to see her. It used to be every other weekend until her involvement in out of school activities had multiplied to such an extent that she seemed to have less free time than he did.

He had always known that this was bound to happen. Jenny had lived almost her entire life as a much-loved member of another family and the next stage would be a growing independence. The main thing was that she was happy and by all accounts she was. He could hardly get a word in when he phoned, she was so full of news and enthusiasm about everything she was doing. He'd given up counting the clubs and societies she belonged to, but thinking about her made him decide to phone her when he got in.

Susan, his sister-in-law, answered and gave him a run down on what was happening in Glenvane and how Jenny was doing at school. 'And now the bad news, Steven . . . she's not in at the moment.'

'Not in?' Steven exclaimed.

'She's over at Jason's.'

'Jason?'

'Her boyfriend.'

'Her what?'

'Steven, she's a teenager. It happens, he's a very nice boy.'

'She's a ch . . .'

'No, she isn't, she's a young woman and a very sensible one if it helps.'

Steven struggled to get over the shock but finally said reluctantly, 'Suppose you're right, you usually are.'

'Thank you, I am in this case.'

Steven looked at his watch then asked anxiously, 'How will she get home?'

'Jason's dad is driving her over.'

'Good . . . shall I try tomorrow?'

'She has karate, but she'll be in by eight.'

'Right,' said Steven distantly. He put down the phone, suddenly feeling very old.

Tally called while he was pouring a whisky. 'How's your mum? He asked.'

'Sober, have you been drinking?'

'How on earth? . . .'

When Tally stopped laughing she said, 'A lucky guess. Susan called me. She was worried that you were upset about Jenny having a boyfriend.'

'Why do I get the feeling the monstrous regiment is ganging up on me?'

'I know she'll always be your little girl, Steven, but she's growing up. She's a teenager and she has started to notice boys. She's also a very well brought up young lady and you have nothing to worry about.'

'If you say so,' Steven conceded.

'I do say so. Mum's fine, I'm planning on coming home tomorrow. Now tell me about your day.'

'Bad doesn't begin to cover it. Barrowman's still missing, John's on a collision course with MI5 and someone planted an idea in my head that just won't go away.'

'Tell me about it.'

Steven told her what Tyler had casually pointed out about Dorothy Lindstrom's post docs.

'Do you think he did it deliberately?'

'Yes.'

'Then that must mean that he thinks there was something dodgy about the American deaths?'

'It was something he mentioned as we parted company so I didn't have the chance to quiz him, but I've asked Jean to dig up what she can.'

'You could also ask her current American post-doc, she must have been there at the time of the fire?'

'You're right. Maybe I'll do that while John is bending the ear of the Home Secretary about Five's refusal to talk.'

'Suppose she refuses too?'

'He won't take that lying down. You know what he's like about Sci-Med's right to investigate without government obstruction.'

'Could be a big day tomorrow,' said Tally.

'It will be, you're coming home.'

'Oh, Mr Smoothie strikes again,' laughed Tally. 'I'm all of a quiver.'

'Love you.'

'Love you too.'

In the morning Steven decided to wait until Jean had come up with a file on the American deaths before talking to Jane Lincoln. He would use that as a primer to highlight any questions he thought needed asking. In the meantime, he would visit Lucy Barrowman who he found alert and looking much better than last time. 'You're a quick healer.'

'Just as well,' said Lucy wryly.

Steven saw once again the strength of Lucy Barrowman's character. She'd had time to think about things and, unlike many women, she wasn't going to search for excuses for her husband's awful behaviour. He sensed that Barrowman had already been consigned to yesterday.

'Have the police found him yet?' she asked.

Steven shook his head. 'He's completely disappeared.'

'Maybe they aren't looking hard enough,' Lucy said with barely disguised bitterness.

'What makes you say that?'

'The whole mess,' said Lucy. 'Secret prisons for the criminally insane that no one – not even the government of the day – is supposed to know about, MPs using leaked information to create a big scandal for their own ends. Liberal lefties full of concern for the criminals rather than their victims. My husband attacking me after getting involved with these people. I'm sure there are those in power who just see it all as a huge embarrassment and who would like the whole damned thing to disappear.'

'I'm sure you're right,' Steven agreed, 'and maybe it will. I hear that Mrs Leadbetter's concern for the denizens of Moorlock Hall is not being shared too deeply by the general public. That being the case, the papers will drop it and move on.'

'Good.'

Steven changed the subject. 'The Lindstrom lab has had a chance to examine Owen's notes and computer files . . .'

'And?'

'The results of his studies on psychopathic killers in Carstairs, Rampton, Broadmoor and all the other places he visited are there with one major exception.'

'Moorlock Hall?'

'Correct. He's obviously hidden anything to do with Lawler.'

'The special one,' said Lucy

'The one he thought was special from the outset,' agreed Steven. 'Dorothy is pleased with what he came up with from his work on the others and thinks it will all be publishable so she's not too concerned that one patient is missing.'

'I take it Owen didn't talk to her about Lawler?'

'Looks that way.'

'Why wouldn't he do that?' asked Lucy looking genuinely puzzled.

'I think he's discovered why Lawler is special – a major discovery that he wants to keep to himself and get all the credit for when it's published.'

'All this is about ego?' Lucy exclaimed.

'It's about people.'

'Yeah, they're great . . .'

'And now for the big question . . . have you any idea where he might have hidden his material on Lawler?'

''If I did I'd gladly tell you, but he didn't confide in me at all. I suppose he must have loaded it on to some computer cloud.'

'Possible,' Steven agreed, 'but I tend to think that he wouldn't put all his eggs in the one basket to quote you quoting him. I think he'd keep something more tangible than a cloud account somewhere.'

'Like a disk in a bank vault?'

'Something like that.'

'I'm not sure if he'd know how to go about that, I wouldn't. It's something you see in the movies.'

Steven smiled. 'Used by rich people to hide money and valuables from the tax man.'

'We never had that problem,' said Lucy with the faintest tinge of wistfulness in her voice.

'Well, if you think of anything let me know,' said Steven getting up to go.

Lucy's expression froze, causing Steven to ask, 'Are you okay?'

'I er . . . don't have your number . . . I mean I don't have your card any more . . .'

'Steven closed his eyes for a moment as the awfulness came back. 'God, I'm sorry,' he said, leaving one on the bedside table.

'Like I said,' said Lucy, 'it wasn't your fault.'

FIFTEEN

Steven accepted the slim file holder that Jean Roberts handed to him on arrival. 'Such a sad business,' she said.

Steven agreed and they spoke for a few moments about the tragedy before Steven asked about the whereabouts of John Macmillan.

'He's with the Home Secretary as we speak.'

Steven nodded and said, 'I'm not sure which one to feel sorry for.' He took the file off to the library and settled down to read.

Under the heading of Yale Fire Tragedy, he read that Dr Paul Leighton and Dr Carrie Simpson, both aged twenty-six, had died in a late-night blaze in the laboratory where they worked as members of Professor Dorothy Lindstrom's research group at Yale University. A photograph of a missing window surrounded by blackened stonework pinpointed the location of a second-floor lab. The cause of the fire was under investigation. Two other newspaper articles reported much the same thing. A smaller article from an inside page and dated two weeks later recorded that the fire department had found a leak in a gas supply pipe to have been the cause of the fire.

Steven continued reading through cuttings taken from provincial papers published in the respective areas where the two had grown up. Both had been the pride of their families, having excelled at high school and college and having gone on to do PhDs and gain prestigious post-doctoral positions at Yale University where a glittering career had been predicted for both. Steven put the cuttings gently to one side, sad stories but nothing to add substance to why Tyler had made the comment he had . . . or maybe it was he who had read too much into it and it had been meant to be taken at face value.

Steven examined the last two cuttings, both written around the time of Dorothy's announcement that she was leaving Yale to move back to the UK. One had gone for the human-interest angle, concentrating on how upset Dorothy had been by the tragedy, fully understanding her desire to move away and start afresh, but the other had chosen to dwell on how upsetting this decision had been for other members of the group who felt let down. One aggrieved student however, had pointed out that something like this had been coming for some time as all had not been well in the lab before the fire: there had, he claimed, been some serious friction between Dorothy and her senior researchers.

'Well, well,' murmured Steven. 'There you are . . .'

Steven drove over to Capital University, ostensibly to ask Dorothy how the trawl through Barrowman's files was going but mainly to engineer the chance to speak to Jane Lincoln. He had expected Dorothy to ask about Barrowman and be anxious to know how the hunt for him was going. Instead, he found her elated that she had uncovered enough data and results in Barrowman's files for at least three papers in decent journals, something she felt her backers would be pleased with.

'Well done,' said Steven. 'that must take some of the pressure off.' *It must be good to know you don't actually need Owen Barrowman in person to secure funding.*'

For one awful moment Steven thought Dorothy had read his mind. She seemed to stare at him before asking, 'Have the police found Owen yet?'

'I'm afraid not.'

'Let's hope he gets the help he needs when they do.'

'Indeed.' Steven put an end to the awkward pause and went on to tell Dorothy that the Sci-Med lab was currently examining the computer Barrowman used at home. 'I'll let you know as soon as they've finished. In the meantime, I was wondering if I might have a word with Jane Lincoln?'

'Of course,' said Dorothy, 'although I don't think she and Owen were great friends.'

Steven was happy with the misunderstanding surrounding his reasons. 'No matter, I don't think I've had a chance to speak to her before. It would be good for me to know all the members of your group.'

Dorothy nodded and went off to fetch Jane. 'You two can use the seminar room,' she said when the pair returned.

'I'm not sure I can help you,' said Jane as they sat down, 'I didn't know that much about Owen's work.'

'Actually, it wasn't that I wanted to talk to you about.'

The smile – which Steven had found open and honest – faded from Jane's face leaving slight bemusement. 'Really?'

'I understand you were with Dorothy's group in the USA at the time of the fire at Yale?'

'Yes, it was my first post doc position, I'd only been there a few months.'

'It must have been a terrible time.'

'It was, but I think Dorothy is the one you should be speaking to . . .'

'I understand she took it very badly at the time and I didn't want open up old wounds. I thought I'd ask someone who was fairly new to the lab and wasn't so personally involved . . .'

Jane swallowed as if going into defensive mode, but Steven suspected this was for ethical concerns rather than anything to do with guilt. 'What is it you want to know?'

'The two senior post-docs who died in the fire, they were working in the lab at night?'

'Yes.'

'Do you know what they were doing?'

'It's not at all unusual for researchers to be in the lab at night,' said Jane. 'We all do it.'

'Can you be more specific about what they were doing?'

'I understand they were repeating some experiments to confirm earlier findings.'

'Earlier findings . . .' said Steven, hoping that the pause might encourage Jane to say more. When it didn't, he changed tack. 'I've been going through the newspaper reports from the time and a few articles written around the time of Dorothy's decision to leave the USA,' he said. 'I came across a suggestion of some bad feeling between Dorothy and her senior post-docs before the fire. Do you know anything about that?'

'These things happen.'

'Do you actually know what the problem was?'

Jane was clearly uncomfortable with the line of questioning and Steven could see that she was struggling with fears of being thought disloyal, but she was on the hook and that was where she would stay until she came out with all she knew.

'Paul and Carrie were excited about their latest work and were keen to publish their findings - they were confident that they'd come up with a major breakthrough, but Dorothy said no.'

'Why not?'

'She didn't believe them.'

'But surely, they must have shown data, facts, figures?'

'They did but Dorothy wouldn't have it. She insisted mistakes must have been made and wouldn't allow them to proceed. She gave them a lecture about how scientists had a social responsibility as well as a scientific one to make sure their conclusions were beyond all doubt. She was adamant she didn't want to be subject to the criticism that scientists often announce findings without any thought being given to the consequences.'

'Handing matches to the baby,' said Steven.

'Exactly.

'So that's why the two post docs were repeating their work in the lab that night?'

'Not quite . . .' said Jane. Dorothy had insisted that their work was flawed and shouldn't be repeated. She asked Paul and Carrie to work on something else.'

'Wow.'

'Paul and Carrie felt sure that their work was watertight but accepted they had to do what they were told. You don't want to make an enemy of someone as important as Dorothy. They started out on a new project but decided to repeat their original work at night, maybe hoping to convince Dorothy to change her mind.'

'Instead they died.'

'Two nice people, two brilliant scientists at the very beginning of their career, an absolute tragedy.'

'Do you actually know anything about the findings that caused all the trouble?' Steven asked.

Jane adopted a reluctant expression but continued. 'Some of us working in neuroscience had known for a while that there was danger lurking on the horizon, especially those of us with a foot in both pharmacology and neuroscience. On the one hand, we studied human behaviour and on the other control of it. Using appropriate drugs, we could make a violent man passive, a calm man aggressive, a sad man happy, a happy man sad. The more we learned the more we could change things through the use of drugs. But of course, science doesn't stop there. We had to know more about what the drugs do . . . what pathways they follow . . . we always have to know more . . .'

'And that's where the danger lies?'

'We may not like what we find.'

'Did Paul and Carrie find out something that fell into that category?' asked Steven.

Jane took a deep breath and said, 'In spades. They came up with a series of results that challenged everything the human race has always believed about itself – that we are all individuals with self-determination and decision-making powers, perhaps made in the image of God and harbouring a soul if you're religious. Their results showed that we as human beings were only individual in the sense that our biochemical make-up varied from one person to another. We were little more than a collection of cells and chemical reactions, something which could be altered at will with the application of the correct knowledge – something which we were fast accumulating. It wouldn't be long before we could alter every aspect of a human being.'

'Maybe even create one?'

'Given time.'

'I can understand why that could upset a whole lot of people . . .' said Steven.

'Dorothy is a committed Christian,' said Jane filling in the blank. 'Paul and Carrie's results contradicted just about everything she's ever believed in.'

'I can understand her reluctance to believe them.'

'I think the questioning of her religious beliefs might have been as big a factor in her mental collapse as the deaths of Paul and Carrie.'

'How about now, is she still a committed Christian? Steven asked.

'I think so . . .'

Steven was interested in Jane's pause. His expression suggested he was waiting.

'A Roman Catholic priest appeared in our temporary lab one day at Yale. He was in Dorothy's office when I came back early from lunch and she was shouting at him.'

'Did you hear what the argument was about?'

Jane shook her head. 'Not really. I just remember Dorothy shouting, "No way." then she saw me through the glass and didn't say any more. The pair of them emerged some ten minutes later looking a bit guilty and Dorothy introduced me to the priest whom she said had been a great comfort to her, Father Liam Crossan.'

'Strange,' said Steven. 'Did Dorothy talk much about her religious beliefs?'

'Almost never,' Jane replied. 'I suppose she knows what most scientists feel about religion. She keeps it as a very personal thing.'

'And then she made her big decision about the future of her research?' said Steven.

'Her big announcement,' agreed Jane, 'A change of field and a move to a new country. Although she never said as much at the time, I suspected she had decided to check out Paul and Carrie's findings by moving the work on to the next level.'

'DNA and epigenetics?'

Jane nodded. 'There was only so far you could go with the techniques involving drugs and volunteers that Paul and Carrie had been using. The genes on your DNA have the capacity to specify all the different chemical substances in your body. If we can link gene products to drug action and find controllers for these genes . . .'

'That's where epigenetics comes into the picture,' said Steven. 'Well, that explains nicely why Dorothy made the move. How about you, why did you come with her?

'I went to Dorothy and told her what I thought she was up to and she didn't deny it. She said that, despite misgivings, she had to know the truth. She invited me to join her in the move to the UK. I agreed . . . providing that no results would be covered up whatever they said.'

Steven smiled and said, 'And I thought science was pretty straightforward.'

'I wish.'

'Where did Owen Barrowman fit in?'

'He applied to Dorothy for a job and was well qualified: she felt we needed his experience. He could bring us all up to speed in the new techniques we'd need Most of us were new to epigenetics and the plan was to investigate as many possible facets of gene triggering as possible, which would be interesting in itself, but would also let us see a way into what Dorothy and I really wanted to work on.'

'Paul and Carrie's findings?'

Jane nodded.

'How did it work out?'

'Everything was fine in the beginning. Owen was a nice guy and taught us a lot. In exchange, Dorothy agreed to him pursuing his own line of research with psychotic criminals, which he was pretty far along the road with. Everyone was happy.'

'But then Owen changed?'

'He became very secretive and seemed to imagine people were conspiring against him. I'm assuming it was some kind of mental breakdown, poor guy.'

Steven nodded.

SIXTEEN

'Dare I ask?'

The length of time taken by John Macmillan to respond suggested to Steven that he wasn't going to like what he was about to hear.

'The Home Secretary and I spoke for half an hour. She did not tell me why Five had blocked funding for Professor Lindstrom and said that she was unable to tell me where Barrowman was being held. She asked that I trust her.'

'And you said?'

'I sort of agreed.'

Steven was openly shocked. 'A politician said, "trust me" and you said yes? That's not the John Macmillan I know.'

'She is the Home Secretary.'

'We also have a shadow home secretary,' said Steven.

The implicit suggestion that the threat of informing Her Majesty's Opposition of a government refusal to cooperate might elicit a change of heart was not lost on Macmillan, but he said, 'It wasn't a complete blank. She didn't deny that Lindstrom's research grant funding was blocked by MI5.'

'Which we already knew.'

'True, but we didn't know that Five carried out the hijack on Barrowman on the way to the hospital. She confirmed that.'

'I'd already reduced the possibilities to a short list of one,' said Steven, bristling at the thought of Sci-Med having given in to a politician. He respected Macmillan more than any man on earth and here he was backing off at government request.

Macmillan conceded the point with a slight raise of his hand. 'Be that as it may,' he said, 'but one thing we didn't know . . . is that Five have lost him.'

Steven was lost for words.

'The hijack was carried out by intelligence officers, but something went badly wrong. The officer charged with delivering Barrowman on the final leg of the hijack was found with his neck broken in a ditch by the side of the road; the vehicle was later discovered as a burnt-out shell.

Steven shook his head in disbelief. 'So, Barrowman could be anywhere. Do we have any details of his last known whereabouts?'

'She didn't have any to hand.'

Steven's look expressed doubt, prompting Macmillan to add, 'She wasn't expecting to be quizzed by me. She wouldn't normally request such details in a situation like this.'

'Fair point

'She did tell me however that the agent had been armed. His weapon wasn't found on his body. His ID and wallet were also missing.'

'It just gets better.'

Both men sat in silence, mulling over the awfulness of the situation until Steven said, 'If the Home Secretary asked you to trust her, she must have given you some reason for doing that . . . otherwise you would have suggested she take a hike – if not in so many words?'

'She made a plea for my – our patience, for the time being. The Intelligence services have been involved in a study for some time, which they believe will have a profound effect on the lives of people, not just in our country but across the entire world.'

'A profound effect?'

'The possibility of a complete breakdown in society, an end to law and order, complete and utter chaos across the globe.'

Steven thought for a moment before saying with some resignation, 'If I hadn't heard what I did from Dorothy Lindstrom's post-doc Jane Lincoln earlier today, I think I would have taken all that with a pinch of salt, but now I can't. Things are coming together.'

Macmillan managed to look pleased and surprised at the same time. 'You can make sense of this?' he exclaimed 'To coin a phrase, make my day.'

Steven told Macmillan what he'd learned from Jane Lincoln about the work of her former colleagues who had died in the fire and their conclusions which had been questioned – perhaps desperately – by Dorothy herself, who, after what must have been a period of deep anxiety, was now resolved to uncover the truth.

'I think they've all been working on aspects of the same thing,' he said – 'the Lindstrom group, our intelligence services, Owen Barrowman . . . they've all been working on the genetic basis of human behaviour – the Lindstrom group are interested in all aspects while Barrowman had focused on psychotic behaviour as I suspect MI5 has.'

'But something has gone awfully wrong for all of them,' said Macmillan.

'Dorothy's people came up with a very unpalatable truth . . . if their results stand up to scrutiny.'

'And Barrowman came up with something which has cost him his sanity. but somehow ties in to what our intelligence services have been up to,' said Macmillan. 'Two dead researchers and one off his head. *Don't put your daughter in a lab, Mrs Worthington.*'

Macmillan's parody of an old music hall song jogged Steven's memory of what Tyler had said about the misfortune of Dorothy's people. It was a thought that just refused to go away.

'Where does that leave us?' said Macmillan.

'With big problems,' said Steven. 'Barrowman is an unstable murderer and he's out there with a gun.'

'And we don't know what his intentions are.'

'At least we won't be the ones looking for him,' said Steven. 'The police and Five will be pulling out all the stops. With one agent already dead I don't give much for his chances of making it to a courtroom.'

'Normally, I might agree,' said Macmillan, 'but they want him alive. They've gone to quite a lot of trouble to get him for their own purposes.'

'True,' Steven agreed, 'whatever they might be.'

Macmillan offered his theory. 'How about, the intelligence community, or more likely their colleagues at Porton Down, have been working on much the same thing as Barrowman and that's why they blocked funding for Lindstrom's research. They didn't want competition?'

'That works for me,' Steven agreed. 'I think Dorothy Lindstrom was only seen as a problem when she took Barrowman on board. Up until then none of her work had been connected with criminal behaviour let alone convicted psychopaths.'

'I think we're getting there,' said Macmillan.

'But we still have to find out who did fund her and why.'

'I don't think the police will be too interested in that, but Five will,' said Macmillan.

Steven thought for a moment before saying, 'You know, I think we know much more than the Home Secretary gave us credit for, which accounts for her reluctance to confide in you. Five probably told her much the same thing as Jane Lincoln told me and she appreciated the enormity of their discovery. If you were to go back to her and bring her up to speed on what we know, perhaps we could all work together?'

'That's a thought,' agreed Macmillan, 'but if what you say is true and Five have come up with the same findings as Dorothy's late colleagues . . .'

'It means they were right,' said Steven. 'It would be confirmation.'

'And if Five or the Home Secretary had any doubts . . .'

'They would be dispelled the moment you tell her and she would be faced with wondering what to do about it.'

'Better her than me,' murmured Steven.

'I take it the police will have put the guard back on Lucy Barrowman.'

'Yes,' said Macmillan, 'although it's hard to see why he'd want to cause her further harm.'

'It's hard to see why he'd want to do anything he's done,' said Steven. 'God knows what's going on in his head.'

Macmillan looked over his glasses to question Steven's choice of phrase and Steven saw the irony. 'Point taken,' he said. 'God's not been playing much of a roll in these proceedings.'

'Unlike the roll his priesthood will be taking when rumours of this gets out,' said Macmillan. 'To continue with inappropriate comments . . . all hell will be let loose.'

'Maybe you shouldn't tell the Home Secretary after all,' Steven suggested.

'Why not?'

'At the moment both parties have doubts about their findings. We should leave these doubts in place. It gives them an excuse for saying and doing nothing until confirmation appears.'

'Good thought . . . devious but good. Plans for tomorrow?'

'I'll go talk to Lukas, see what he's come up with from Barrowman's computer, but I'm not expecting much. I'm also going to ask Jean if she can come up with anything else on the Yale fire.'

Macmillan seemed surprised. 'I thought you'd checked that out.'

'I have, but it's like an itch, I've scratched it but it keeps coming back.'

'Your instincts have always paid off in the past.'

'What exactly am I looking for?' asked Jean.

'Can you see if you can get your hands on the fire investigators' report and maybe the police one if it was separate.'

'I'll do my best, anything else?'

After a slight hesitation Steven said, 'Yes . . . see what you can come up with on a Roman Catholic priest named Father Liam Crossan. He came to see Dorothy Lindstrom in her lab at Yale after the fire, no further information I'm afraid, but he could have been Dorothy Lindstrom's parish priest, if they have such a thing in the states, or maybe he's attached to Yale in some pastoral capacity.'

'You think he's a baddie?'

'Dorothy told one of her colleagues he was a great comfort to her, but this was just after the same colleague had heard them having a shouting match.'

'Could have been telling a porky pie,' said Jean with a smile.

'Could have been,' agreed Steven with an even bigger one.

Tally was in the flat when Steven got home. She had just got in and smiles and hugs took priority over anything else. 'So good to have you back,' said Steven.

'So good to be back, you look tired.'

'So do you,' said Steven, 'you've been under a lot of strain. I take it your mum's okay?'

'She's had a real shock, but there were no complications and the break should mend given enough time and good behaviour.' Tally yawned and said, 'You know, I think an early night could be on the cards.'

'What a lovely thought,' said Steven, holding her close. Hungry?'

'What do you have in the fridge?'

'Cheese.'

'And?'

The silence was broken by, 'There's some bread in the cupboard . . . or we could go out?'

Tally put her finger on Steven's lips. 'Cheese on toast sounds just fine. I'm going to shower.'

'Tea or wine?'

'Silly question.'

As they lay in the darkness, Tally with her head resting on Steven's shoulder, Steven tracing patterns lightly on her skin with his fingertips, Tally murmured, 'That was nice,'

'Yep,' Steven replied, 'when it comes to cheese on toast . . . I'm your man.'

Tally slapped the palm of her hand on Steven's thigh. 'Why must you always play the fool?' she demanded through giggles.

'It's a gift.'

Another slap.

'I love you.'

'I love you too.'

Steven drove over to the Lundborg labs in the morning and accepted Lukas' offer of coffee. 'Espresso?'

Steven took a sip and murmured his appreciation before asking about progress.

'It's a good, solid piece of work,' Lukas replied. 'I expected a hard time after what you said about the guy, but his entire project was laid out in such a clear way that even a lay person could get the gist of it. He found significant differences between certain areas of the genomes of convicted killers in his study and what we would regard as normal among the general population.'

'Publishable work?'

'Absolutely.'

Steven nodded but remained silent until Lukas said, 'You don't seem happy. Something wrong?'

'Your findings match those of his group leader who's been examining what's on his work computer.'

'Oh, good . . .' said Lukas, softening the sarcasm with a smile.

She was delighted because publication of Barrowman's work should ensure continued funding for her group.'

'Group leaders have to think that way.'

'Okay, I'll level with you, There's something missing.'

'It seemed pretty complete to me.'

'It was meant to,' said Steven. 'When Barrowman wrote this up he was already totally paranoid; he thought everyone in the world was hell bent on stealing his work. Everyone, including me, feared he would go to enormous lengths to conceal his findings and were prepared to find nothing on his computers. Instead we find what you've just seen for yourself, the results of a successful project perfectly presented.'

'He's thrown a sop to what he sees as the chasing pack . . . so there must be a reason?'

'I'm certain there is. He deliberately left one patient off the list, Malcolm Lawler, the Moorlock Hall prisoner he thought was special. He told me that when we first met and said much the same to his wife who watched him fall further and further under Lawler's spell. She said he claimed to loathe the man but was still mesmerised by him. The more time he spent with Lawler the more distant he became to those around him until he lost all reason and became a killer himself. I take it you didn't find any mention of Lawler on Barrowman's computer or in his notes?'

'None at all.'

'Neither did Professor Lindstrom, but it didn't worry her greatly, for her it was just a matter of having one fewer subject in the study than there might have been. Not a problem, there were already enough in terms of numbers to make the study significant.'

'She didn't know anything about this Lawler being special?'

'Barrowman didn't confide in her.'

'So, what happens now?'

'Unless we can find out what he's done with the data he collected on Lawler we may never know what he discovered.'

'He didn't confide in his wife before he lost his mind?' asked Lukas.'

Steven shook his head. 'He saw her as one of the enemy.'

'If they take him alive, the intelligence services will interrogate him.'

'Like I say, we may never know what he discovered.'

SEVENTEEN

Steven made the promised call to Neil Tyler to bring him up to speed on what had been gleaned from Barrowman's home computer and lab notes.

'Pretty much the same thing as Dorothy found,' he reported. 'Our man found a nice piece of work with several interesting observations about differences in the genomes of psychopathic killers.'

Tyler made affirmative noises as if this was what he expected to hear, but then asked, 'When we met with Dorothy you asked her about a prisoner whose samples seemed to be missing from the report. Was the same man's data missing this time?'

'It was,' Steven confirmed, 'Malcolm Lawler, the prisoner from Moorlock Hall – there was no mention of him.'

'A deliberate exclusion. What do you make of that?'

'Should I make anything of it? Maybe the study on Lawler wasn't complete: he was the last one to be added.'

'I don't think you believe that any more than I do,' said Tyler. 'Barrowman was very reluctant to speak of anything to do with Moorlock Hall or who he was working with. I picked up on that straight away. Now Lawler is missing from the report.'

Steven decided to put his cards on the table, but first he asked a couple of questions. 'You said you'd never heard of Moorlock Hall before Barrowman mentioned it. Was that true?'

'Yes, but when I did hear about it, I became very interested indeed.'

'Is that a personal interest or are you asking on behalf of your anonymous clients?'

'Personal. I'm sure my clients will be well satisfied with the work found on Barrowman's computer when I put in my report. It's an excellent piece of work.'

'But you and I both suspect that what Barrowman found out about Lawler may be even more interesting?'

'When someone with Barrowman's ability hides something it automatically makes it interesting,' said Tyler.

'All we have to do is find out where he's hidden it. Any ideas?' Steven asked, tongue in cheek.

'The digital world is his oyster.'

'About sums it up.' Steven agreed. He decided that things between he and Tyler had been going well. He took a gamble and asked, 'You once pointed out that Dorothy had been having bad luck with her post-docs; was that just a casual observation or was there more to it?'

Tyler drew breath and paused before saying, 'I attended an international scientific meeting at Yale around the time of the fire. It was a meeting about the determinants of human behaviour – the reason I was there. The usual topics were covered, nature versus nurture, the influence of religion, scientific progress in gene studies, what makes one man a saint and another a terrorist. Dorothy Lindstrom was one of the speakers: being a Christian she acted as a sort of bridge between science and religion and was there to provide support for a Roman Catholic bishop who did his best to give credit for all the good in the world to God while all the blame for the bad things was laid at the door of the human race.'

Steven made a face and Tyler responded with a wry smile. 'That's what most of the delegates thought,' he said. The bishop was given a hard time, particularly when he tried to blame Islamic terrorist behaviour on false promises made to the faithful regarding the ready availability of virgins upon their demise. Some delegates pointed out that afterlife promises made by Christian leaders aren't that different.'

'Sounds like a bad day to have worn your collar back to front,' said Steven.

'Dorothy did her best to make the case for religion being perfectly compatible with science – it was all a matter of open-minded interpretation, she claimed and, to be frank, she did well, but there were questions about what she might do if she actually came up against scientific facts that utterly disproved all religion.'

'A toughie.'

'You'd think so, but she simply replied that she thought that would never happen. But, if it did – and this was a bit of a show stopper – she maintained that she, as a scientist, would have to accept proven scientific facts.'

'Wow,' said Steven, 'good for her.'

'Mm, but things went a bit downhill after that. An angry young man asked her if that were the case, why had she blocked the submission of his work to the scientific journals.'

'One of her post-docs?'

'Paul Leighton.'

'What a moment, how did she handle it?'

'Really well, she came over as an indulgent mother dealing with the impetuosity of the young. All it needed was a bit more work, she lectured, and everyone laughed. I think the guy wanted to say more but the moment had gone.'

'So, you and Dorothy knew each other before you turned up as advisor to a bunch of lawyers?'

Tyler shook his head. 'No, there were hundreds of delegates at the meeting. I was just a face in the crowd near the back. I did seek out the post-doc who asked the question afterwards however. He told me that Dorothy had pulled the plug on his work, but our conversation was interrupted by the bishop joining us: he seemed intent on urging the lad to open up his mind to the holy spirit. A few days later he was dead along with Dorothy's other post-doc.

'Carrie,' said Steven. 'Carrie Simpson.'

'It sounds like you've been making a few investigations of your own.'

'I've requested copies of the police and fire department reports from the US,' Steven admitted. 'Maybe you've already seen them?'

'Chance would be a fine thing,' laughed Tyler. 'I'm a loner, a freelancer, I have no official position and no access to official documents. I depend on friends.'

'I'll let you know if I find out anything.'

Steven found John Macmillan looking despondent and asked why.

'Sometimes I feel like I'm running in mud. I ask the police and MI5 if they've caught Barrowman yet and I'm told not, but I don't know whether I believe them. They haven't exactly been open and honest about anything in recent times and that breeds suspicion. Even the Home Secretary is playing silly buggers. I'm beginning to think we're turning into East Germany before the wall came down.'

'We're not,' Steven assured his boss. 'Sci-Med wouldn't have lasted five minutes with the *Stasi* around.'

Macmillan gave a small embarrassed smile at Steven reminding him of the much-feared East German police and conceded, 'Perhaps I was exaggerating a little.'

'But I share your frustration,' Steven added. 'For what it's worth, I don't think they have caught Barrowman yet and they're finding it humiliating. They don't understand why with the combined resources of the Met and MI5 hunting him down he's managed to evade capture. He may have been transformed into a psychotic killer, but he has no background as any kind of criminal. He's never been on the run before so it's hard to see how he could have gone to earth so easily. Where would he go? Who would he turn to for help? Who would give it to him?'

'All good points,' said Macmillan. 'All he has going for him is that . . . he's bright . . . armed . . . psychotic . . . Have I missed out anything?' said Macmillan.

'Purpose,' said Steven as if it had just occurred to him. 'We don't know what's driving him. His research was the most important thing in his life; nothing was allowed to get in the way of it and suddenly it's gone. He has lost what he cared about most and this has left him feeling . . . what?'

'Angry, confused, filled with hate, fear, loathing, a desire for revenge against those who conspired against him, of which . . . you are one, the man who met with his wife behind his back on the night it all went wrong.'

'A happy thought.'

'I suggest you pay a visit to the armourer,' said Macmillan in a tone that made it more than a suggestion.

'Will do,' said Steven reluctantly. He hated this moment. He knew it was a sensible precaution, but he always saw the moment he felt the presence of a pistol under his left arm as being symbolic of distancing himself from everyone else in society, a feeling he didn't like, not least because Tally loathed the idea of it too. He had always gone to great lengths to assure her his job was nowhere near as dangerous as she feared – he was simply an investigator engaged in finding out the truth – but a gun hanging over a chair in the bedroom always suggested, mutely but very loudly, that there might be more to it.

Steven told Macmillan about his conversation with Tyler and what he'd learned about the Yale meeting before the fire.

'It would appear that Professor Lindstrom's open-mindedness might be subject to question,' said Macmillan thoughtfully.

'She did assure Jane Lincoln that the truth, whatever it turned out to be, would be submitted for publication.'

'Mm.'

'God, I could do with some good news,' said Steven. 'You're not the only one who feels he's running in mud.'

'I think I can help there,' said Macmillan. 'It would appear that the public aren't the slightest bit interested in Moorlock Hall and its inmates and the press have had to give in to public opinion for fear of damaging their circulation figures. Their attempts to whip up outrage have been dismissed as "liberal leftie crap" to quote one of my sources and there's been a bit of a rush by MPs to distance themselves from the whole thing too with an election coming up next year. They don't want to be found disagreeing with a public who think the bastards have got exactly what they deserve if a noose wasn't available.'

'Does that mean they're going to leave things as they are?' asked Steven incredulously.

'In a word, yes, but they can't all be seen to be walking away. My source tells me that the redoubtable Mrs Leadbetter has been left holding the baby. She has been tasked with fact finding, compiling a comprehensive report and making recommendations which will be considered in due course by committees yet to be set up.'

Steven broke into a smile. 'Serves her right,' he said. 'Does that mean that Groves, the superintendent, won't be retired after all?'

'My source didn't say.'

'Actually, I think he was looking forward to it.'

'I can't see anyone else wanting the job, can you?'

Steven shook his head.

Steven checked with Jean that no information had come in from the USA before going off to the armourer to be issued with a 9mm Glock pistol and Burns Martin shoulder holster.

'It's been a while,' said the armourer, checking the record book.

'Not long enough,' Steven replied.

'Better safe than sorry.'

Steven gave him a look that suggested clichés were neither required nor welcome.

'I see it's also been a while since you visited the range.'

'I just don't feel at home there . . .' said Steven but the joke fell flat and the armourer continued, 'I recommend a session.'

Steven was about to decline when the armourer added, 'We don't want the public being at risk from stray bullets, do we?'

Steven felt he had no option but to go downstairs to the range to be issued with ammunition, sign for it and don ear protectors after hearing what was required of him.

'In your own time.'

Steven pumped rapid fire shells into the bad guy dummy and waited while it was reeled back for examination.

'Good grouping,' murmured the range commander. 'Pop-ups next.'

Steven reloaded the pistol and took a firm stance, holding the weapon up in front of him in both hands. 'Ready.'

A series of figures popped up at the far end of the range at one second intervals and in random positions along a twenty-metre horizontal stretch before disappearing again. A woman carrying a shopping bag . . . a man with a briefcase . . . a woman pushing a pram . . . a child with a toy gun . . .a masked man pointing a gun at him. *bang, bang, bang.* A boy with a football . . . an old woman leaning on a stick . . . a man putting up an umbrella . . . A man reaching for a *bang,* mobile phone . . . *'Bugger.'*

'You put two in the baddie, pity about the guy with the phone,' said the range commander. 'But you'll do.'

Steven left the building knowing that men reaching for mobile phones were going to be uncommonly safe from him for some time to come. He was still dwelling on his mistake when his own phone rang, it was Lucy Barrowman.

'Steven, do you think you could come and see me?'

'Of course, how about now?'

Lucy laughed and said, 'It's nothing urgent but there's just something I'd like to run past you when you have some free time.'

'That's now, see you in thirty minutes?'

'Great.'

Steven wasn't sure if Lucy had been told about her husband killing the MI5 officer so he phoned Jean and asked if she would check with the police. She called back to report that Lucy knew Owen was still at large but had not been told about the murder. Five wanted to keep it under wraps.

Steven found Lucy alert and feeling better although her eyes betrayed a sadness he suspected might not leave any time soon. 'How are you?' he asked.

'I'm well,' she replied. 'I'm pain free and looking less like a panda each day. I've decided to stay with mum and dad for a time when I get out.'

'Sounds like a good idea.'

'I understand they haven't caught Owen yet?'

'That's my understanding too.'

'How can that be?'

The question was direct and Steven could see that Lucy had been thinking along the same lines he had. 'I honestly don't know,' he replied. 'It's not as if he has any great experience of lying low and avoiding capture. Where would he go?'

Lucy took time to ask, 'You don't think he's . . . he's done anything . . . silly.'

Steven suddenly realised Lucy was thinking about suicide, something that hadn't even occurred to him and, feeling foolish, he admitted as much.

'He's got himself into such a mess he might not be able to see any way out,' said Lucy.

'I suppose it's a possibility,' Steven admitted – even more of one when the murder Lucy didn't know about was added to the equation. It might also explain why he hadn't been caught if his body was lying at the bottom of the Thames.

'Is that what's been on your mind?' he asked.

'No, that's not why I wanted to see you,' said Lucy. 'It may be nothing but I've remembered something.'

Steven felt a small adrenalin surge. Could Lucy be about to give him the break he so desperately needed to make progress?

'An old friend of Owen's from his time at Edinburgh University, Dan Glass, came to give a seminar at Capital a few weeks ago, Owen must have sent him something a few days later.'

'What makes you say that?'

'I took a phone call from Dan at home a week or so after his London seminar. Owen was working late at the lab as usual, Dan asked me to tell him the package had arrived safely.'

Steven felt genuine excitement. 'But you don't know what was in it?'

'I'm afraid not, but I thought I'd tell you.'

'Absolutely,' agreed Steven. 'Do you know which department Dan works in at Edinburgh?'

'Human Genetics at the Western General Hospital.'

EIGHTEEN

'Will you be staying up in Scotland to see your daughter?' asked Jean when Steven told her he wanted to fly up to Edinburgh in the morning.

Steven said not. 'I'm hoping it's just going to be a flying visit. The plan is to get my hands on the package and get back to London in time to deliver it to Lukas at the lab. This could be the break we've been hoping for.'

'Does this Dan Glass know you're coming?'

Steven said not. 'I'd like it to be a surprise.'

'Good luck.'

Tally loaded her fork with the smoked fish risotto ready-meal that Steven had prepared for dinner, but paused to ask, 'Don't you like using the telephone, or do you just fancy a jolly to Edinburgh?'

'I just fancy a jolly to Edinburgh,' Steven replied, filling both their glasses and pretending to concentrate on his plate.

Tally looked at him suspiciously. 'You're lying, aren't you?'

Steven smiled and said, 'I don't know what the arrangement was between Barrowman and his friend, Glass. Assuming the package contains what we hope it does and holds data on Lawler, there may be some arrangement in place as to what to do if some stranger starts asking questions. I want to be a surprise visitor.'

'I see.'

'Eat up.'

'My compliments to Monsieur Tesco.'

'Are you taking that thing with you? asked Tally, inclining her head to where Steven left the gun in its holster.

'No, I'll put it in the safe. I should manage a trip to Edinburgh without a gunfight.'

Tally gave him an unsmiling stare, reminding Steven he should never make jokes about guns.

Next morning, Steven took a British Airways shuttle flight to Edinburgh which landed just after ten. The morning rush hour was largely over, allowing him a clear taxi ride from the airport, which lay to the west of the city, to the Western General Hospital which was to the north west. As they drew near, the driver asked which ward or department he was going to. Steven told him and the man replied, 'That's on the east side, I'll drop you at the Crew Road entrance. It's a modern building, a concrete and glass box like all the rest.'

'You're not a fan,' said Steven.

This was the trigger the driver needed to unload his misgivings about modern architecture. 'It's the only field of human endeavour I know that's gone backwards,' he maintained. 'You'd think these people had never seen a cathedral, never learned anything from guys who lived hundreds of years ago. All you get these days is concrete boxes and weird looking crap they get prizes for. See that boiler house over there . . .'

Steven looked over to a tall chimney.

'Bugger got a prize for that.'

Steven tipped him well and took comfort from having provided the man with a release valve for his anger. Apart from that . . . he had a point.

Steven took a seat while the receptionist made a phone call. He heard one side of the conversation. *Dr Dunbar . . . Steven Dunbar . . . Didn't say, do you want me to ask him? . . . Right, I'll tell him.*

'Dr Glass is coming down.'

A man wearing jeans and a black tee shirt bearing the name of a pop band he didn't recognise duly appeared. He looked to be around the same age as Owen Barrowman.

'I'm Dan Glass, how can I help?'

'Steven presented his ID and expected the usual questions about Sci-Med. He was pleasantly surprised when Glass said, 'I've heard of you, you're a sort of scientific police force?'

'Sort of,' Steven agreed. 'I'd like to talk to you about Owen Barrowman, I believe he's a friend of yours?'

'We were students together,' Glass replied with a smile. 'What's he been up to? Not in any trouble, is he?''

'Maybe we could speak somewhere more private?'

'Let's go upstairs.'

'Steven took Glass's relaxed demeanour and slight air of puzzlement as a sign he had no idea what had been going on. This was a bonus. 'I'm afraid your friend's in a great deal of trouble,' he said. 'He's had a serious mental breakdown.'

'Owen? You're kidding.'

'I'm afraid not, he completely snapped, attacked his wife and injured her badly. She's in hospital: he's on the run from the police.'

Glass was dumbstruck until he eventually managed, 'Christ almighty, that's beyond belief.'

Steven accepted that Glass's shock was genuine. After a suitable pause he said, 'Barrowman sent you a packet sometime after your recent visit to Capital in London?'

'He did.'

'I must ask you to hand it over please.'

'I'm afraid not,' replied Glass, still appearing shocked.

'It's not a request, Doctor . . . I do have the authority . . .'

Glass appeared to come to his senses and said apologetically, Oh, no, sorry, I'm not being awkward, I don't have it any more.'

'Where is it?'

'Owen has it, he asked me to send it back to him.'

'I'm sorry?'

'He asked me to send it back to him.'

'What?' exclaimed Steven. 'When?'

'Yesterday.'

Steven had an image of Barrowman floating up from the watery grave he imagined him to be in. Questions tumbled out. 'Where was he? Where did you send the package? What did he say?'

'He sounded like he was in a bit of a hurry and didn't have much time to talk,' said Glass, 'He apologised for messing me around and asked that I send the package to the address he gave me. I said, no problem, I'd do it right away.'

'Do you still have the address?'

Glass looked round at the surface of a cluttered desk. 'I think so.' He got up and started rummaging.

'Did he tell you what was in the package?' Steven asked.

'He didn't.'

'And you didn't ask?'

'He was a friend asking for a favour. If he'd wanted me to know he would have told me. Ah, here it is . . .'

Glass handed Steven the piece of paper he'd found.

'A post box number in London' Steven exclaimed, 'nothing else, did he say where it was?'

'He had no reason to, I suppose I assumed it was a box used by the university. What was in this packet anyway?'

Steven ignored the question and said, 'Dr Glass,' he said, 'Owen Barrowman is a wanted man with serious charges pending against him.' He handed his card to Glass. 'Please call me immediately if you hear from him again. In the meantime, I'd rather you didn't mention our conversation to anyone.'

Glass looked as if something was troubling him. 'Of course not,' he said hesitantly . . . 'But you know, Owen didn't sound as if he were suffering from a severe breakdown . . .'

'Maybe I chose the wrong words,' said Steven. 'I think experts might call it a severe personality disorder.'

'I'm struggling to believe it.'

'So is Lucy in her hospital bed.'

'I'm sorry . . . give her my best.'

Steven called Jean on the way to the airport and asked if she would try to get information on the post box number. 'It could be one that Capital University uses,' he added. But maybe not.'

'No package?' she asked.

Steven said not. 'Barrowman phoned Glass and asked him to send it to the number I've just given you.'

'So, he's still alive.'

'And with a plan apparently.'

Jean said, 'My God, his life is in ruins, he's on the run from the police for murder and he's still piddling around with this research data nonsense. It's unbelievable.'

'For a normal person, Jean, but he's not normal. He's devious, cunning, totally unpredictable and completely devoid of compassion or sympathy. What we mustn't do is underestimate him. He may be a nutter, but he's a nutter with a PhD who believes he is on some kind of mission.'

'And with that happy thought . . . 'said Jean, 'I can tell you that the stuff you asked for from the US has come in. I'll leave it on your desk along with anything I find out about the box number. I'll be leaving a bit early tonight.'

'Choir?'

'We're giving a concert.'

'Have a good one.''

The news that his flight back to London had been delayed because of engine problems did little to improve Steven's mood. It darkened further when the aircraft eventually took off only to be put in a holding pattern over West Drayton an hour later while it waited for a revised landing slot at Heathrow.

'We'd like to apologise for the slight delays you've suffered today . . .'

Passengers exchanged glances at the word 'slight'.

'and thank you for flying British Airways today. We hope to see you again soon.'

Next time I'll use a pogo stick.

Steven found the office empty when he got back to Whitehall. There was an envelope on his desk containing the information he'd asked for from the US and a note from Jean stating that she had 'hit the wall' in her efforts to find out where or what the post box number was linked to. The 'wall' appeared to be Royal Mail security.

Steven swore under his breath, but noted that Jean had enlisted John Macmillan's help in resolving the problem before leaning back in his chair and rubbing his eyes while he considered the world's obsession with what they imagined was security. People were becoming afraid to say or do anything. It was really blame that they feared most. Lawyers and the threat of litigation stalked their every move and listened to every word. Steven checked his watch and decided to take the US material home.

'Hi Tally,' he called out as he unlocked the front door. He was slightly out of breath after choosing to run up the stairs rather than take the lift, a habit he adopted when opportunities for planned exercise were curtailed. He'd never liked the idea of 'going to the gym', preferring to run through landscapes rather than gaze out of a window while on a treadmill – even if the landscape happened to be the hell of sand dunes or rain-swept mountains.

As he turned after closing the door, a small white object caught his attention and he bent to pick it up . . . it was a card . . . a business card. The blood drained from his face as he read the name on it . . . Dr Owen Barrowman. On the back was written, 'Sorry you were out'.

Steven remained frozen to the spot. Barrowman had been here. All he could think was that the card was the psychotic weirdo's idea of a joke. His own presence at Barrowman's flat had been given away by him leaving his business card and this was some kind of what? A warning that more was to come? Tally wasn't home . . . but she could have been.

Steven found his mouth dry and his throat tight as he walked slowly through the flat, checking the rooms, reassuring himself that there was nothing amiss. He was in the bedroom when he heard the key go in the lock and Tally's voice asking if he was home.

'In here.'

Tally came in and smiled. 'There you are,' she said, 'What's wrong? You look strange . . .'

'Just pleased to see you.' He gave her a hug.

'I'm really not that late, Steven,' said Tally. It was a joke, but she was clearly concerned.

Steven flirted briefly with the idea of trying to hide what had happened but didn't feel comfortable doing that. He showed her the card.

Tally's normal air of self-confidence collapsed. She took a series of deep breaths before exclaiming, 'He's been here?'

'He put it through the letterbox.'

'Why? What did he want?'

'He's off his head, Tally, it was some kind of a sick joke. He found my card in his place . . .he was letting me know what it felt like . . .'

Tally looked at Steven accusingly. 'Is that how you see it? Is that how you really see it, Steven?' She took a step back. 'That sick creature nearly beat his wife to death, he goes on to murder an intelligence officer and he came here as a joke? If I'd been here . . . If I hadn't been held up at the last moment this evening, I might have answered the door to him . . . I could have *died* laughing at that joke, Steven.'

'I'm so sorry.' Steven's tone had changed. He'd given up on hiding the truth from Tally. She'd always hated his job and this kind of situation was why. It wasn't a flaw on her part, far from it; she was a decent, normal human being who loathed violence and anything to do with it. Her job involved doing her level best to make sick children well again and give them the best possible chance in life. She couldn't come to terms with his world because, despite his protestation that Sci-Med investigations were largely routine, the threat of danger and violence was ever present at the back of her mind or, as in this instance, the front.

'He won't be back.'

'How do you know?' Tally's voice had dropped to a whisper.

'The flat will be put under twenty-four-hour surveillance and you'll be given police protection from now on until this is over.' Steven knew he sounded cold and dispassionate, but, for the moment, this was what was required

'And who is going to protect you?' Tally asked.

'I am. I can call for police assistance any time I need it.'

'He obviously blames you for all that's happened. He wants revenge.'

'Doesn't seem right,' said Steven. 'You'd think looking for revenge would be way down his list of priorities in his situation.'

'You'd think getting his hands on his research data would be even further down,' countered Tally.

'Good point.'

'Supposing it comes down to you versus him?'

'I'll win.'

Tally looked at Steven, feeling that she was seeing a side to him she'd never seen before.'

'He's spent his life as an academic, I haven't. If it comes down to him taking me on, he'll wish he'd stayed home and played with his train set.'

'I'm sorry,' said Tally softly. We've been here before, I'm giving you a hard time and you don't deserve it. It's probably the last thing you need after finding that thing.'

'You've every right to be upset and I'm so sorry that something that shouldn't involve you at all has come so close.'

'I guess it's always a bad idea to bring your work home,' said Tally, with a smile that competed with tears.

Steven wiped the first teardrop away with his forefinger before saying, 'The world needs people like you, Tally; unfortunately, it also needs people like me.'

Tally took a deep breath. 'We'll make the best of it.'

'I'll make some phone calls.'

NINETEEN

Steven's final call was to John Macmillan who heard him out before saying, 'Interesting.'

'Not exactly what Tally said,' said Steven, feeling a bit nonplussed at Macmillan's response.

'I can imagine.' said Macmillan. 'She must have been very upset.'

'Try bloody angry,' said Steven, adding what sounded like an afterthought but wasn't, 'Why did you say you found it "interesting"?'

'Man on the run . . . wanted for murder . . . hunted by police and security services, but takes time out to come into central London and do something like that. I think we can learn from that.'

'I put it down to the arrogant single-mindedness of the psychopath,' said Steven. 'They're known for showing off how smart they are and are always keen to expose the foolishness of the authorities.'

'A reasonable hypothesis,' agreed Macmillan.

'But not shared by you?'

'I see someone who has found safety and security. I don't think he's on the run any more. If he feels confident enough to take risks playing silly games, he's doing it from a secure base and he probably has support. He's not alone.'

'Respect,' Steven murmured after a long pause. 'I read the text book, you read the man.'

'I take it you've arranged to have police protection for Dr Simmons and your flat?'

Steven confirmed that he had and asked about progress with the PO box number. The short silence that ensued suggested that more bad news was on the way.

'I'll be seeing the Home Secretary in the morning.'

'The Royal Mail didn't play ball?'

'The box has something called private security status. No one I spoke to could tell me anything about it because they maintained that they personally didn't know. They don't have a list of these numbers.'

'This is crazy,' said Steven. 'Royal Mail security doesn't know where their PO box is, but Barrowman does. He gets someone in Edinburgh to put a package in the post with a number on it and obviously expects it to reach him. How in God's name does that happen? Does he have some kind of diplomatic immunity? A personal courier?'

'I'm looking forward to the Home Secretary telling me,' said Macmillan.

Steven flopped down in his favourite chair feeling exhausted. He swung his feet up on the windowsill and closed his eyes, intent on escaping the windmills of his mind for a few minutes, but Macmillan's theory about Barrowman's circumstances put a stop to that. What kind of friend would still be a friend after hearing what Barrowman had done. How could anyone bring themselves to offer him shelter knowing that? At least, if Macmillan was right, earlier suspicions that Barrowman might not be on the run at all but was being held by security services could be discounted; they would hardly be letting him out to roam around central London.

Steven was interrupted by Tally's hand on his shoulder. She handed him a glass of malt whisky and said, 'I'm going to bed, don't stay up too late.'

Steven took the whisky and kissed her hand.

The welcome fire in his throat helped him find momentary distraction and allowed him to concede that he wasn't going to get anywhere wondering about Barrowman or who might have helped him. He turned his attention to the reports Jean had obtained from the U.S.

After forty-five minutes of concentrated reading Steven put the papers down on the floor by his side and put his head back on the chair to look out at the night sky. Both reports were detailed and well presented. Any question he might have asked had been answered and the conclusions that foul play could be ruled out and the fire had been the result of a tragic accident seemed sound.

This in itself was a relief, something he knew he should feel pleased about as just about every other aspect of his investigation was clouded in uncertainty . . . and yet something was wrong. He tried telling himself it might just be his natural suspicion and the knowledge that people compiling reports often tended to see what they and everyone else expected them to see before reporting accordingly. This wasn't conscious bias, it was human nature and had to be guarded against, but he still couldn't shake the feeling that something wasn't quite right. Coffee might help.

A double espresso did the trick. It was the bodies; the position of the bodies was telling him something. A gas leak from a main supply pipe had been the cause of the fire but there had been no mention of an explosion so why had there been no sign of the victims fighting the fire or attempting to escape? Much mention had been made of the flammable substances in the lab like ether and ethanol, which no doubt had contributed to the ferocity of the fire, but still . . . if the pair had been drunk, shocked, confused . . . fair enough, but they weren't. They were young, alert and wide awake, working on something exciting and of huge importance to them.

The position of the bodies, or what was left of them after the fire, suggested that they had been overcome by smoke and fumes at the bench where they were working. The question nagging away at him was simple. Had they been conscious when the fire broke out? If they hadn't . . .

Steven baulked at the thought of another layer of complexity appearing. He thought about John Macmillan's assertion that he was running in mud and acknowledged that he was just about to add another half-ton to the mix, but, having thought of it, he'd have to give the possibility due consideration.

It was obvious from the fire department's photos that the state of the bodies precluded any possibility of forensic examination. Proving that the pair had been drugged was a world away from thinking it. Apart from that, the remains would have been disposed of a long time ago after release to the families by the police.

It would be a long shot, but the only way he could see of making progress would lie in establishing the movements of the pair before they went back to the lab on that fateful night. That is when they must have been given some sedative compound – maybe a one to two-hour window? Where were they? Who were they with? So much time had passed that it seemed unlikely anyone connected to the Lindstrom group would remember where or when they had last seen the pair. On the other hand, people often did remember where they had been around the time of something awful happening. It would be worth talking to Jane Lincoln again.

Steven checked the door locks and turned the lights off before looking out of the window and spotting an unmarked vehicle down in the street which he decided was police protection. 'Stay awake, gentlemen,' he murmured. 'Stay awake.'

Tally left for work with a discreet police presence in attendance while Steven left some time later with his 9mm Glock for company. He thought he'd take the opportunity to go see Jane Lincoln while John was having words with the Home Secretary. Protocol demanded that he approach Dorothy Lindstrom first so he did. They exchanged pleasantries and puzzlement over the continued failure of the authorities to find Barrowman.

'I've been preparing his results for publication,' said Dorothy, 'but it's giving me a bit of a problem . . .'

'In what way?'

'In normal circumstances, Owen's name should go on the paper as first author, but the circumstances are far from normal and I'm not sure what I should do about that.'

Academics are truly wonderful, thought Steven, she wants to leave him off.

'I'm not sure I can help you there, Professor.'

Dorothy gave a half smile and asked, 'Is this a formal visit or did you just pop in to say hello?'

'Actually, I was hoping to have a word with Jane Lincoln if that's all right and she's around?'

'I'm beginning to wonder what you two are cooking up,' said Dorothy getting up from her chair.

'No need,' Steven assured her, 'just a couple of details I forgot to ask her about last time.'

'Hello again,' said Jane, 'Any news of Owen?'

Steven said not.

'I still can't believe what happened to him and thinking about it is making me worry about the rest of us.'

'Really?' Steven exclaimed. 'None of you has had any sustained contact with the sort of people Owen worked with, have you?'

'No, it wasn't so much that I was thinking about . . . we have a young group member who has been working with suicidal people and I've noticed her become more and more withdrawn. She says she's fine, but I'm not so sure.'

'Have you spoken to Dorothy?'

Jane nodded. 'She's keeping an eye on her.'

The look that passed between them suggested that might not be enough.

'It's difficult,' said Jane. 'Everyone has their career to think of so she won't want to admit to having problems which might be construed as mental frailty. That sticks, no matter what people might pretend otherwise, it sticks. The situation has made me think about the whole concept of normality. If you are surrounded by ten people who see things differently from you, like it or not, you are the abnormal one. It's all very well thinking that there are thousands of people out there who think exactly like you, it's the people around you who will eventually get you to establish a new norm.'

Steven nodded, impressed by Jane's analysis.

'Anyway, I'll keep trying to get her to open up on a personal basis,' said Jane. 'As they say, it's good to talk.'

'You're a good woman, Charlie Brown,' said Steven. 'We need more of you.'

'And what can this good woman do for you, Dr Dunbar?'

Steven took a deep breath as if concealing embarrassment to come. 'This may sound like a crazy question, but have you any idea what Paul Leighton and Carrie Simpson might have been doing in the hours leading up to the fire?'

'Doing in the lab?'

'Before they went back to the lab that night'

Jane's eyes roamed round the room as if searching for inspiration and failing. 'I really don't know,' she said. 'Is this important?'

'Very.'

Jane took that on board and said after a moment's thought, 'Let me see, I was quite late in leaving myself that night so most people including Paul and Carrie had already left before I did. If they were planning to come back later – as they were – they would probably have gone to grab a bite to eat, but that's about as far as I can take it.'

'Any idea where?'

'Probably Romero's, but that's a guess.'

'Romero's?'

'Most of us used McDonalds or Wendy's if we were planning to work late, but Carrie was a vegetarian; she preferred Romero's because they made proper veggie dishes rather than put out tubs of salad.'

'A small place?'

'Yes.'

'And they would go directly back to the lab from there?'

'I think so. They were intent on getting through the repeat experiments as quickly as possible. I can't see them being distracted by anything else.'

'Would they be known to the staff in Romero's?'

'I guess there's a good chance,' said Jane, 'they were working late a lot so they might even have been seen as regulars, but, in any case, I'm pretty sure the restaurant would have thought about them when they heard about two people dying in a fire that night,' she added, seeing where Steven was going with his questions. 'And now, are you going to tell me what you really want to know?'

Steven smiled. 'I really want to know if they were alone and, if not, who was with them.'

'Are you going to tell me why?'

'You were honest when I came to see you last time when you could have blanked me so I'll be straight with you. I think there's a possibility that Paul and Carrie's deaths were not the result of a tragic accident. I think they were drugged or sedated in some way so they were unconscious when the fire started.'

Jane looked as if this was a bit too much to take in. 'Oh my God,' she managed before shaking her head slowly. 'How awful.'

Steven waited for more to come. He thought the flood gates might open when Jane started wondering why anyone would want to murder her colleagues and she started answering her own question. Eventually she said quietly and in trepidation, 'Surely you don't think Dorothy was involved, do you?'

'Do you?'

'No, no, no,' said Jane in a hushed voice, 'She's a top scientist, a committed Christian, she may have been shaken to the core to see the results Paul and Carrie came up with and not have wanted to believe it without seeing absolute proof – maybe even to the point of delaying seeing it – but we all know that murdering the messenger never changed anything. The message stays the same.'

'How true.'

'The very reason that she invited me to come with her and work here in the UK was to establish the truth . . . whatever it turned out to be.'

Steven nodded. 'Okay, I can't say I like the woman, but I think I have to go along with what you say. That's not an entirely happy conclusion however . . .'

'How so?'

'If Dorothy had nothing to do with the Paul and Carrie's deaths, someone else did and, if it was because of their research, you and Dorothy are working on the same thing.'

Jane made a face and found an argument. 'Not exactly the same, we may be asking the same questions, but, by changing fields to epigenetics, we're approaching from a different angle and that means we're a long way off being able to refute or verify Paul and Carrie's findings.'

'And in a different country,' Steven added.

'Science on the run,' said Jane, managing a smile. How about you, where do you go from here?'

'The Romero's lead you've given me is all I've got so I'll have to find a way of checking it out, see if anyone remembers the couple being there that night. I take it Romero's is close to the department where you all worked?'

Jane said that it was. 'It's in Kelman Boulevard, would you like me to help?'

'In what way?'

'I was friendly with one of the technicians in the lab at Yale; she got a job in one of the other labs when Dorothy left; we exchange emails now and again. Cindy liked Romero's – she's a veggie too and presumably still goes there – I could ask her to try and find out if anyone remembers Paul and Carrie being there that night and who they were with, if anyone.'

What at first sounded like music to Steven's ears quickly became concern about putting Jane's friend in danger. He said as much to Jane who considered for a few moments before concluding, 'I don't really think so; it's all a very long time ago and no one ever imagined that any kind of crime was involved . . .'

Steven was happy to go along with this.

'What did you tell Dorothy about my last visit?' he asked.

'I told her pretty much what you told her, that you were gathering information on the group to get a feeling for the research we were doing. I didn't lie to her; I told her you had asked about the fire and that you'd asked me as a relative outsider at the time rather than her out of respect for her feelings.'

'Good.'

'I didn't admit to telling you anything about the rift between her and Paul and Carrie or what it was about.'

Steven nodded and said, 'That's also good, but I don't think I should come to the lab any more, it's going to require too much explanation. If Dorothy asks about today, it wouldn't be a lie to tell her that we spoke more about the changes that overcame Owen Barrowman and how you told me you were concerned about another of your colleagues.'

Jane was comfortable with this and Steven gave her a series of contact numbers to call when she had any news.

TWENTY

John Macmillan was still with the Home Secretary when Steven got to the Home Office so he decided to touch base with Neil Tyler. His call went to voicemail.

'Neil, I've been through the police and fire reports. We should talk. Are you free for lunch today? Give me a call.'

Half an hour later, Tyler returned the call. 'As luck would have it, I've just spent the morning with my legal retainers. Lunch would be a good idea.'

Steven suggested The Moorings, the same riverside pub he'd used for meetings with Barrowman and they agreed to meet at one o'clock. His liking for the place had little to do with the service or the food – which was fine – but simply because it afforded good views of the Thames and its bridges. Somehow, that was important.

'You were right to draw attention to the fire deaths,' said Steven.

'I'm not sure I should be pleased to hear that,' said Tyler.

Steven explained how he'd become suspicious after viewing the fire department photographs.

'Why didn't they pick up on that?' Tyler murmured.

'I didn't at first, but I kept going back to them until it struck me that I was looking at two people who had died without any apparent attempt to fight the flames or escape the building and that didn't seem right. The difference between me and the authorities was that I set out to look for something wrong and they didn't.'

'They saw what they expected to see,' Tyler agreed, 'They'd identified the cause of the fire – a gas leak – a tragic accident with no sign of foul play suspected . . . or looked for to any great degree.'

Steven told him of his earlier meeting with Jane Lincoln and her offer of help in tracing the last movements of Paul and Carrie.

'That's a bit of luck, I thought you were about to tell me you were going there, in which case I was about to suggest I come too,' said Tyler.

'Does that mean you got the sack from the lawyers this morning?' asked Steven.

'Far from it,' said Tyler. 'A few days ago, I submitted my report on the work found on Barrowman's computer on the make-up of psychopathic criminals and they seemed very satisfied – or rather the people behind them are.'

'No objections to the publication of these results?'

'None at all.'

'Dorothy will be pleased, but will they be happy to continue funding now that Barrowman's out of the picture?'

'Barrowman may be out of the picture, but they see him as having come up with the goods – a nice piece of work – and now they're looking forward to seeing what the others in the group come up with.'

'Happy bunnies all round,' said Steven, 'but where does this leave you? Will they still need you to ride shotgun on Dorothy's group and keep an eye on what they're up to?'

'Apparently yes, they'd like me to continue with monthly reports on the group's progress and to hear my assessment of where it's going. It might have been Barrowman's research on psychopaths that drew their attention to the Lindstrom group in the first place but obviously they're interested in everything else that's going on.'

'Interesting,' said Steven. 'I get the impression that they don't know anything about Moorlock Hall and Barrowman's studies on Lawler?'

'When you think about it, there was nothing to tell,' said Tyler. 'You and I both think he's hiding something but the fact that Lawler doesn't rate a mention in his results is not much to build a case on.'

'True,' Steven conceded. 'He told a few people he thought Lawler was special, but never said why. He didn't confide in Dorothy or his wife apart from telling Lucy he found him mesmerising or words to that effect. What do your employers know about Barrowman?' he asked.

'Just what Dorothy told them,' Tyler replied. 'They know of course that he had some sort of a breakdown recently, something being put down to long term exposure to the type of people he was associating with and they know he attacked his wife and had been referred by the police for psychiatric assessment.

'But they have no suspicion he was sitting on something important?'

'I don't think so; they were worried when they thought he might have destroyed his data because of his mental state and were relieved when that turned out not to be the case. They know about Moorlock Hall of course, because it was in the papers, but, like Dorothy, they took the view that one subject more or less was no big deal when there was enough data already to warrant publication.'

'You look as if you're trying to solve Fermat's last theorem,' said Tyler when Steven had stared unseeingly into space for at least thirty seconds.

'Sorry, I'm just trying to put pieces on the board in the right order.'

'And?'

'Let's go through it . . . we think that Barrowman has discovered something big but Dorothy doesn't know about it.'

'Agreed.'

'The same goes for the anonymous people you work for, but both are happy with what Barrowman did come up with, something which Dorothy sees as part of an overall understanding of what makes people tick,

'Agreed.'

The UK security services tried to block funding for Dorothy's group and were particularly interested in Barrowman and what he was doing to the extent that they kidnapped him from the police, possibly because they have people working on the same thing'

'If you say so.'

'Dorothy's group continues trying to unravel the mysteries of what controls our genes and how, but there's also a background agenda to prove or disprove what their two dead colleagues came up with before they died.'

'And who may have been murdered to prevent these findings being made public,' Tyler added.

'So where does that leave us?'

'Puzzled.'

'Steven raised an eyebrow.

'Don't get me wrong, epigenetics is an exciting field, but it's in its infancy. It will be one thing establishing which genes are subject to switching but quite another figuring out the details of how it works and how we can influence and eventually control it. I'm sure Dorothy and her co-workers are going to come up with a lot of interesting findings along the way but it's going to take a long time before the Americans' findings are confirmed or not.'

'Point taken,' said Steven, 'and maybe that suits Dorothy, but of course, lucky breaks sometimes happen . . . which brings us to Barrowman.'

It was Tyler's turn to look surprised. 'Do you think he knows how it all works?' he exclaimed.

'I think he learned something from Lawler that puts him way ahead of the field. Lawler was his lucky break, one that made his previous work almost irrelevant – he was happy to share all his other results, but went to enormous lengths to keep the Lawler discoveries to himself, presumably until such times as he could claim all the credit and go down in scientific history.'

'I still can't figure where your employers are coming from,' said Steven. 'They fund research anonymously and then sit back monitoring it. Why?'

'After what you've told me,' said Tyler cautiously, suppose . . . just suppose . . . they are the same people who were behind the murder of the two Americans . . .'

'Wow, talk about biting the hand that feeds you . . .'

'You know the old saying, keep your friends close and your enemies even closer?' said Tyler.

'Go on.'

'If Dorothy's two post-docs were murdered to stop them making their findings public, maybe the murderers thought that the same findings might surface again albeit from a different angle.'

'So, they fund them in order to keep an eye on things?'

'And to put a stop to things if they feel the time is right.'

'Well, Machiavelli has nothing on you, doctor,' said Steven, 'but funding an entire research group is not done with small change. We're talking big bucks here.'

'Which limits the field,' said Tyler.

'To whom?'

'People with big bucks.'

'If you keep this up, we're going to get our own radio show,' said Steven, 'I'm thinking US intelligence. UK intelligence blocked initial funding for Dorothy, maybe US intelligence took a stronger line?'

'A depressing thought.'

'The intelligence world is a very depressing place,' said Steven.

'You sound like you know it well?'

'Our paths have crossed.'

'Do you think MI5 are hiding Barrowman? Tyler asked.

Steven shook his head and told him about Barrowman's 'little joke' with the card.

Tyler was shocked. 'Jesus,' he murmured. 'Is that why you're carrying?' He nodded towards Steven's left shoulder, causing him to adjust his jacket. 'Don't worry, the weapon's not visible. I take it you don't do this often enough to warrant the attention of your tailor?'

'Quite,' said Steven. 'John Macmillan is convinced Barrowman has been given shelter by person or persons unknown. I wasn't so sure, but just when I was beginning to think he might have committed suicide, he phones a friend in Edinburgh, asking him to forward a packet he'd been keeping for him.'

'Scary stuff . . . Tell me about this packet.'

'There's a good chance it contains the data on Barrowman's work with Lawler.'

'Where was it sent?'

'Good question, John Macmillan was seeing the Home Secretary this morning with a view to finding that out.' Steven told Tyler of the PO box number problem.

It was agreed that Tyler would concentrate on trying to find out more about who was funding the Lindstrom group and Steven would let him know if and when Jane Lincoln had been back in touch.

Steven walked back to the Home Office feeling uncomfortable with the idea that U.S. intelligence could have been involved in the deaths of the two young scientists. This was not because he didn't think intelligence services could resort to murder when there was plenty of evidence to the contrary – a CIA plan to murder the Cuban leader, Fidel Castro with an exploding cigar, A Bulgarian agent using the deadly poison, ricin via a scratch from the tip of an umbrella, Russian radio-active polonium being added to tea for a

London assassination – but more the thought that intelligence services could be interfering in front-line scientific research. In his book, the search for truth should be above and beyond whatever else the human race got up to. Ivory towers should be sanctuaries for the gifted few capable of asking the right questions and seeking out truth to expand human knowledge. *Dream on Dunbar.* He took solace from the thought that the only reason for bringing up possible US intelligence involvement was the large amount of money required. There was absolutely no evidence that they were . . . for the moment.

'The police have been trying to contact you,' said Jean when Steven got back to the Home Office.

Steven took out his mobile and turned it back on. 'I've been having lunch with Neil Tyler,' he explained. 'We were discussing the probable murder of Dorothy Lindstrom's two American post-docs.'

'Oh no,' Jean whispered, 'Not good . . . and the news from the police isn't going to help.'

'Do you want to tell me first?'

'It's Lucy Barrowman, she's been attacked.'

Steven was shocked. 'What? But she's staying with her parents down in Eastbourne,' he protested.'

'Apparently such things happen even in Eastbourne,' Jean replied, 'The house was subject to a break-in while they slept. Poor girl, after all she's been through you'd think life would give her a break.'

'Steven called the police to be given details of the sexual assault carried out on Lucy Barrowman while she slept in her parents' home.'

'I take it she wasn't under police protection?'

'That was withdrawn when she left hospital and we thought Barrowman had gone to ground.'

'Was it him?'

'Mrs Barrowman says not.'

Steven didn't ask for details, his mind was reeling from the awful news.

'There was a second casualty,' the policeman continued. 'Her father woke up and disturbed the intruder. He was just pushed out the way but suffered a heart attack shortly afterwards. Both are in hospital. We'll keep you informed.'

Steven put down the phone just as John Macmillan came in to the office.

'Bad news?' he asked after seeing Steven's face.

Jean, who had heard the phone call, gave Macmillan details while Steven tried to think things through. He was struggling to accept the attack on Lucy had been some kind of horrible coincidence, but if Lucy had told the police it wasn't Barrowman . . . what was he left with?'

'Are you all right?' asked Macmillan.

'I knew life was a bitch, I just didn't realise how big a one.'

'I'm older, I knew.'

Steven asked, 'What news?'

'A convoluted tale,' said Macmillan. 'Many years ago our intelligence services set up a Post Office box number system, which could be used in times of emergency to send material securely through the post.'

'So far so good,' said Steven.

'It worked a bit like a Russian doll, one number led to another which led to another and so on.'

Steven frowned.

'The package sent from Edinburgh was addressed to a box number in London. The box number would not mean anything to the receiving office and would be put aside as improperly addressed mail. Someone – presumably senior and who had signed the official secrets act – would see it and forward it to another PO box number where the same thing would happen. This would go on as many as four times until it reached a final destination where it would be collected by someone giving a password.'

'So where was this final destination?' Steven asked.

'We don't know.'

'You are joking,' exclaimed Steven, feeling as if some celestial being was having a laugh at his expense.

'I'm afraid not. The Home Secretary was as angry as I was. She called in the heads of Royal Mail security and MI5 while I was there and demanded to know what the hell was going on. In a nutshell . . . they didn't know either. She sent them away with a flea in their ear and ordered them to find out. Two hours later MI5 came back with an answer, thanks to someone with a historical interest in the service. The system was devised during the Second World War when there was a fear that we might be invaded. It was assumed, rightly or wrongly, that the mail service would still operate and so a plan using box numbers was devised, which would allow the resistance to use it without suspicion.

Although it was never used to any great extent, the box number system was never fully disabled. Trusted people who'd signed the act and been sworn to secrecy would still know what to do when one of these box numbers appeared in their sorting office. When they left or retired, a new trusted individual would be appointed and so it has gone on.'

Steven shook his head. 'Are you saying that when someone is appointed to some senior role in a sorting office they are asked to sign the Official Secrets act, sworn to secrecy about an archaic box system and told never to divulge details to anyone?'

'Apparently.'

'Talk about a love of historic ritual,' said Steven.

'Have you seen the opening of parliament?' said Jean.

'But the bottom line must be that we can now find out where Barrowman's package ended up?' said Steven.

'In theory,' said Macmillan. 'In practice, it's going to involve questioning people who have been sworn to secrecy and who believe they're doing their duty by denying all knowledge of what we want to know.'

'Oh God,' sighed Steven, feeling the will to live drain from him.

'They'll probably think they're being tested,' added Jean less than helpfully.

Macmillan said, 'The Home Secretary has asked Special Branch to deal with it.'

'Special Branch?' exclaimed Steven, unable to hide his surprise.

'MI5 thought they should do it and I objected, maintaining it should be left to Sci-Med as it was a medical science investigation. They didn't want to admit that they were involved in the same thing so they maintained it was part of a murder inquiry – one of their own for good measure. In the end, the Home Secretary decided that Special Branch should carry out the PO box number business and inform both Five and Sci-Med so that we can both be present when the final box is opened.'

'Could be a rather grand opening of an empty box,' said Jean, voicing what they were all thinking.

'It's true we might be too late for the Scottish packet, but he may be using the box for other things and he might even be picking up stuff himself,' said Macmillan.'

'I don't think we should give up entirely on the Edinburgh packet not being in the box,' said Steven.

'Really? I thought the Scottish chap said that Barrowman was keen to have it back.' said Macmillan.

'He did, but it's possible Barrowman just wanted it put in the post as soon as possible,' said Steven. 'Knowing what we know now about the box system, he may have been moving it to what he thought would be a safer place in case someone started snooping around in Scotland.'

'Someone like you,' said Macmillan.

'Exactly, I missed it by a day, but once it was in the post it would be on its way to a post box in a secret place where it could lie for ever if necessary, away from prying eyes and, if he didn't get the credit for his work, no one else ever would. He was hardly going to need it while he was on the run for murder.'

'Good thinking,' said Macmillan.

'I'll see your "good" and raise it to brilliant,' added Jean.

'Well, folks,' said Steven getting to his feet. 'It's been a long day, time to go home.'

'Did you learn anything from the American reports?' Macmillan asked as he headed for the door.

'Yep, it was murder.'

TWENTY-ONE

'How are you today?' asked John Macmillan.

Steven recognised there was more to the question than a polite enquiry.

'Sorry, I was a bit abrupt last night,' he said, 'I couldn't face going over all the events of the day. The attack on Lucy was the final straw.'

'Understandable, no one saw that coming.'

'Thanks.'

Steven went through everything that had happened on the previous day, how his suspicions had been aroused by the photographs from the US fire department, moving on to his meeting with Jane Lincoln and her offer of help in establishing who might have been with Paul Leighton and Carrie Simpson immediately before the fire on that awful night and ending with his conversation with Neil Tyler.

'It was Neil who brought up the possibility that his employers might have been implicated in the American deaths,' he added, 'Now the fear is that they are monitoring what Dorothy's new group comes up with before . . . putting a stop to it.'

Macmillan leaned back in the chair and interlaced his fingers across his stomach before saying, 'Assuming that what you and Tyler are suggesting is true, it would seem to suggest that Professor Lindstrom's backers are not scientists and, by association, neither are those behind the American murders.' You're a medic, Tyler's a scientist; you both could see that the professor's plan to replicate the work of her dead colleagues would take a long time; that's something the anonymous backers clearly didn't take into account.'

'That is a very good point,' Steven agreed. 'and happily, it may also take US intelligence out of the frame.' He answered Macmillan's inquiring glance by pointing out how much it would be costing to fund Dorothy's research. 'They'd be one of the few candidates capable of financing it anonymously, but, of course, they would have the scientific nous to realise how long something like that would take and would keep watch from the side lines rather than rush in.'

'Well, I think we can call that progress,' said Macmillan, 'Mind you, I'm keen to call anything progress these days.'

'We can safely adopt the politicians' gambit,' said Steven.

'Which is?'

'Blame other people.'

Macmillan grinned. 'I think in this case we may have good cause. Have you informed the US police about your suspicions?'

'Not yet,' said Steven, hoping he might be able to leave it at that, but Macmillan expected more.

'I thought I might delay until we see if Jane Lincoln comes up with anything.'

'Can I ask why?'

'We're working in the dark. If the US police agree there might be something wrong with their original conclusions and instigate a full-scale murder – or should that be homicide – investigation, it will alert people we don't want to alert and maybe scare them off.'

Macmillan accepted this but pointed out, 'We don't want to end up investigating an American murder; that's way outside our remit.'

'Agreed, but if Jane should come up with the identity of a third person present in the restaurant that night, it would probably mean more to us than it would to the local police and might even help with our inquiry if we could see a connection.'

'Fair enough.'

'How long is it since you last spoke to your daughter?' Tally asked.

'A couple of weeks,' Steven replied, 'I couldn't get a word in edgeways for hearing about the wonders of Jason,'

Tally smiled. 'You should call her,' she said, 'Play her at her own game, tell her how wonderful I am.'

'Everyone knows that,' said Steven.

'Maximum brownie points,' said Tally, slapping a phone into his hand. 'Go on, call her.'

Steven was surprised when Jenny herself answered. 'Hi nutkin, how are you? I wasn't expecting you to pick up the phone.'

'I'm waiting for Jason to call, Dad.'

'Oh, I'm sorry, maybe I should call back?'

'Don't be silly, Dad, he can wait.'

This cheered Steven. He deliberately extended the call by asking every conceivable question he could think of about school and life in general, happy in the knowledge he would be keeping Jason waiting. Eventually, he gave in and said, 'Well, I'd better go and let you speak to your beau.'

'My what?' Jenny exclaimed.

'Sorry, it's an old-fashioned word for boyfriend.'

'Dad?'

'Yes, nutkin?'

'I love you.'

Steven felt himself choke and struggled to manage, 'Love you too, nutkin,' before ending the call.

Tally took the phone from him, 'Well, my big, brave warrior,' she said, 'that wasn't so hard, was it?'

Steven smiled.

Next morning, the sun shone from a clear blue sky after having been absent for several days. Steven took the opportunity to walk by the river and enjoy the warmth of its rays on his face as he thought about Jenny and how grown-up she'd sounded the night before. It made him reflect on how quickly life was passing by. In an ideal world there would be a slow-down or pause button somewhere. A rewind would be a step too far – what was gone was gone – but it would be nice to have just a little more time to cherish things that really mattered.

The beep of an incoming text message interrupted his reverie, especially when he saw it was from Jane Lincoln. It said, 'Can we meet? Reply by text.'

Steven replied, asking where and when and was told, 3p.m. Rose's coffee shop in Cedar Avenue. He had to look up the address and saw it was quite a long way away from the university. Was there a reason for that? he wondered.

The reason became clear when they met. Jane told Steven that she shared a flat around the corner in Cedar Crescent and had taken the afternoon off. 'I didn't want to meet you anywhere near the university,' she said, 'or even have you call me there.'

'Okay,' said Steven, not understanding but hoping this was about to be put right.

'I've got some news.' Jane paused when Steven's espresso and her own latte arrived along with two pieces of chocolate cake which Jane insisted he must try. Steven could see by the smiles being exchanged that Jane was a regular.

'I heard back from my friend . . . there were three people at the table in Romero's that night.'

'Excellent, this could be a big piece in the puzzle.'

'There's more.'

Steven felt the hairs on the back of his neck rise.

'I asked her if she knew who the third person was and she said, no.'

The hairs settled.

'But she could see what he was.'

Steven rubbed the back of his neck. 'And what was that?'

'A priest, a Roman Catholic priest.'

'Well, well, well,' murmured Steven, but feeling unsure why he'd said it or what to think about it.

'There's more. Thinking ahead, I asked if she could describe him and she did, not all that well – she had no reason to pay him close attention – but well enough for me to think he might have been the same priest I saw with Dorothy in the lab in the days following the fire – short, paunchy, clean-shaven, balding at the front. My friend said they all seemed very friendly and remembers that the priest left with Paul and Carrie: they went off in the direction of the lab.'

'That could be so important,' said Steven.

'Could it?' asked a troubled looking Jane. 'If that man had anything to do with the fire and then turned up in the lab to see Dorothy, it could mean that Dorothy was involved after all.'

'Point taken.'

'That's why I didn't want to be seen talking to you or have anyone thinking it was you on the phone.'

'You did right, but let's not implicate Dorothy just yet . . . for all the reasons we spoke about before.

Jane nodded. 'It's still a worry.'

Steven agreed that it was, but asked her to carry on as normal for the time being. He promised to get in touch when he had any news and she did likewise. As he got up to go, he said, 'That was the best chocolate cake I ever tasted.' He left two smiling women behind.

When he got back to the Home Office, Jean told him that John Macmillan had been called to a special meeting by the Home Secretary. Steven told her what Jane Lincoln had come up with and her eyes widened in surprise, 'A priest?' she exclaimed, 'what do you make of that?'

'Jane thinks there's a good chance it was the same priest who came to see Dorothy Lindstrom at the university after the fire,' said Steven, 'the one I asked you to run a check on.'

'I remember,' said Jean.'

Steven confessed that he hadn't got round to taking a look at the file. He'd been distracted after seeing the fire department photographs.

'Can you remember if he came up as part of the pastoral care team at Yale?' he asked.

'Actually, no, he didn't. I half expected him to be one of the chaplains but he didn't appear on the list.'

'I know they have a department of Religious Studies,' said Steven. 'He could be a faculty member.'

'I'll check.'

'He might even be a local priest'

'Dorothy's local priest perhaps?' Jean suggested. 'Do we know anything about the area where she lived while she was at Yale?'

'I could find out discreetly from Jane Lincoln, but I don't want Dorothy to know we're sniffing around,' said Steven. 'Maybe Neil Tyler might be able to help out. He was actually there at the time of the fire.'

'Do you really think this priest was involved?'

''Right now, he's our prime suspect, however unlikely it sounds.'

'In that case . . .' said Jean, pausing to look through papers on her desk, 'Time to bring in the big diggers for . . . Father Liam Crossan.'

John Macmillan returned from his meeting with news that Special Branch had identified the first two transfers in the chain Barrowman's packet had taken. They were confident of coming up with the other two within the next twenty-four hours.

'Progress at last,' said Steven.

'We have the Home Secretary to thank,' said Macmillan. 'She made it very plain to a number of very senior people that they should start checking their pension arrangements if they didn't pull their fingers out.'

'Good for her. Did you discuss the opening procedure?'

'The final box is not to be opened until you and Five's appointed representative are both present. The Royal Mail's security man will do the opening.'

'And then what?'

'That, of course, will depend on what the contents are,' said Macmillan. 'But if, as we all hope, the packet posted from Scotland should still be there and found to contain what seems to be data sources – disks, memory sticks, whatever – they should be copied there and then and shared between ourselves and Five. Lab notes are to be photo-copied and shared.'

'This requires the presence of suitable hardware,' said Steven.

'I thought of that,' said Macmillan. 'The Home Secretary has agreed that both MI5 and Sci-Med can take along one extra person with the skills and equipment to carry out the copying and sharing.'

'Lukas,' said Steven.

'Lukas,' Macmillan agreed.

'I'll call him,' said Steven, 'put him on stand-by. In fact, I'll go over and see him, tell him what's been going on. Was this all the special meeting was about?' he asked.

Macmillan moved uncomfortably in his chair – only momentarily but Steven noticed.

'There were a couple of other things,' Macmillan said, making as if to get up.

Steven didn't move and Macmillan sank slowly back down. 'All right,' he said, 'we shouldn't have secrets from each other.'

'Would you like me to go?' asked Jean.

'No, I wouldn't,' Macmillan responded – a bit too loudly for Jean who was startled. 'No, I wouldn't,' he repeated more softly. 'You are an invaluable member of our team and contribute to it greatly.'

'Thank you, Sir John.'

'The Home Secretary's main reason for calling the meeting was to inform us that Mrs Lillian Leadbetter has gone missing.'

'The MP who broke the Moorlock Hall story?'

'Yes.'

'She was treated pretty shabbily by her fellow MPs when they discovered the public didn't give a damn and the press followed suit,' said Steven.

'Exactly, said Macmillan. 'Her husband says that she was angry at first but then became depressed, especially when colleagues started avoiding her and it began to dawn on her that her career might be over, just when she'd been led to believe that promotion was on the cards and a glittering tomorrow was about to unfold before her.'

'Poor woman,' said Jean.

'Don't feel too sorry for her,' said Steven, 'the whole thing was about her career, just as it is for those avoiding her now.'

'Oh, Steven,' said Jean.

'Sadly, he's right,' said Macmillan. 'The woman left a trail of wreckage behind her in her quest for advancement. She destroyed the career of medical director, George Groves, without a second thought,'

'How long has she been missing?' asked Steven.

'Three days,' said Macmillan, 'and just before you say that's not long, the Home Secretary called the meeting to appraise us of events in case things should turn out badly and there was a press frenzy.'

'What does missing mean exactly?' Steven asked.

'Her husband came home and found her gone, no note.'

'Car?'

'She'd taken her car but no overnight bag – or any clothes as far as he could see although her briefcase had gone – but he says that it might have been in the car anyway. She was a bit careless about leaving it there.'

'I take it someone brought up the possibility of suicide?'

'Her husband was adamant that she wasn't suicidal. He agreed that she'd been very low, but she'd been getting back to being angry again and was determined to "show these bastards" as she put it.'

Steven thought for few moments before asking, 'Did he know what she meant by that?'

'He didn't elaborate, why do you ask?'

'I was just wondering if it had been an empty threat or if she actually had some plan of action to get back at those she felt had wronged her.'

'What could she do?' asked Jean.

'Who knows . . . a couple of barrels of gunpowder in the boot of the car and little boys could be celebrating Lillian Leadbetter Day in centuries to come. Penny for the Lillian, mister.'

Macmillan shot Steven a look that discouraged further black humour.

'Maybe she's gone to see her sister in Wales?' Jean suggested, feeling the diplomatic need to move the conversation on.

'Has she got a sister in Wales?' asked Macmillan.

'Er, I don't actually know, Sir John,' I was just sort of making a general suggestion as it's only been three days and there may be a perfectly innocent reason for Mrs Leadbetter's absence.'

'Quiet,' Macmillan agreed, 'and we have plenty of other things to keep us occupied. Any progress?'

TWENTY-TWO

'You did well,' said Macmillan when Steven had finished telling him what Jane Lincoln and her friend had come up with, but we're sailing ever closer to the wind by withholding information from the US police.'

Steven was tempted to point out that the American police actually had the information in front of their noses but failed to see it, but didn't. He knew Macmillan was right.

'It's just a question of how we go about it,' said Macmillan. 'Our own investigation is important too.'

'I think we should get as much information as we can to further our investigation before handing anything over. I don't honestly think we are delaying anything. If I were to notice something odd in the photographs next week instead of last week . . . would it really make any difference to a police investigation?'

'I suppose when you put it that way . . .' conceded Macmillan. 'What did you have in mind for the time being?'

'Dorothy,' said Steven. 'I'd like to tackle her head on, maybe even tell her everything we know and see what happens.

'Light blue touch paper and retire immediately,' said Jean, remembering advice that used to be printed on firework wrappings.

'That would be taking a step there's no coming back from,' said Macmillan. 'We must be able to see a clear gain before we risk it.' He looked to Steven to make the case.

'We should be able to establish whether or not she had any direct involvement in the deaths of Paul and Carrie. If it turns out that she had, we immediately hand the whole lot over to the U.S. police and inform our own police of what's been going on. As a *quid pro quo*, we could ask the US cops if they might give us anything they come up with on Father Crossan.'

'You've obviously given this some thought,' said Macmillan, 'and if you conclude that she's not guilty of direct involvement?'

'We ask her what was going on between her and Crossan. Why was he in the lab after the fire? What were they arguing about?

'Well,' said Macmillan, 'You seem to have covered all the bases as our American friends might say, wouldn't you agree, Jean?'
'Absolutely.'
'I think we can risk one more week.'

Steven decided it was too late to tackle Dorothy; he'd do that in the morning. In the meantime, he would go over to see Lukas in the labs in Crompton Lane to warn him that his services were about to be needed again.

'Are you telling me that you've come up with Barrowman's missing data?'

'We're hoping so.'

Steven told him about the secret Post Office box system.

'Hey! John Le Carré stuff,' Lukas exclaimed. 'Is the exchange going to be made on London Bridge at midnight?'

'We think a sorting office somewhere in south west London is more likely,' said Steven. 'MI5 are coming to the party too.' He went on to tell Lukas of the agreement that all material was to be shared on site. 'Can you bring along everything you might need to make copies from a range of data sources?'

'No problem. What's between you and Five, I thought we're all on the same side?'

'We think Five, or more likely Porton Down, have been working on the same thing Barrowman has and maybe they'd like to keep it all to themselves.'

'For reasons connected with defence of the realm,' Lukas said with the merest suggestion of sarcasm.

'What else?'

'OK, I've got the picture, but what happens then?'

'I'm not with you,' Steven confessed.

'We both leave with the data. Presumably you'd like me to examine it and interpret it if I can?'

'There's no one better.'

'But from what you've said it sounds like it's some sort of race. You don't think there might be . . . interference?' I mean, if Five really doesn't want to share Barrowman's data . . .'

'Sir John obtained an assurance from the Home Secretary herself that no such "interference" would be tolerated,' said Steven. 'Sci-Med is off limits to the intelligence services.'

'A comfort,' said Lukas, 'but maybe I should increase our fire insurance cover just in case a freak lightning storm should strike the area.'

'Wouldn't do any harm,' agreed Steven, 'nor would making some extra copies of everything to be kept at an undisclosed location.'

Before leaving for Capital University in the morning, Steven sent a text to Jane Lincoln to warn her he would be coming, but not to see her. He planned to interview Dorothy.

'I take it you're her to see Jane,' said Dorothy Lindstrom when she saw him appear in the lab. She said so without smiling and Steven replied in the same way, 'No, Professor, it's you I'd like to speak to.'

For a moment, it looked as if Dorothy might dig in her heels to make a point, but Steven's unsmiling countenance changed her mind. 'If you can just give me a moment.'

'Of course.'

Dorothy finished briefing the student she was with and invited Steven in to her office. She parked herself behind her desk as if establishing the rules of the game and invited him to sit with a wave of her open palm. Before he did so, Steven challenged the rules by taking out his ID and laying it open on the desk. He informed Dorothy that this was a formal interview, he was not interviewing her under caution, although he had the right to do so and, if she preferred, they could continue at a local police station.

Dorothy's eyes opened wide in amazement. 'Good heavens, couldn't we just talk?' she asked.

'Professor Lindstrom, I have reason to believe that the fire which took the lives of two of your young colleagues at Yale University may not have been an accident. I think there's a very real chance that they were murdered.'

Dorothy searched for words. 'But this is . . . an outrageous suggestion,' she stammered. 'It was an accident . . . a tragic accident . . . the fire department, the police . . . they all agreed it was an accident.'

'They did,' Steven agreed, 'but they could have been wrong.'

'But why? Why would anyone want to kill Paul and Carrie?'

'To make sure what they had discovered would not be made public.'

Dorothy reacted by staring down at her desk.

'You weren't happy with their findings either, were you, Professor?'

'It's true I found their conclusions . . . very difficult to accept.'

'To the point of preventing their publication.'

Dorothy shook her head as if dismissing a ridiculous suggestion. 'That's going too far,' she said. 'I . . . we all had to be absolutely sure before allowing such findings to be made public. Paul and Carrie were young; they were impatient and impetuous; they gave no thought to the possible repercussions of what they were intent on announcing.'

'So, you put a stop to that.'

Dorothy took two or three deep breaths before saying quietly, 'I suppose you could say that. I just needed time to be sure. We all had to be sure.'

'Did you know they were repeating their experiments in the evening in the hope of convincing you they were right?'

'Of course, I did.'

'But you didn't want to know.'

'They were rushing, doing the same thing all over again in the same way, that's not what was needed.'

'So, you murdered them to put a stop to it.'

'No, a thousand times no,' Dorothy spluttered, shocked to the core. 'They were my colleagues, my friends, brilliant young minds. I wanted them to slow down, think things through and use a different approach to asking the same questions.'

'They thought you were blocking their findings for your own selfish reasons.'

'If by "selfish reasons" you mean my faith, you're right, that has always been very important to me. I certainly didn't want it damaged by findings which subsequently turned out to be flawed. I didn't want to hide the truth, I just had to be sure it was the truth.'

'Outside your lab . . . who knew about the findings?'

'No one.'

'You didn't tell anyone at all?'

Steven noticed a slight flicker in her eyes before she repeated her answer. 'Are you . . . absolutely sure?'

'I was deeply troubled,' said Dorothy. 'I . . . I did unburden myself at confession, but that is sacrosanct. It's not the same as telling someone.'

Steven thought privately it was exactly the same but asked, 'Who took your confession, Professor?'

'Bishop Charles Stanley.'

'Was he the cleric who spoke at the Yale conference on human behaviour?'

Surprise registered on Dorothy's face. 'Yes, we have been friends for some time. How did you know about that meeting?'

Steven told her that Neil Tyler had been present at the conference.

'I see. Bishop Stanley and I both believe that there is no need for science and religion to be at war with each other. They have more in common than most care to admit.'

Your post-doc, Paul Leighton, openly accused you of blocking the publication of his work at that meeting.'

'He did,' Dorothy responded quickly. 'Paul was upset, he was a young man in a hurry to receive scientific acclaim, without subjecting himself to rigorous examination from all angles.'

'And Carrie?'

'Paul could be very persuasive. He probably convinced her she could be the next Marie Curie.'

Steven relaxed his demeanour: he believed what he was hearing. 'So, Professor, if you weren't involved in the deaths, who was?'

'I can't believe anyone was. I'm still convinced it was an accident, an awful accident.'

'A priest came to see you at the university a few days after the fire, who was he?'

Dorothy paused as if wondering where Steven was heading. 'Father Liam Crossan.'

Steven was forced to prompt for more. 'The priest at your local church?'

Dorothy shook her head. She did it absent-mindedly as if thinking about something else, but when she became aware that Steven was waiting patiently, she said, 'Bishop Stanley asked him to come and see me. He was worried about my state of mind and thought I might benefit from counselling.'

Steven noted a slight edge creep into her voice. 'And did you?' he asked.

'No . . . Father Crossan came across as a friendly, charming man, but, after a short conversation, it became apparent that he was more interested in my future plans than in my then state of mind . . .'

Steven was excited by the comment, but concentrated on not showing it.

'When I told him that I intended to pursue the research Paul and Carrie had been engaged in by using an alternative approach, he tried to dissuade me. At first, he said that he understood that my faith must have been shaken by what had happened, but it would recover and perhaps it would be for the best if I moved away from that type of research altogether. When I told him I was determined to pursue the truth and that I owed that to Paul and Carrie . . . he became quite aggressive and insisted that I would only end up damaging the church I loved . . . I should reconsider . . . and desist.'

'I see,' said Steven. He could see that Dorothy was now thinking what he was thinking.

'Oh, God, surely not . . .' she murmured. 'He's a priest!'

Steven considered calling a halt, but then risked one last prod. 'Tell me about Bishop Stanley.'

The gamble worked. Dorothy escaped from the agony of suspicion to concentrate on her friendship with the bishop.

'He was my rock when I was in the USA. It's not easy being a scientist and keeping a strong faith. Charles is very old school and often disagrees with what he sees as pandering to popular taste. Despite the dangers of defying papal authority, he continues to hold mass in Latin. He saw that as a great unifying factor; you could experience the same service all over the world and feel equally at home attending mass in Paraguay or wherever as you would in Rome. He regarded saying mass in the language of the country as divisive populist rubbish. I agreed with him.'

'A man of strong conviction,' said Steven.

Dorothy gave Steven a suspicious look.

Before she could mount any kind of pre-emptive defence of her friend, Steven asked, 'What was his connection to Father Crossan?'

'I don't know.'

'Presumably they knew each other if your friend asked him to come and see you and offer counselling. Was he part of some official support group for VIP Catholics?'

'VIP?' Dorothy exclaimed.

'Well, as you pointed out yourself, it's unusual for a high-profile scientist to be a committed Christian or to follow any faith for that matter. You would be seen as an important ally – witness the Yale meeting where you and the bishop spoke in supportive style instead of knocking lumps out of each other.'

'I suppose.'

'At some stage soon, I am going to have to hand over what I've come up with to the American police,' said Steven.

Dorothy pursed her lips but said, 'Of course, it's the right thing to do. I just feel for Paul and Carrie's parents; coming to terms with a horrific accident must have been bad enough, but murder . . .'

On the spur of the moment Steven decided on a course of action he might have difficulty explaining later, but it felt right. He said, 'I could delay for a while longer . . . or maybe even indefinitely.'

'Why would you do that?' Shock had reduced Dorothy's voice to a whisper.

'To give you time to contact your friend the bishop and ask him about Liam Crossan, you want to know who he is and what he is . . . and if he stalls, you want to know exactly why he discussed the substance of your confession with him.'

Dorothy seemed stunned, but after long consideration, she nodded and said quietly, 'Very well.'

* * *

'You did what?' John Macmillan exclaimed when Steven told him what he'd done. 'Have you taken leave of your senses? This is a matter for the American police not Sci-Med. It's their job to trace this Crossan character and find out what's been going on and bring him to justice if that's warranted.'

Steven waited until Macmillan's anger had subsided a little before saying, 'I don't think the American police will be able to do anything at all.'

'I'm waiting,' said Macmillan.

'They'll have absolutely nothing to go on in the way of solid evidence.'

'They'll see what you saw in the photographs when you point it out to them.'

'And they may well agree there's a strong possibility the pair were drugged, but they won't be able to prove it. It's too late. Again, Crossan was with them in the restaurant but there's no evidence he drugged them. He left the restaurant with them but there's no evidence he went back to the lab with them and there's no evidence anyone started the fire deliberately.'

Macmillan looked as if he was facing up to an unpleasant truth as did Jean Roberts who had remained silent throughout.

'We think we know what happened. We're even pretty sure, but we'll never be able to prove it and neither will anyone else,' said Steven.

'The police will find this Crossan character,' said Macmillan.

'And maybe even question him as a murder suspect, which he'll deny, calling it outrageous and demanding to know what possible motive he could have had: he's a priest, not a killer.'

'And that will be the end of it,' said Jean, 'It does sound ridiculous when you look at it all that way.'

'Whereas . . . it's the motive that *we* are really interested in,' said Steven. 'We think Crossan killed the two Americans to prevent their findings being made public and he didn't do that as some unbalanced lone wolf. He was known to Bishop Charles Stanley and sent to 'counsel' Dorothy Lindstrom, but really to dissuade her from continuing her line of research. This morning, after talking to Dorothy, I thought her friendship with the bishop might make her more successful in uncovering Crossan's background connections than the police might be . . . That's why I took the decision I did.'

Jean gave Steven an encouraging glance while Macmillan contemplated a portion of humble pie. Eventually, he said, I'm sorry I jumped down your throat, Steven, I should have known better after all these years.'

'Nothing to be sorry for, John, you've always had the best interests of Sci-Med at heart.

'So have you.'

'God, I think I'm going to cry,' said Jean, making light of the whole thing. Coffee anyone?'

TWENTY-THREE

Dorothy Lindstrom cleared her throat nervously as she waited for her transatlantic call to connect.

'Bishop Stanley's secretary.'

'Hello, this is Professor Dorothy Lindstrom calling from London, England, I'd like to speak to Charles please.'

'One moment please professor, I'll see if he's free.'

'Dorothy? What a wonderful surprise,' came the familiar booming voice, 'I was just thinking about you the other day, how are you?'

Dorothy had to swallow again before replying, 'I'm well, thank you Charles, I have a question for you.' She had to hold the receiver away from her ear as booming laughter threatened her hearing before Stanley said, 'I hope I can answer it if it merits a transatlantic call.'

'It concerns Father Liam Crossan.'

No laughter this time. 'What about him?' came the flat question.

'Who is he and what is he?'

'I thought he might be able to help you come to terms with the loss of your young people, Dorothy. It was clear you were taking it very badly – and understandably so, it was tragic. Father Crossan is a skilled counsellor, trained in helping people through difficult times in their lives.'

'He wanted to put a stop to my research, Charles,' said Dorothy, biting her lip afterwards.

'I'm sorry you see it that way, Dorothy, maybe you took it the wrong way, he probably thought it would do you good to get away from everything for a bit, re-charge your batteries, that sort of thing.'

'No,' said Dorothy decisively. 'He wanted an end to my research, full stop. You say he is a skilled counsellor, attached to what, where? Where exactly does he fit into the Church, Charles?'

'Why are you asking all these things, Dorothy?'

'Because I want to know the answers.' Dorothy put staccato on her words: her nerves had disappeared. She wasn't going to be fobbed off.

'All right . . . I admit I haven't been completely honest with you . . .'

The pause became so long that Dorothy started to think the connection had been lost.

'It can be no surprise to you to hear that I am unashamedly conservative in my views. There are a number of us within the Church who feel that way. We stand for the old values and spurn the fashion for making constant concessions to the latest pressure group to emerge from the woodwork. Father Crossan belongs to a group of fellow sympathisers who go under the Latin name, *Fidei Defensores*. They regard themselves as defenders of the faith, the true faith. It is their sworn duty to protect the Church from outside threats wherever and whenever they might occur.'

'And they saw me and my group as a threat?'

'A possible challenge.'

'After you told them about what my research group was working on.'

'And why you were deeply upset. They knew you were a practising Catholic and hoped they might be able to persuade you to . . . change tack.'

'I'm also a practising scientist, I seek truth wherever it takes me.'

'I'm truly sorry you're upset, Dorothy, I understand you have to be true to yourself and your principles. I can only apologise for the slight deception on my part . . .'

Slight deception? . . . He doesn't know, the man doesn't know, he doesn't know Paul and Carrie were murdered, He doesn't understand what he did. He betrayed me and my confession and he calls it a slight deception.

She didn't know what to think or what to say so she said nothing and ended the call. She sat staring at the receiver as she was slowly surrounded by the ashes of a former friendship and maybe the ruins of a crumbling faith.

When she had recovered some composure, Dorothy called Steven and gave him the information he'd asked for. She did it as briefly as possible and without further comment before telling her staff she wasn't feeling well and going home.

Steven passed on the information to Jean who, to his surprise, appeared to recognise the name *Fidei Defensores*.

'You know . . . this begins to make sense,' she murmured. 'I haven't been able to trace Father Crossan on any clerical list: I was beginning to think he must be going under a false name, or even someone pretending to be a priest, but now I understand why he's not on any official list. *Fidei Defensores* is not recognised by the Roman Catholic Church. They're reputed to be a pretty right-wing lot and not averse to bending the rules to achieve their aims.'

'Which are?'

'To protect the reputation of what they see as the true church at all costs and stop its erosion as they see it. You won't find abortion, contraception and gay marriage on their to-do list.'

'They do the dirty work and the church pretends to know nothing at all about them?'

'Allegedly,' said Jean.

'And now they may have added murder to their repertoire,' said Steven, 'I'm impressed, how come you know about them?'

'I'm asking myself the same question,' said Jean. 'I must have come across them recently when I was looking for something else.'

'If anyone can cross-reference her thoughts, you can,' said Steven. 'It'll come to you.'

'As will arthritis and old age,' said John Macmillan, emerging from his office. 'What news?'

Steven told him about Dorothy Lindstrom's phone call. 'She must have contacted the bishop as soon as I left her. She was obviously upset to think he had betrayed her confidence, but didn't think he was directly involved in anything Crossan planned to do.'

'I trust Professor Lindstrom didn't mention anything about your suspicions surrounding the fire deaths to the bishop?'

Steven said not. 'I asked her not to. She said she was pretty sure he believed that Crossan was just going to reason with her and try to persuade her to change the direction of her research.'

'Poor woman,' said Macmillan. 'She's had a lot to cope with recently.

'I've got it,' Jean exclaimed, 'I've remembered where I came across the name. It was when I was looking for information on the lawyers representing the people who are funding Professor Lindstrom's research group. I discovered the firm was retained for the defence of a number of priests charged with the sexual abuse of a large number of children back in the seventies and eighties. No one was convicted.'

'Why not?' asked Macmillan.

'The trial collapsed. Officially, the defence based its case on so much time having passed – thirty years or more. Memories could be unreliable and there were serious inconsistencies in the stories of the witnesses. Unofficially, the prosecution noticed that many of the inconsistencies had appeared rather suddenly as had a certain financial improvement in the circumstances of a number of the would-be leading witnesses for the prosecution.'

'They'd been got at.'

'Nothing was proved along these lines but there was suspicion surrounding the involvement of a certain group of priests, ostensibly there to provide comfort and support, which I remember was called . . . *Fidei Defensores*.'

'Well done, Jean,' said Steven.

'Absolutely, Macmillan agreed. 'Although I'm not sure if I should thank you for just opening a great big can of worms.'

'Really?' Jean asked.

'We have the link,' said Steven. '*Fidei Defensores* were involved in blocking the Lindstrom group's research in the US and now we know the same legal firm that fronted their defence of the paedophile priests are fronting the funding of Dorothy Lindstrom's research here in the UK and monitoring it, presumably with a view to blocking it when the time seems right. John was quite correct, the people coming up with the money are not scientists.'

'But a small group of extremists couldn't possibly afford to do that,' said Jean.

'Exactly,' said Macmillan. 'That's where the can of worms comes in. Their church may have disowned them publicly . . . but.'

'Oh dear,' said Jean.

'They're not averse to putting a few bucks their way,' said Steven.

'More than a few in this case,' said Macmillan.

'You know, I just can't understand what all the fuss is about,' said Tally when Steven told her what had been going on. 'Even if science provides incontrovertible evidence that there is no such thing as the soul, the self or the individual and we're all really just the result of a bunch of chemicals reactions . . . society won't collapse. Most people will choose not to believe it.'

'How can they if the naked truth is put before their eyes?'

'The way they do at the moment!' Tally insisted. 'People will continue to believe what they want to believe; that's always been the case. The Pope isn't going to appear on the balcony in St Peters Square to announce to the masses it's all been a terrible mistake, is he? BBC Radio two isn't going to be broadcast from minarets instead of the morning call to prayer.'

'You have a point,' Steven conceded, 'but it's not the response of individuals I'm concerned about. 'Religion will continue to have its adherents as it always has. Darwin's theory of evolution will continue to have a tough time in certain parts of the USA. Space and time can warp all it wants to but mom will still be up in heaven looking down.'

'So, what is it you're so worried about?'

'It's not the public's view of religion I'm worried about, it's the massive organisation behind it. All these people, all that infrastructure, all that money, power and influence, they won't like it at all . . . It will be seen as a threat to their very existence and they will react accordingly.'

'As you and your colleagues have just found out,' said Tally with a slight shiver, but it's not as if the men in robes have large armies to call on.'

'Think again, Tally, these people influence millions of others. For many, they are infallible, their word is law. Their followers will do as they are told.'

'A scary thought.'

'Scary is the word.'

Tally hesitated before changing the subject and asking, 'Have you been to see Lucy Barrowman?'

Steven shook his head.

'Don't you think you should?'

'I've thought about it . . . and decided against. Steven grimaced in discomfort before continuing, 'However much I care about what has happened to her – and I do care – there is nothing I can do to help in any practical sense. I could take flowers and say how sorry I am, ask if there's anything I can do, make all the right noises, but the truth is I was part of her whole nightmare, I was instrumental in starting the whole damn thing off. My continual turning up would remind her of that and stop it fading. I don't want to interfere with the healing process. As for the latest attack, I find it beyond belief that anyone could be so unlucky and wouldn't begin to know what to say.

'You really have thought about this, haven't you,' said Tally.

'Do you have anything to say about it?'

'I love you.'

TWENTY-FOUR

'Only in the UK,' stormed John Macmillan.

Jean Roberts smiled sympathetically, 'Is Something wrong, Sir John?' she asked. 'Anything I can do?'

'The bugger's on holiday.'

'Which particular "bugger" are we talking about, sir, asked Jean, tongue in cheek.

Macmillan was overcome by embarrassment. 'Sorry, Jean, the fellow who is supposed to be at the end of the PO box number trail is on holiday. Apparently, he has a *bolt hole* in Scotland. He uttered the words with distaste. 'The stress of working for the bl… the Post Office seems to require a bolt hole and no one knows where it is.'

'Who is working on it?

'The police, MI5, Special Branch, you name it. They're combing the country.'

Jean had an image of horizontal lines of policemen carrying out a fingertip search of the Scottish Highlands and had to turn away.

'It's not funny, Jean,' said Macmillan who had noticed anyway. 'Have you seen Steven this morning?'

'I think he was planning to see Neil Tyler, he's been working on the identity of the Lindstrom funders too.'

'The Home Secretary would like to see both of us this afternoon.'

'I'll make sure he knows.'

Steven and Tyler had arranged to meet in Green Park at Tyler's request, but only if the weather permitted and it did. It wasn't overly warm but the sky was clear with only a slight breeze bringing a chill to the air.

'This was one of my wife's favourite places,' said Tyler 'She always said she felt she was at the beating heart of England.'

'It is nice,' Steven agreed, 'and next to all the levers of power.'

'Everything that keeps the country running like a well-oiled seagull,' said Tyler.

Steven was glad of the joke. He had feared that things might get a bit maudlin.

'Any luck?' he asked.

'I figured my best chance of getting to the providers of Dorothy Lindstrom's funding was through my legal eagle employers, Scarman and co. It turned out that I wasn't the only one taking an interest in them, which was a bit of luck as it turned out. I recognised one of the investigators as a forensic accountant I met a few years ago when we were both on the trail of terrorist funding flowing into the Middle East.'

'I'm hoping you're not going to tell me that Islamic terrorists are funding Dorothy Lindstrom,' said Steven.

'Far from it,' Tyler replied. 'Marco was looking for money haemorrhaging from the Vatican.'

Steven looked at him as if he couldn't believe his ears but desperately wanted to. 'I think this is where I shout bingo and jump up in the air,' he said.

'Glad that makes someone happy,' said Tyler, waiting for an explanation.

'No, go on,' said Steven.

'Apparently there's a bit of a rift going on in the Vatican at the moment. A number of cardinals are being less than respectful to his holiness because they don't like the way the church is moving. They would prefer to see a return to a more traditional approach as opposed to what they see as leftist-leaning anathema.'

'Ah, the poor are all very well, but let's keep them in their place.'

'Quite. Money has been going walkabout and the fear is that it's being used to fund the ambitions of the rebel cardinals.'

'Wonderful,' said Steven. 'He told Tyler all about Father Liam Crossan and *Fidei Defensores*.

'Maybe I'll join you in a jump up and down,' said Tyler.

They exchanged a high five.

'First time I've done one of these,' said Steven.

'Me too.'

'Well, I think we can agree, Vatican money is funding Dorothy Lindstrom's research,' said Steven. 'officially or unofficially and, in our case, we know why.'

'That just leaves Barrowman's secret to uncover.'

'And we're getting closer.

Steven got Jean's text as he left Green Park. He acknowledged it and saw that he had plenty time to grab something to eat at The Moorings before heading back to the Home Office. It had just gone noon and that meant that there would still be room at the outside tables to sit and watch the river for a while. He felt good, Neil and Jean between them had come up with the evidence that the Vatican was involved and the fact that it was through the actions of an unsanctioned group rather than the real deal was the icing on the cake. It was going to make it so much easier (for others!) to deal with and probably put an end to without undue repercussion. It would be in everyone's interest to cover it all up.

There would of course be problems for Dorothy Lindstrom when her funding suddenly stopped, but letting it be known to Dorothy that it had been the British intelligence services who had stopped her being financed through conventional government sources should provide her with enough ammunition to turn such funding right back on again. Life was looking much better.

Steven had just asked John Macmillan what the meeting was going to be about when Macmillan's phone rang. When he'd finished taking the call he turned to Steven and said, 'They've found Mr Simon Stratford.'

'Good . . . who's he?'

'Sorry, he's the missing link in the PO box number saga. They found him in a cottage on the Moray Firth coast in the north east of Scotland . . . or at least that's where he was. He's now on his way to Lossiemouth where the RAF are going to bring him back to London. I hope he had a light lunch.'

'Couldn't he just have given us the information we need?'

'Seemingly not, there's procedure, he insists he should be there.'

'Fair enough,' said Steven, wondering how long it might take the UK to launch a Cruise missile and then thinking that might be a good thing anyway.

Steven suspected that the Home Secretary had called the meeting in response to what Macmillan had already told her about the possible murder of Dorothy's two post-docs in the US and what possible dangers lay here. He was not wrong. She had invited along two senior intelligence officers, a shadow cabinet minister and a number of church leaders to discuss the 'current situation with particular regard to epigenetic research'.

'The current situation is highly volatile,' she announced, but I am determined that government funded science will not be permitted to openly attack religion – any religion, and religion – any religion, will not be permitted to deliberately interfere in scientific research.

Steven interrupted. 'With respect, Home Secretary, the situation is perhaps not as volatile as you feared. We have today established that attempts made in the USA to interfere with Professor Lindstrom's research were the work of a small but powerful dissenting faction within the Roman Catholic Church – a group called *Fidei Defensores*. The same group are behind what was until now the anonymous funding of Professor Lindstrom's group in the UK. Their plan was to monitor it and put a stop to things should it come up with anything not to their liking. While it's true that Vatican money is being used, it seems certain that this has been siphoned off illegally by senior figures within the group – a number of cardinals with extreme traditional views. The Vatican are currently investigating this. I can provide you with details at some other time if you'd like.'

'Well, thank you, Dr Dunbar. It's not the first time Her Majesty's Government has had to cause to thank you for your efforts. We are most grateful.'

Steven nodded and sat down. He noticed Macmillan looking pleased; he loved it when Sci-Med looked good.

The Home Secretary seemed relieved that resolution had been brought to a complicated situation and, probably more importantly, it could be left to the church to sort out its own mess. No mention was made of the UK intelligence services' earlier interference in research funding, but Steven decided to leave that to Dorothy to bring up. The Home Secretary limited what more she had to say to warning science and religion to keep out of each other's way and the meeting was over.

'Mr Stratford has arrived in London,' said Jean when Steven and Macmillan got back to the office. An RAF Typhoon delivered him . . . I understand his stomach will be forwarded later, poor man.

'I take it the police are taking him directly to his sorting office?' asked Macmillan.

'Where they will wait until all concerned from Sci-Med and MI5 have turned up.'

'I'll call Lukas,' said Steven.

Despite having been allowed to tidy himself up, Simon Stratford managed to look as if he had been put through a wash cycle and tumble-dried. His repeated attempts to flatten his hair failed miserably and tugging at his tie did little to straighten it. He made a valiant attempt to display gravitas when he said, 'I understand you are trying to trace material sent to a confidential box number, one which I am sworn to secrecy about.'

'We are.'

'Your ready access to an RAF Typhoon FGR4 Euro-fighter suggests to me that you possibly have the right to do so.'

Steven and Lukas exchanged glances. Stratford did actually look like a plane spotter.

'We have. How does the system work, Mr Stratton?' asked Steven.

'We are a main sorting office; if something comes in addressed to a secure box number care of our sorting office I will check the number to find out whether it is to be redirected to another main sorting office via a new box number or kept here in storage until claimed. I will have no idea of where it came from other than it would be another UK main sorting office. If it's to be stored, it will remain here until collected by someone giving the appropriate password.

'How do you decide the password?'

'It's given to me when I check the box number.'

'How do you do that?'

'Online.'

'I thought this was a Second World War system,' exclaimed Macmillan.

'I suppose we've moved with the times.'

'Are you saying that this system is still used regularly?' Steven asked.

'Not infrequently.'

'Is anything being stored here at the moment, Mr Stratford?' This was the big question that stopped everyone breathing.

'There was when I left for my holiday.'

'Are you saying that someone could have collected it while you were away?'

'Oh yes, at this stage it's just a case of someone picking up a parcel by giving a password. I would give the password to my deputy before I left.'

'But he knows nothing about the box numbers?'

'You've got it.'

Steven felt like he'd just completed the Times crossword. 'Could you check please?'

'This way.'

Macmillan, Steven and the MI5 agent followed Stratford into his office where he used his keys to open a cupboard door, behind which stood a large floor-standing safe. He entered the combination and swung back the door.

'Still here,' said Stratford. He brought out two packages, one large, one small. 'I will need receipts.'

'Of course,' muttered Macmillan.

'Official Government receipts,' Stratford reminded him.

Steven picked up the smaller package and looked to the MI5 man who nodded. Steven opened it to reveal a number of computer disks and four memory sticks. 'I think we're in business,' he said. Turning to the others, he said, 'You folks can set up your gear.'

Lukas and the woman accompanying the MI5 agent readied their copying and scanning gear while Steven finished emptying the package of several sheets of folded A4 paper. 'Barrowman's notes on Malcolm Lawler,' he announced to the others. 'Oh, happy day.'

Macmillan took Stratford aside to explain to him that there would be an official presence at his sorting office until such times as someone came to pick up the packages that were currently being opened. 'Either Special Branch or intelligence officers,' he said. 'They will be in plain clothes and armed but it's important that everyone behave as normal and go about their business.''

Steven meanwhile had finished opening the larger package. It contained a number of chemicals contained in large bottles, small ones, phials, packets, tubes and all with long sounding names that meant little to Steven or apparently to the others when they took a look and shook their heads.

'What do we do with these?'

'Make a note of the names,' said Steven thinking ahead. 'We can investigate later.' He turned to the MI5 man and said, 'I suggest we re-pack the box and leave it here. If someone comes to pick anything up, Mr Stratford can stall by giving him this rather than saying that there's nothing. It should start a discussion about a missing second package and will give the plain clothes guys more time to react.'

Steven drove back to the Crompton Lane labs with Lukas; he was anxious to get a first look at what they had recovered.

'What did you think about the chemicals?' he asked, knowing full well that they would have meant something to Lukas even though he had shaken his head along with the others.

'Someone has a molecular biology lab,' Lukas replied. 'It looks like Barrowman must be in a position to carry on his research.'

'Bloody hell,' Steven muttered.

'Norma Kellerman would have known that too.'

'Who?'

'Norma Kellerman, the woman Five brought along, I've come across her before; she works at Porton Down.'

'Did she recognise you?'

'Oh, yes,' Lukas replied.

'Oh, well,' said Steven, 'good to be *transparent*.'

Both men smiled. They shared a sense of humour.

'First impressions?' Steven asked as Lukas went through Barrowman's notes, pausing every now and then to make reference to his computer screen and occasionally changing the input source to find what he wanted.

'This looks big, but it's going to take a while . . . maybe a long while. Barrowman has been able to assign function to large areas of what we've been calling junk DNA for years. Look at this section here . . . it doesn't code for proteins, but if you fold it this way and then that . . . and then do this . . . you get this configuration . . .' Lukas' fingers danced over the keyboard. 'which he claims can act as either a trigger or suppressor of these genes. It's a controller.'

'A switch?' Steven murmured.

'Let's not run before we can walk. 'I'll call you as soon as I figure out more.'

Tally was in bed reading when Steven got home. She put down her book and smiled as Steven lay down beside her fully clothed. 'You smell like a lab,' she complained.

'That's just where I've been.'

'Can I take it from your cheesy grin that you've had a good day?'

'You certainly can. Want to hear about it?'

'Sure do.'

TWENTY-FIVE

In the morning, Steven controlled his urge to drive directly over to Crompton Lane to find out how things were going, knowing that Lukas needed time to go through Barrowman's results and wouldn't welcome someone standing over him while he worked. He knew that they weren't in a race with MI5, but there was that feeling about it when, in fact, it was more complicated. It didn't matter who managed to interpret Barrowman's findings first as long as both of them succeeded in doing it. Things might start to get awkward if Five succeeded and Lukas didn't because Five's findings would almost certainly be smothered under a security blanket for as long as it took Five and probably Porton Down to assess any discovery in 'defence' terms. Success for Lukas would mean any important findings being added to scientific knowledge and made accessible to all.

Steven was beginning to relish the idea of a day off when his mind begged to differ – it pointed out he had things to do. Nothing needed urgent attention, but they still had to be done. Dorothy Lindstrom and Jane Lincoln had to be told about the extent of *Fidei Defensores'* activities both in the USA and here at home in the UK and how it would almost certainly lead to an immediate stop to funding when the leak to Vatican resources was plugged. He was still intent on advising Dorothy how they might be restored through revealing in the right circles that she knew who had blocked her Research Council funding at the outset. The Home Secretary could hardly lecture the churches about interfering in scientific research when she had done exactly that herself.

After mulling this over, Steven changed his mind. He wouldn't tell Dorothy about Five's involvement after all. Dorothy might be a fine scientist but she was no diplomat. John Macmillan was, and he knew the value of letting people work things out for themselves. He would ask John to right the wrong and look forward to hearing from him that the Home Secretary had expressed her gratitude for his suggestion and that Government funding would indeed be found to enable Professor Lindstrom to continue her exciting work. This would be preferable to Dorothy phoning the newspapers.

Although Steven had decided not to visit Lucy Barrowman, he still had an interest in finding out how much progress the police had made in catching her attacker. He was on the point of calling them when John Macmillan phoned him.

'Bloody Keystone Cops,' stormed Macmillan.

'What's happened, John?'

'He got away, that's what's happened. He turned up at the sorting office and he got away. Can you believe it?'

Steven had little choice. 'Was it Barrowman himself who turned up?'

'No, it was a postman.'

'I'm sorry?'

'A cheerful postman came into the office and gave the password. Special Branch's finest thought it was Barrowman dressed as a postman and pinned him to the floor. Turns out it was a real postman. A man in a car down the road had stopped him and offered him ten pounds to collect his parcels for him – said he was recovering from a knee operation and it was playing up.'

'And by the time they ran to the car it was gone?'

'Correct.'

'And it's not even the pantomime season,' said Steven.

'At least we have his data,' said Macmillan.

'Yep, all of us can have a bad day.'

For Steven, the feel-good factor of the day had completely disappeared, but he pressed on with his plans and phoned the police, asking to speak to the officer in charge of the Lucy Barrowman case. As soon as he heard Detective Inspector Morris speak he knew something was the matter. There was an apologetic tone to his voice.

'I'm sorry . . . I've been meaning to phone you,' said the DI.

'You've not made an arrest,' Steven suggested.

'I'm afraid not. To be quite frank we were hoping for some forensic help but somewhere along the line it went wrong.'

This was a new one on Steven. You either had forensic evidence or you didn't; it didn't "go wrong". 'In what way?'

'We got a DNA match but it was wrong.'

'You mean it was contaminated?'

'Yes, I suppose that's the word.'

Steven knew how sensitive modern methods for DNA fingerprinting were. Part of the process involved amplifying the tiniest trace found at the scenes of crime. Great care had to be taken that none of the investigators contaminated the scene with their own DNA.

'One of the officers?'

'No, actually . . . we matched it to er . . .Malcolm Lawler, which of course is impossible. He's been inside for years.'

Steven shuddered at the name.

'To be quite frank,' continued the DI, 'there must have been a cock-up at the lab. Samples from the first assault on Mrs Barrowman must have got mixed up with those taken from the second . . .'

'Where does Lawler's DNA come into it?' snapped Steven.

'Mrs Barrowman's husband had been to see Lawler on the day he attacked her. He probably had traces of Lawler's DNA on him which transferred during the assault . . . on to Mrs Barrowman and her clothes.'

'I see,' said Steven. It was the best he could do. A few skin cells would have been enough . . . that and, of course, the most appalling bad luck that they were picked up by the police forensic people.

'I'll keep you informed,' said the DI.

'Thanks.'

Steven fidgeted away the rest of the day, feeling that the whole world was against Sci-Med if not him personally. His earlier resolve not to interrupt Lukas weakened and finally gave way to a need to hear something positive. He drove over to Crompton Lane. His fear that Lukas might not have been too pleased to see him disappeared when he was met with a big smile and the words, 'This is amazing.'

'Tell me.'

'I know a lot of people think that junk DNA is there to stop too many mutations accumulating in the coding stuff – it takes the hits that life throws at it rather than the vital regions – and I'm sure they have a point, but when you think that over seventy percent of the human genome is what they're calling junk and has no function, well, you have to think . . .'

'And you think he's shown it's involved in switching mechanisms?'

'Yes.'

Steven smiled, but had the impression that Lukas was sitting on something else. 'Anything more you'd like to share?' he asked.

'Somewhere along the line Barrowman came across something he refers to as "a great danger". If I'm reading it right, he thinks there is one particular switch sequence which, if triggered the wrong way, can lead to absolute disaster. A number of genes are involved; some are turned on and others off.

'What sort of disaster?'

'His lab notes suggest that, if switched one way, you get evil incarnate, a personality devoid of all empathy and sympathy, no trace of decency, no vestige of what we like to call humanity. Barrowman actually refers to it as the Satan Switch in his notes.'

'Can I take it this is where Lawler comes into the picture?'

'Lawler has the capacity to control this switch at will.'

'Did Barrowman find out how he did it?'

'It's not recorded in his notes, but one of the disks is encrypted and I haven't found a way to crack it.'

'You've no idea yourself?' Steven asked.

'Come on,' laughed Lukas. 'I suspect people will be applying for five-year grants into the foreseeable future to figure that out if we can't get into that disk.'

'Do you think that's what happened to Barrowman himself, he inadvertently triggered the switch?'

'There's a long history of scientists trying out their discoveries on themselves,' said Lukas.

Steven considered for a moment then said, 'If this were all true, it would mean that every now and then in the normal way of things, a baby would be born with a mutation that causes the sequence to trigger the wrong way . . . and he or she would grow up with a psychopathic personality?'

'That's exactly what would happen in the normal way of things and what I was thinking as I read through the notes,' said Lukas. ''But . . .'

'But what?'

'Barrowman believes it's the other way around. He thinks that the evil state was the norm in early human beings and the switching mutation occurred to introduce decency and care and empathy and sympathy and so on.'

Steven felt stunned. 'He's suggesting that human beings are naturally evil but have mutated to become . . . better?'

'And stay that way unless the genome reverts to its original state, in which case you get a psychopath, not the other way around.'

'It sounds as if there was an ancient battle between the forces of good and evil and, in the end, good won?'

'As a broad general statement . . .'

'There's more?'

Barrowman goes on to speculate that the evil state is stronger than the mutated one: evil people are liable to be more powerful and are capable of exerting great influence over others. The ones we are aware of in society tend to be criminals who get caught committing horrific crimes and get locked up, but he suggests there are others.'

'Others?'

'Psychopaths who are clever and cunning enough to rise to the top in whatever field they choose to be in . . . including government, where they can exercise their power . . . to great and often horrifying effect.'

'You mean people like Hitler, Stalin, Pol Pot . . .'

'And throughout history, Attila the Hun . . . Caligula . . . Vlad the Impaler . . . Idi Amin . . . the list is endless. People who will do the unthinkable because they see nothing to stop them and can influence others to follow them without question.'

'Well, at least that answers my mother's question,' said Steven. 'She always used to ask, how do such awful people get into positions of power?'

'I don't think she's the only person to ask that,' said Lukas.

'If Barrowman threw the switch in himself it would suggest he knows how to do it: That's the knowledge the intelligence services and Porton Down will be after.'

'I can't argue with that,' said Lukas, 'much as I'd like to.'

'How do you think they will be getting on with analysing Barrowman's data?'

'Pretty well,' said Lukas. 'Barrowman kept good notes and has lots of data. It's not difficult to work your way through it.

'Pity,' said Steven, forced to imagine a city where the switch was thrown in an entire population and the resulting mayhem. 'You've been brilliant,' he said to Lukas.

Steven didn't know what to feel as he drove home. He had hoped to feel cheered by hearing how much Lukas had been able to decipher but the opposite was true. He felt as if he wasn't a real person at all, the real him was hidden under some kind of genetic sedation, as was everyone else . . . apart from creatures like Lawler. Tally would make sense of it, he decided. She was good at finding the common-sense view of all situations. He looked forward to being told to get over himself.

He glanced at his watch as he slowed and turned into the down slope to the entrance of the underground garage, deciding that Tally would probably be home. He parked the car and made for the stairs. The only thing blocking his way were two dead policemen.

Steven froze and stared at the tableau of death. He hadn't known the men personally, but had seen them often enough over the past week or so, they were part of Tally's protection detail; their throats had been cut.

Steven hurtled up the stairs, to find his fingers all thumbs as he fought against the effects of adrenaline rush to get his key in the lock. The door flew back and he stopped dead in his tracks. He waited until his breathing had subsided, took out the Glock from its holster and started moving through the flat slowly and silently. He completed the search; there was no sign of the killer . . . and no sign of Tally either.

Still breathing calmly but slightly irregularly, Steven put the pistol back in its holster and took out his phone. As he did so, he noticed the note lying on the table: it wasn't written in Tally's handwriting. He picked it up.

I want my stuff, Dunbar. Your woman will provide entertainment until I get it. Wait for a call.

Steven remembered that Barrowman had his mobile number from earlier times. He called the emergency number made available to all Sci-Med investigators engaged on live investigations and listed what he needed and what he wanted to happen. This was acknowledged without question. He asked that the police protection unit be informed sensitively that they had two officers down and where they could be found – it was too late for an ambulance – MI5 should be informed of the situation – CCTV footage covering that past two hours was to be made available for examination and John Macmillan was to be informed as was Jean Roberts. Both should be asked to return to the Home Office as quickly as possible. He called Lukas using the house phone and was relieved to find he was still in the lab. Without explanation, he asked what had happened to the original disks and memory sticks containing Barrowman's data.

'I've got them,' Lukas replied.

'And the notes?'

'Yes, them too.'

'Thank God. Barrowman's got Tally. He wants his data back.'

'Oh man, I'm so sorry. Just say where you want me to bring them.'

'The Home Office, we're all going to meet there.'

'On my way.'

The phone rang again as soon as Lukas had rung off, it was Macmillan. 'What's going on?'

'He's got Tally.'

The wail of sirens announced the imminent arrival of the police with two ambulances following behind. Steven looked out of the window, thinking again that there was no hurry for the ambulances as the awful image of the two dead officers added to the turmoil that filled his mind. He stared at his mobile, knowing that this was now his one link to Tally; he put it gently in his pocket. He went downstairs to speak to the policemen and saw that the senior man was the officer he'd spoken to when setting up protection for Tally. He was doing his job, issuing instructions, but was clearly upset. Steven read it his eyes when he came over to speak to him.

'I'm so sorry,' said Steven.

'They were good men.'

This was the wrong time for Steven to have this conversation. 'He's taken Tally.'

'Jesus Christ,' muttered the policeman. 'What a mess.'

'I've got to get to the Home Office,' said Steven, 'to decide what we're going to do.'

The policeman nodded. 'Of course.' He turned to look back at his two dead colleagues and said, 'These guys were the best. For what it's worth . . . there must have been more than one of them.'

TWENTY-SIX

Steven thought about what the policeman had said as he made his way to the Home Office. The man had just lost two of his close colleagues, probably friends, who had died suddenly and horribly, but somewhere among the grief would be the fact that they had failed to do their job. The had failed to protect Tally and that would add discomfort to the mix. The DI would want to minimise any damage to their reputation if he could. Could Barrowman really not have been alone? It seemed unthinkable to imagine he'd had an accomplice to murder, but the fact that he was still at large seemed ridiculous too. A wave of anger aimed at the police and MI5 threatened to challenge his judgement, but he rose above it. Any kind of emotion in the current situation would be counter-productive. He needed to be at his cool, calculating best – so why was a tear running down his cheek?

'Have you heard anything?' Macmillan asked as Steven entered the office to find everyone there except Lukas.

Steven said not.

'Time enough yet,' said Macmillan, making everyone wonder what that meant.

'The trace is on your phone,' said Jean before she handed him a new one with a new number. 'Everyone has a note of it. 'No one will call you on the old one.'

Lukas arrived, apologising for being last. He handed over the packages they had intercepted at the sorting office. 'I've done my best to re-pack everything the way it was. Maybe he'll think we haven't had a chance to look at anything yet. Not a lot of time has passed.'

Steven didn't believe that for a moment, but thanked him.

I suspect what he's really after is the one disk that is protected by encryption. I'm sorry, I haven't been able to crack it,' said Lukas.

Steven nodded, adding, 'Can't be helped.' This was for the benefit of anyone who was about to suggest they should give Barrowman a false one in place of it. That was a non-starter.

He let the police and intelligence services representatives have their say about what should happen before saying, 'There are a number of agendas present here. We all want Barrowman for our own reasons: a dead MI5 agent and two dead policemen have to be avenged, but the bastard has my lady and I want her back alive. That takes priority.'

There were no dissenting voices.

'Barrowman is a psychopath and a very clever man. I don't want anyone coming up with cunning plans designed to trap him – think what happened at the sorting office. He's been running rings round us so we will respect that while I do whatever he says to get Tally back. There will be no interference from anyone, absolutely none. I will keep Sir John and Jean advised and call on the Sci-Med back-up service if I need anything. Everyone else should stay out of it.'

'I understand how you must feel, doctor, but kidnap is really a matter for the police . . .'said the senior policeman present, but Macmillan shut him up with a look and the words, 'Not this time.'

Steven went home to his flat. He sat in his chair by the window, watching as the sky darkened. He held his phone lightly in his hand willing it to ring and he had pen and paper at his side ready to jot down instructions. The phone call when it came wasn't going to last long enough for anyone to trace the origin. He expected a simple directive, probably to call another number from another phone. He would comply.

The minutes passed . . . the hours passed . . . the stars came out and the call didn't come. Steven's angst was becoming unbearable . . . and then he worked it out. Barrowman was orchestrating his misery. He was torturing him by deliberately not calling, letting his own imagination do the job for him. 'Oh, Tally my love, he sighed . . . where are you . . .'

By two in the morning Steven had drunk so much coffee that his nerves were jangling. He paced up and down for close to thirty minutes before going through to the bedroom and throwing himself flat on the bed to lie in the darkness, allowing thoughts to come and go and reappear again in a varying order to form a changing mental tapestry which rivalled the flickering shadows on the ceiling as occasional car headlights passed along the street below . . . Macmillan's assertion that Barrowman had found somewhere secure . . . somewhere he wasn't alone . . . somewhere he felt so secure that he had started to think about science again. He wanted his data disks and a batch of chemicals . . . The forensics mix-up over Lucy Barrowman and the police failure to find her attacker, the disappearance of Lillian Leadbetter . . . and their current failure to find her either . . . the policeman's assertion that Barrowman hadn't been alone in carrying out the murder of his officers.

Steven suddenly sat bolt upright; his breathing had quickened to shallow, short breaths. He knew what was going on. He knew where Tally was.

He was surprised at how quickly Macmillan answered his home phone at that hour in the morning. 'Has he rung?' Macmillan asked.

'No, but I know where she is and I know where Barrowman is. They're in Moorlock Hall.'

'How on earth . . .'

'Barrowman must have gone there after killing the MI5 officer. Groves, the medical superintendent, wouldn't have known anything about that so he allowed him in, assuming it must have something to do with his research project. Barrowman was armed with the gun he had taken from the MI5 man and had the element of surprise on his side; he probably forced Grove to free Lawler and the pair of them took over the place after doing God knows what . . . Since then, they've been enjoying trips up to town in a staff car to leave business cards, pick up parcels . . . and assault Lucy Barrowman!' Steven exclaimed as he suddenly realised it could really have been Lawler who attacked her; it wasn't a forensic mistake. 'Oh my God.'

'Some other things make sense now,' said Macmillan. 'The Post Office box system must have been used by Moorlock Hall when it was still a secret. Groves must have told Barrowman and Lawler about it under duress and they've been using it to order in what they wanted.

'I can only imagine what they did to Groves to get the information,' Steven murmured. 'Oh, God, Tally's their prisoner too.'

'You say he hasn't phoned?' asked Macmillan quickly.

Steven told him why he thought he hadn't. 'He's got me dangling on a hook; he's enjoying my suffering.'

'If you're right about all this we have the advantage,' said Macmillan. We have the time between now and when he phones to get organised.'

'We can't risk a full-frontal assault,' said Steven. 'These animals have nothing to lose, they're already serving life. There will be no possibility of negotiation either.'

'I'm thinking anti-terrorist squad.'

'I'm thinking the Regiment, said Steven, using the nickname of the SAS, but Moorlock is not an ordinary building, it's a high security prison. There are no windows, no openings for stun grenades, no weak doors.'

'And on top of that we don't know how much time we have to set up anything at all,' said Macmillan. 'It all depends on how long Sonny Jim gets pleasure from making you sweat.

'He's doing well,' said Steven bitterly.

'We have to regard this as a full hostage situation, but not necessarily one the police can handle. I'm going to call the Home Secretary and brief her along with our recommendation. I'll get back to you as soon as I hear from her, but, rest assured, I'm very much aware that Barrowman could call at any moment.'

'The moment he does we revert immediately to the original plan,' insisted Steven. 'I do whatever he says and make the exchange without interference from anyone.'

'Of course, but in the meantime, there's no harm in getting things moving. We can get SFO police officers in position at a safe distance. They could at least report on anyone leaving the building and perhaps even intercept when they're well away.'

'The priority right now is Tally,' insisted Steven.

'I absolutely agree,' said Macmillan, but the longer he keeps you dangling the more it works in our favour. It will take a while to get an SAS troop there from Credenhill assuming permission is given.'

'I want to be near Moorlock Hall,' said Steven.

'Not a good idea,' said Macmillan. 'Barrowman will assume you are waiting for instructions at home. You don't want to be a two-hour drive away when he gives you details of the exchange.'

'You're right. God, I just need to be doing something.'

'I know, but sit tight and I'll get on with the organising things. Let me know as soon as you get the phone call and I'll freeze everything until Dr Simmons is safe.'

If Barrowman suspects for a moment that we know he's at Moorlock Hall . . .'

'I'll make it crystal clear that that mustn't happen.'

Steven called Sci-Med support and requested an old car be made available. 'Anything as long as it goes.' He didn't want to use a high-profile car like his Porsche. If there were to be a rendezvous, he would rather he spotted what the opposition was driving rather than the other way around. The old car was to be left in Maple Street, neighbouring Marlborough Court: the keys should be left under the passenger seat.

'Understood.'

The hours continued to pass but, at least, Steven's anguish was now mitigated by the knowledge that Barrowman's tactic might be working against him. At a quarter to four the phone rang but it was his new mobile. Macmillan reported that permission had been given for members of 22 SAS regiment to be deployed from their base at Credenhill in Herefordshire. An initial team of six were already on their way to appraise the situation, Police Specialist Firearms Officers were already in position at a discreet distance. No one had left Moorlock Hall.

Steven drifted off into an uneasy sleep in his chair around five thirty but woke with a start an hour later. The dawn of a new day demanded that he get himself into gear. He still had some Benzedrine tablets in the bathroom cabinet from an occasion in the past when it had been essential that he keep awake and alert for long periods. He took two, put on some coffee and made himself two slices of toast to give an impression of breakfast.

Macmillan called at seven. 'No phone call?'

'No,' Steven replied, irritated that he'd been asked '

'Strange.'

Steven had to edit his reply. He knew he was incredibly on edge.

'Yes.'

'No one has left Moorlock. Any thoughts?'

'I'll get back to you, John.'

Steven needed to end the call because the stimulant he'd taken was allowing a succession of nightmare thoughts to enter his head. One emerged as a clear favourite. Barrowman hadn't called because . . . Barrowman wasn't going to call . . . Barrowman had never intended to call. He just wanted to torture him for as long as possible . . . maybe until he had worked this out for himself and . . . now that he had . . . there was worse to come. Barrowman didn't want his data back because he didn't need it. The proposed exchange for Tally had been an elaborate hoax. There never was going to be an exchange . . . Tally could be dead.

Steven struggled to face the big question. Was he going to gamble everything on what he'd just imagined to be the case and give up on waiting for a phone call that he now believed wasn't coming . . . or should he concede that he could be wrong and wait for the call, leaving the others to mount an inevitable assault on Moorlock Hall when time and their patience ran out?

Steven called Macmillan to say he was on his way to Moorlock. He cut off any argument by asking where Macmillan actually was.'

'We've set up headquarters about two miles past the entrance to the lane leading to Moorlock. There's an old abandoned farm building off the main road to the left. You'll find a police mobile unit round the back.'

Steven grabbed the keys for the Porsche then thought better of it. He didn't want a Porsche being seen anywhere near Moorlock in case it aroused suspicion – unlikely, but he would take no chances. He ran around to where he'd asked for an old car to be left and saw the Land Rover Defender. It was old, filthy and ideal. Defenders were as anonymous as grass in the countryside. Every farmer and his dog had one. Steven smiled at the noise of the engine – no sound-proofing, no concession to comfort, the only thing Defenders had going for them was that they could go absolutely anywhere and keep going. Steven permitted himself a small smile before turning his attention to just how they were going to break in to a maximum-security prison. By the time he'd found what looked like a large black horsebox at the back of the farm building and noted that there was another Land Rover parked beside it, he'd had an idea.

TWENTY-SEVEN

'What possessed you, man?' asked Macmillan as Steven entered the mobile command centre and was stopped by a gun in his face. 'This is Dr Steven Dunbar,' said Macmillan.

'Hello,' said the man lowering the gun.

Eight other men were there, two were in black, police Special Firearms Officer gear, the other six were dressed in variations on a camouflage theme and appeared more relaxed.

In answer to Macmillan's question, Steven told him how he'd come to his conclusions and of the gamble he'd just taken.

'Then we should all pray your phone doesn't ring,' said Macmillan.

Macmillan did the introductions to two police commanders and six SAS soldiers who had travelled as an advance party from their Credenhill base. Steven nodded and said hello.

Macmillan said to one of them, 'Dr Dunbar was with your lot.'

'We heard,' said the soldier, introduced simply as Andy. 'Mark Leyden said to say hello.'

Steven felt embarrassed at not recognising the name.

'He says you saved his life.'

'He's probably exaggerating,' said Steven.

Smiles all round told him it was the right thing to say.

'I think we're all agreed this isn't going to be easy,' said Macmillan. 'Nobody breaks into a high security prison. We've been trying to scale down our thoughts from rocket-launchers and bulldozers.'

'I had an idea on the way down,' said Steven.

All eyes turned to him.

'Moorlock is a high security unit but it was built as a self-contained module inside the ground floor of an old, derelict hospital. It is very secure, but I've been in there and I think there may be an Achilles heel.'

'Give that man a bow and arrow,' said one of the policemen.

Steven continued, 'The medical director's office is attached to the secure unit but it's not actually inside it and not that far from the prison entrance although that certainly is secure.'

'How does that help?'

'The ceiling,' said Steven. 'When I was sitting in the director's office I noticed that the ceiling was very high, very dirty and cracked in places. That suggests it's the original hospital ceiling in that room.

'Got you,' said one of the soldiers. 'If we could get access to it from the floor above, we could get down into the office.'

'Okay, that gets us past the front entrance, but we'll still be outside the main unit,' another of the soldiers pointed out.

'It's the unit director's office,' Steven emphasised, 'there's a chance we'll be able to lay our hands on the codes for the alarms and doors. It's just possible we might be able to get into the secure unit without a shot being fired.'

'Brilliant.'

Questions followed thick and fast.

'Why is this guy's office outside the unit?'

'I'm no psychiatrist, but having met him, I think it would be his choice,' said Steven. 'Although the room's attached to the unit, it's outside it and I think that would be important to him – a sort of psychological barrier between him and them. It certainly wasn't because it's a pleasant room, it's grotty.'

'Does the secure unit extend back through the entire width of the old building?'

'I think not,' said Steven. 'It extends along most of the front elevation, but looking at the side elevation of the original building, it probably only reaches half way back.'

'I tried to get plans. No luck,' said Macmillan.

Macmillan summarised. 'Entry through the back of the building should be achieved with the objective of gaining access to the first floor. Once there, it would be a case of . . . moving to where it's thought the room above the office is situated. How do we know that?

Steven said, 'Without plans, I agree that could be a problem. All I can suggest is that I make a rough sketch of the layout as I remember it and we wing it from there.'

'Sounds good,' said Andy, 'we'll have to drill small holes in the floor anyway to see what's below, whether there's a light on, whether it's the right room, whether there's anyone in it.'

Steven accepted the pen and paper Macmillan found for him in his briefcase while the others discussed what they would need for the operation and who should do what. He thought carefully through his one and only visit to Moorlock, trying to remember in detail his route through the main gate, the pause at the first security halt, the entrance to the main hospital building, the walk along a short corridor parallel to the front elevation . . . how long? . . . twenty metres, thirty metres? The right turn into Groves' office just outside the modern, combination-guarded entrance to the secure unit.

Steven said, 'You know, it would help to have a photograph of the hospital building.'

One of the police commanders radioed Steven's request and a photograph was transmitted back within eight minutes.

'Just one man on the ground who knows what he's doing,' said the commander, noticing the look on Steven's face, which seemed to question the wisdom of anyone getting too close to Moorlock.

Steven nodded and accepted the photo. He matched his calculations to the first floor of the building and found his best guess took him along to the third window in from the corner at the east end. That room would not be directly above Groves' office – his office had no window facing the front – it would have to be the room on the other side of the corridor. He said so to Macmillan.

'Providing it is a room,' said Macmillan, 'It's an old hospital, the window might well be in what was an open ward.'

Good point,' said Steven. He did another calculation in his head and said, 'Okay, as we don't know what's behind the third window on the first floor, it would be safer to say that the area we are looking for should be around fifteen to twenty metres back from it in a straight line.'

With this clear objective established and general agreement that everyone had what they needed in terms of equipment and personnel – Andy reported back to his unit that no back-up was required – attention turned to details. After a short discussion, Macmillan listed them.

The operation would begin at midnight. Those detailed to enter the building – Steven and the six soldiers – would be dropped off at the end of the lane leading up to Moorlock by the army Land Rover and left to make the final approach on foot. On achieving a successful entrance to Groves' office, two of the soldiers would deploy to explore the possibility of opening up the front entrance – hopefully armed with codes and combinations obtained either from the office or the security stop just behind the entrance. Steven and the remaining four soldiers would effect entry to the secure unit. Again, it was hoped that this would be achieved with codes found in the office. If not, the explosives expert of the group, Luke, would do his thing and the others would follow up with stun grenades.

If they did manage to enter the secure unit without the use of . . .

Steven's old mobile phone rang and caused a heart-stopping interruption. His blood turned to ice as he faced his worst fears – Barrowman wasn't in Moorlock at all, he was somewhere else entirely. He was about to give instructions for an exchange meeting he couldn't possibly keep.

Everyone seemed hypnotised, rendered immobile like figures in a renaissance painting.

Steven snatched at the phone. 'I'm here, Barrowman.'

'You took your time, Dunbar. And here was me thinking you'd be worried out of your mind.'

'Where's Tally? What have you done with her. If you've hurt her I'll . . .'

'Don't be ridiculous, Dunbar. You're in no position to do anything . . . Oh, and if you have a little squad of elves trying to trace the call, tell them not to bother, I'm using a shielded satellite job.'

'What's the deal?' asked Steven with his eyes tight shut and afraid of the coming reply.

'There is no deal, Dunbar. There never was. I must say I like your lady a lot, I'm enjoying her . . . and I'm going to keep her, I just thought I'd give you a bit of a whirl on the old mental roundabout.'

'You bastard.'

'Tut tut.'

'You need your data.'

'No, you do. It's true I'd rather you lot didn't have it, but maybe you'll never break it. I don't need to. I already know what I know and how to apply it.'

'Is there no decency left in you, Barrowman? No hint of the person you once were? Is there really no way back?'

'Boring. Bye.'

Steven was left staring at a silent phone. He felt as if he'd just cut his one and only lifeline to Tally.

Macmillan quickly broke the silence. 'Let's concentrate on the positives. He didn't ring to make a rendezvous you couldn't keep and Dr Simmons is still alive. What's more, you could still be right about Moorlock Hall and surprise is still on our side. Until we know different, nothing changes.'

'Absolutely,' agreed one of the policemen.'

'We'll get her back, mate,' said Andy.

Macmillan's briefing resumed. 'We can assume that members of staff, if alive, are being held under lock and key. Any man moving around freely can be regarded as the enemy and shot without question – all the inmates are killers. We know that Barrowman is armed. It's reasonable to assume that any firearms normally held on the premises are now in the hands of the prisoners. No chances are to be taken. Armed police officers will continue with their cordon round Moorlock and deal with any escape attempt should things go wrong. The same policy will apply. Shoot to kill.

The relief at finally being on the move after what seemed like an eternity waiting for darkness to fall and the midnight hour to register was almost palpable in the long-base army Land Rover taking them up to the end of the lane. The moon wasn't full but it gave them some light when clouds weren't passing across it. Two SAS men equipped with night vision equipment led the way and the others, carrying a variety of equipment, followed along in their footsteps, listening out for murmured warnings of any major obstacle. Steven was excused donkey work – one of the soldiers suggesting this was in deference to his age to the amusement of the others. He affected a half-hearted laugh, so half-hearted that Andy said, 'Don't worry, mate, you wouldn't be with us if we thought you couldn't cut it.'

Steven had dressed in the clothes he'd brought with him, close fitting black gear, and balaclava and his shoulder holster promoted to the outside of his clothing. Lightweight Berghaus hill boots gave him security underfoot.

They circled the building at a distance and approached the back fence where they found no great effort had been made to secure it; any security measures had obviously been saved for the prison unit itself. The hospital was just a crumbling shell around it.

'Piece of cake,' muttered one of the soldiers as he checked the wire for electrification and found none. He snipped through old wire to give them entrance to the grounds.

They made their way through knee high weeds to the rear elevation of the building where the moon allowed them to examine the wall.

'Spoilt for choice,' said one of the soldiers. 'Pick a drainpipe . . . any drainpipe.'

'He was detailed by Andy to climb a pipe that ran in close proximity to a first-floor window with an almost horizontal section leading off under it. It would provide something to stand on. He had a coil of rope over his head and shoulder. 'Got the tape and diamond?' Andy asked.

'Affirmative.'

Steven watched as the man tried to open the window and failed. It wasn't unexpected, the old, rotten sash and case windows were probably never going to open again. The soldier moved on to scoring the lower pane with a diamond point cutter. He marked out a square, tracing the edge of the frame and then attached strong, sticky tape at strategic points before elbowing the glass smartly until it gave way and parted company with the frame. The soldier loosened the tape carefully from the frame and fed the pane slowly inside the window opening to lower and prop it up against the inside wall before climbing in himself and finding a secure anchor for the rope. A minute or so later he lowered the other end to start pulling up the equipment bags. They were followed by the men themselves. All seven of them were standing inside on the first floor of the hospital building inside eleven minutes. None of the soldiers showed any signs of exertion, Steven felt as if his arms had become six feet long.

They were in a large, narrow room with a row of sinks against the wall they just climbed. The horizontal section of the pipe they'd used to stand on was the waste pipe from the sinks leading to the down pipe. 'Looks like a laundry,' Andy suggested.

'It was probably the sluice room,' said Steven, 'waste from the ward would be washed away here. I think we'll find there's an open ward out here . . .' He made his way over to the door and the others followed.

'It's a bloody ballroom,' said one of the soldiers as moonlight lit up a long open ward where rows of beds on either side would once have stood in days gone by. It was empty.

'Right,' said Andy. 'We should be heading over this way 'We need to find the ward on the other side of the building.'

They exited the ward into a short corridor running at right angles to it and shared between the ward they'd just left and the one next to it, the one that they found faced the front of the building.

'Yo!' said Andy.

'And it stretches right up to the east wall,' said Steven. He pointed to the third window along on the far wall. 'That's what we're looking for.'

Steven approached the window, turned his back and measured out seventeen walking paces. He traced a circle in the air with his finger as he turned around in a full revolution. 'I think the office is down there,' he said, pointing at the floor.

One of the soldiers got to work with a small-bore drill, constantly sensing the resistance of the floor until he felt it lessen. He stopped before the drill bit had gone right through the ceiling below and withdrew it to be replaced by what looked to Steven to be a rod with a needle point on the end. The soldier pushed the needle through the remaining plug in the drill hole and then withdrew it to look down through shielded eyes. 'No light on,' he said. Steven understood that the soldier hadn't wanted a small plug to fall from the ceiling into an occupied room. He watched as the drill was allowed to finish its job. A flexible cable camera was inserted in its place.

'Desk . . . couple of chairs . . . books . . . picture on the wall, boats.'

'That's it,' said Steven. 'Can you point to where the desk is?'

The soldier indicated and Steven chose an area where he thought it would be clear to drop down.

'Couldn't we drop down on to the desk without using ropes?' Andy asked.

Steven said not. 'The ceiling's too high. Even hanging at full stretch, we'd still have a six foot drop on to the surface of the desk.'

'Broken leg territory,' said Andy. He set about looking for a rope anchor while two of the others set about cutting a circular hole in the floor. Steven expected noise but, whatever they were using, it made very little and even less when it came to cutting an opening in the ceiling below. 'Bit of a tight squeeze,' said one. They had to make the opening between joists.

'This is where we find out who ate all the pies,' said Andy who had come up with an old iron bed frame they could press into use as an anchor.

All seven made it down safely although Steven felt his rib cage had been pushed through his spine He resisted a strong desire to hug himself.

There were no windows in the office so shielded torches could be used to search for useful information. This was made more difficult however, by the room having been searched already and its contents scattered everywhere.

'Christ!' exclaimed one of the men. He said it in such a way that everyone spun round sensing something approaching panic. 'There's a bloke in the corner,' said the soldier.

Torches lit up the figure of a man sitting propped up in the far corner. He was dead and his ears and nose were missing.

'It's Groves,' said Steven. I recognise the suit . . .'

The search continued in silence, but all were considering what they were up against, Steven more than most.

'How about that?' said Andy, pointing at the wall to the right of the door.

Steven looked at a card with seven four number sequences printed on it. 'One for each day of the week,' he said.

'We can get in the easy way,' said Andy to sighs of relief all round.

'Maybe,' Steven cautioned, 'we don't know what day of the week the inmates took over the asylum.'

'Does that matter?'

'They might not have bothered changing the entry code after that and we don't know what day of the week they stopped doing it,' said Steven. 'We might punch in the wrong code. We'll probably get away with one wrong entry, but two or more and we'll probably trigger an automatic lock-down with alarms going off.'

'Right, we give it two tries but won't risk a third,' said Andy. 'We'll blow the door and follow up with stun grenades. 'Are there any coded doors inside the unit?'

'There are, but somehow I don't think they'll be operational. If you'd been locked up for years I think an open-door policy might be very popular.'

'Good point. Beats me why they haven't all hit the road anyway.

'The two guys in charge are clever,' said Steven. 'If they let the others scatter to the four winds without a plan, they'll be picked up within a few days and the cat would be out of the bag about Moorlock. As it is, they have what they believe is a safe and secure hideout for the time being where they can plan their next move.'

'Only . . . they're wrong,' said Andy. 'Time, guys.'

The soldiers picked up their weapons and readied themselves without comment. The man Andy had detailed to carry out a quick reconnoitre – specifically to see if anyone was in the gatehouse – stood ready by the door. Torches were extinguished, Andy opened it a fraction and listened before nodding and letting him out. He was back within four minutes. 'Empty, boss.'

Andy nodded to the two men detailed to investigate the opening of the front entrance and they slipped out. After a few more moments he turned to Steven and the four remaining soldiers. 'Show time.'

The five men left the office silently. Andy switched his torch back on and highlighted the electronic main entrance keypad on the wall while the others crouched down, one holding stun grenades the others pointing weapons at the entrance. Steven entered a four-number sequence he'd taken from the card. He hadn't chosen it at random, but had deliberately picked Thursday's number because he remembered it had been a Thursday when Barrowman had escaped in the car belonging to the MI5 agent he'd murdered. If he'd driven straight to Moorlock and initiated the coup, the code might not have been changed after that. Wrong. A red LED flashed and nothing happened.

Very aware that he was about to make his second and last attempt before explosives came into play, Steven entered the code for Friday. The LED stayed dark and, after an agonising pause, mechanical levers obeyed electronic instructions and the door opened.

Andy held his hand up as it became apparent that the well-lit corridor stretching out before them was empty. He and Steven exchanged glances that spoke of good fortune. They could hear voices, but they were coming from the far end. Laughter was present in the sound, another good sign. Andy signalled to the soldiers that they move along both sides, listening at doors. He and Steven led off.

Steven was first to hold up his hand. The others came to a halt while he listened more intently. He turned and silently mouthed the words, 'A woman.' Putting his left hand on the door handle and holding the Glock pistol in his right he waited for a soldier with an automatic weapon to sidle into place beside him. The door wasn't locked. It swung open to reveal a single occupant, a weeping middle-aged woman whose clothes were ripped and her hair a tangled mess. She turned her tear-stained cheeks towards the two armed men, her eyes wide as if expecting some new horror to unfold.

Steven replaced his weapon and approached the woman. 'Who are you?' he asked gently.

The woman appeared surprised at the question, her eyes examining Steven's face as if totally confused.

'You're safe now,' Steven assured her. 'Who are you?'

'Lillian Leadbetter.'

'MP?'

The woman nodded.

Steven questioned the woman as quickly and as kindly as he could. He asked if Lawler and Barrowman were in charge.

'They killed Dr Groves in front of my eyes. 'Animals . . . sheer bloody animals . . . I hope they rot in hell.'

'Is there another woman here?'

'A doctor, yes, the woman Barrowman brought here. She's been forced to treat Lawler.

'Treat him?'

'He was attacked by two of the others and badly injured. They were drinking. Barrowman was furious, he shot them both.

'Where is she treating him?'

'I don't know.

'Everything's going to be all right but we need you to keep quiet. Okay?'

The woman nodded.

'We can hear voices, where are they all?'

'End of the corridor, to the right. They drink and play cards . . .'

'Steven whispered what he'd learned. 'Andy said, 'You look for your lady, we'll spoil the party.'

They made their way to the end of the corridor where the soldiers turned right and Steven went left, listening at each of the four doors he found there. He thought he heard movement behind the third door and readied his weapon before opening it quietly. Tally turned to look at him, turning away from the unconscious man she had been tending to and whom he presumed was Lawler. Her face was pale and withdrawn. She looked as if she hadn't slept for days and wouldn't have known what day of the week it was. She stared at him as if wondering if she was seeing things.

'Hello,' he said softly.

'I knew some day my prince would come . . .'

'Always the smart one-liner,' said Steven, his face breaking into the first genuine smile for days. He holstered his weapon and moved towards her, but, as he did so, the deafening sound of prolonged gunfire broke out. Lawler was shocked out of sedation and took in the situation quickly. He pulled Tally across the bed on top of him, holding her neck in the crook of his arm as Steven levelled his pistol at him.

'Drop it.'

Steven hesitated, his mind furiously assessing the situation. Lawler was weak and he was unarmed . . .

'Drop it or I'll bite her throat out.'

Steven looked at Lawler's snarling mouth and saw it was all too close to Tally's neck. He dropped his shoulders in resignation and made to drop the gun on the floor, but, at the last moment, he spun the Glock in his hand and shot at Lawler's feet in one clean movement. Lawler screamed in pain as a bullet smashed through his metatarsals and Tally took advantage of his distraction to break free and fall down flat on the floor. Steven's second shot killed Lawler . . . and, if it didn't, his third certainly did. Steven helped Tally to her feet and wrapped his arms around her.

After a few moments of just holding each other Steven said, 'I think it's all over, but I have to check.' He let Tally go and took out the Glock again before slowly opening the door and risking a quick look out to find a man pointing a gun at him. It was Andy, taking the same precautions over someone who was opening a door. 'All right?' he asked.

'All over,' came the reply. 'You?'

Steven brought Tally out to receive an impromptu round of applause from the soldiers who had joined Andy. Tally looked beyond them and asked, 'Does anyone need my help in there?'

The soldiers looked at each other before Andy said, 'That's a very kind thought, doctor, but no . . . no one.'

They were joined by armed police officers who had been let in by the soldiers who had uncovered the code for the front entrance and opened it.

After brief discussions, reports were called in by the senior men to the Home Office, the Ministry of Defence and other involved parties interested in hearing that a dangerous and hugely embarrassing situation had been resolved.

Despite Steven's protestations Tally insisted on comforting Lillian Leadbetter while they waited for an ambulance to arrive. She however, declined medical attention for herself. Steven called John Macmillan to give him the information he would require for a clean-up operation to be launched. Of necessity, he had to limit details to the number of dead and leave it at that apart from highlighting the particular horror of Groves' death and the murder of all staff save for Staff Nurse Clements who was with the inmates when the soldiers intervened. He had died with them.

'The police have been detailed to take you and Dr Simmons home while I see to things.'

'Thanks.'

'Are the soldiers from 22 SAS still there?'

Steven looked round and saw only policemen. 'No, they've gone.'

'It was ever thus,' said Macmillan.

Steven and Tally were taken back to London at high speed in a comfortable five series BMW using blues but with no need for twos. Tally slept with her head on Steven's shoulder for the whole journey while Steven's eyes remained wide open, transfixed by thoughts of the past few days.

'We're home,' he murmured as the car slowed and turned into Marlborough Court.

'Are we . . . are we really?' Tally whispered sleepily.

Steven thanked the driver with a nod and the man responded in kind.

Tally seemed to recover some energy when the door closed behind them. 'I think we could both do with a drink,' she said. When she didn't get a reply, she turned to find Steven looking at her. He wasn't smiling. 'What's wrong?' she asked.

'When are you going to stop?'

'Stop what?' she asked.

'Playing the brave little lady who takes everything in her stride, it doesn't wash with me . . .'

A number of expressions tried to appear on Tally's face before they all failed and she lost all vestige of control. 'Oh, Steven . . .' Tears flowed freely down her face as an emotional dam burst inside her. 'Oh Steven . . . hold me, hold me, hold me.'

Steven did. 'I'll never let you out of my sight again . . .'

'Even Tally in her current state couldn't stop a slight splutter at Steven's ridiculous promise. 'Oh God,' she stammered. 'I never guessed human beings could be like that . . . vicious loathsome animals. No, they were worse than animals: they tortured and killed for fun.'

'Pure evil is something that most people never come across,' said Steven.

'But it fascinated Barrowman,' said Tally.

'A victim of his search for truth.'

'Is he dead?'

'They're all dead.'

'Somehow . . . I find that a great comfort.

'I suspect Mrs Leadbetter may find similar solace.'

'Poor woman, I'm sure she thought she was doing the right thing.'

Steven gave Tally a look that left her in no doubt about his disagreement.

'Oh, Steven, you and politicians.'

'Let's not go there.'

'Okay, do I get that drink now?'

When the hour of the day and the day of the week began to recover some relevance, Tally insisted that she'd be fine if Steven left her to go to the Home Office for a debriefing session. He telephoned Jean to say that the following morning would be good and asked her to make sure that Lukas would be there.

Steven talked everyone through the re-taking of Moorlock Hall and Macmillan said, 'Are we to assume that Barrowman's secret died with him?'

'We know what the secret was,' Steven replied. 'He found the switching mechanism for controlling genes in a number of regions on the human genome. He found it in regions of the DNA previously described as junk, but there's more. Maybe Lukas should take over.'

Lukas nodded and said, 'Barrowman not only described switching mechanisms in stretches of DNA we've been calling junk, but he came across a bank of genes which determine in broad general terms whether a person is what we might call a normal decent human being when its controlling switch is turned one way, but when it's reversed, we get a psychopath who is as far from being decent as you can get. I think the details of how you can turn this switch on and off are on a protected disk we found among Barrowman's stuff, but I haven't been able to break into it.'

Steven took over again. 'I'm pretty sure that Barrowman believed he was on the brink of being able to manipulate the switch in psychopathic killers and turn them into normal people, but somewhere along the line, he screwed up and flicked it the wrong way in himself. He turned into a complete monster.'

'Do you think he was working on turning it back in himself?' Jean Roberts asked. 'I was thinking about the chemicals he ordered.'

'It would be nice to think so,' said Macmillan.

'Having read his notes, I think it far more likely he was intent on creating more monsters,' said Lukas.

'Which brings us to our intelligence services,' said Steven. 'Does anyone know if they have succeeded in breaking the code to get into Barrowman's last disk?'

'I've not had confirmation of that,' said the Home Secretary.

'Well, if we see the Queen's own regiment of psychopathic killers trooping the colour next year we'll know that's a yes . . .' said Steven.

The Home secretary made a face but didn't take Steven to task. As he left the room, she said to Macmillan. 'He did a magnificent job.'

'We can agree on that, Home Secretary.'

'The way he planned the assault on Moorlock Hall and the danger he put himself in to rescue Dr Simmons was quite extraordinary.'

'I suspect he doesn't know he's just a collection of proteins and chemicals, Home Secretary . . .'

Before leaving for home, Steven called Neil Tyler to tell him all that had transpired.

'I think you've just told me I'm out of a job.'

'Sorry about that.'

'No problem, it was Barrowman's work I was interested in, but I'd like to be kept in the loop if any progress is made with understanding his switch mechanism.'

'If I hear it, you'll hear it'

'Thanks, Steven. By the way, did you contact the Americans with your thoughts on the Yale fire?'

'Not yet,' Steven confessed.

'If it helps your decision, the New Haven Connecticut police found the body of Father Liam Crossan hanging under a bridge last night. You might say justice has been done.'

'Wow.'

'There are some tills you just don't put your fingers in.'

* * * *

'How did it go?' Tally asked.

'It's over and that's all I care about right now. We should go away, take a holiday, sunshine, blue skies . . .'

Steven stopped when he saw Tally shake her head. 'No,' she said, 'I want to go and spend some time with Mum, tell her all the things I should tell her before it's too late. You should go and see your daughter before she's completely grown up. You can meet Jason . . .'

'Mm, right.'

Tally hid a smile. 'Steven?'

'Yes?'

'You did give that gun back, didn't you?'

THE END

REVIEWS for KEN McCLURE

'His medical thrillers out-chill both Michael Crichton and Robin Cook.'

Daily Telegraph.

'McClure writes the sort of medical thrillers which are just too close to plausibility for comfort.'

(Eye of the Raven) *Birmingham Post.*

'Well-wrought, plausible and unnerving.'

(Tangled Web) *The Times*

'A plausible scientific thriller . . . McClure is a rival for Michael Crichton.'

(The Gulf Conspiracy) *Peterborough Evening Telegraph.*

'Contemporary and controversial, this is a white-knuckle ride of a thriller.'

(Past Lives) *Scottish Field.*

'Ken McClure looks set to join the A list at the top of the medical thriller field.'

The Glasgow Herald.

'McClure's intelligence and familiarity with microbiology enable him to make accurate predictions. Using his knowledge, he is deciding what could happen, then showing how it might happen . . . It is McClure's creative interpretation of the material that makes his books so interesting.'

The Guardian.

'Ken McClure explains contagious illness in everyday language that makes you hold your breath in case you catch them. His forte is to take an outside chance possibility, decide on the worst possible outcome . . . and write a book.'

The Scotsman

'Original in conception . . . its execution is brilliantly done . . . plot and sub plot are structured with skill . . . the whole thing grabs the attention as it hurtles to its terrifying climax.'

(Requiem) *Independent Newspapers (Ireland).*

'Absolutely enthralling.'

(Crisis) *Medical Journal*

'Pacey thrillers from Scotland's own Michael Crichton.'

Aberdeen Evening Express

'Fear courses through the narrative, unhinging the characters. It leaks through the government, corrupts the body politic and infects the nation. It is fear, too, tinged with curiosity, that keeps the reader turning the pages.'

(White Death) *The Independent*

Printed in Great Britain
by Amazon